Ezra offered a sprig of pussy willow to Callie with a bow. "I wish this were a rose."

"A kind thought, sir. But I prefer the pussy willow."

When their hands touched, Callie's fingers trembled and Ezra stepped closer.

"Callie..." Her name was a hoarse whisper, a question.

She stepped back. "Thank you, Ezra." She turned toward the hotel.

Ezra's pulse quickened as they approached the steps. He would take her elbow and help her up to the porch, bid her good-night at the door.

But Callie stopped short at the base of the stairs.

"Good evening, Ezra."

The finality of her tone made her meaning clear—he was to come no farther. She climbed the steps and crossed the porch.

Ezra waited until she was safe inside, then exhaled a long breath. He was accustomed to young women welcoming his slightest attention, not turning their backs on him. Courting Callie Conner could prove to be more costly to his pride than he imagined.

Books by Dorothy Clark

Love Inspired Historical

Family of the Heart
The Law and Miss Mary
Prairie Courtship
Gold Rush Baby
Frontier Father
*Wooing the Schoolmarm
*Courting Miss Callie

Love Inspired

Hosea's Bride
Lessons from the Heart

Steeple Hill Single Title

Beauty for Ashes
Joy for Mourning

*Pinewood Weddings

DOROTHY CLARK

Critically acclaimed, award-winning author Dorothy Clark lives in rural New York, in a home she designed and helped her husband build (she swings a mean hammer!) with the able assistance of their three children. When she is not writing, she and her husband enjoy traveling throughout the United States doing research and gaining inspiration for future books. Dorothy believes in God, love, family and happy endings, which explains why she feels so at home writing stories for Love Inspired Books. Dorothy enjoys hearing from her readers and may be contacted at dorothyjclark@hotmail.com.

Courting Miss Callie

DOROTHY CLARK

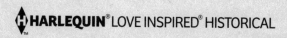

HARLEQUIN® LOVE INSPIRED® HISTORICAL

™ LOVE INSPIRED BOOKS

Recycling programs
for this product may
not exist in your area.

ISBN-13: 978-0-373-82952-1

COURTING MISS CALLIE

www.LoveInspiredBooks.com

Printed in U.S.A.

A GOOD name is rather to be chosen than great riches, and loving favor rather than silver and gold.
—*Proverbs* 22:1

This book is dedicated with love
and deep appreciation to my church family.
To those prayer warriors who faithfully
seek the Lord on behalf of my writing—thank you.
I love and appreciate you all.

And, again, to Sam. Thank you is such a
puny expression of my appreciation, but it will
have to do—unless that fertile mind of yours can
come up with better words. Blessings, my friend.

*"Commit thy works unto the Lord,
and thy thoughts shall be established."*

Your Word is truth. Thank You, Jesus.

To You be the glory.

Chapter One

March, 1841
Pinewood Village, New York

Callie Conner propped the full basket on her hip, closed the door of the buttery and started toward the hotel, then stopped and stared at the man limping up the path toward her. A logger by the looks of him. She sighed, looked down at the ground and waited. She hated meeting new people—especially men. There was always the staring, and then the profuse compliments about her beauty, and then—

"That basket looks heavy for you, miss. May I carry it for you?" She lifted her head and it happened—just as it always did. The man's eyes widened. He stared, blinked and stared again. He gazed into her eyes, and she heard his breath catch. She frowned, but held back the refusal that rose to her lips. If he was Aunt Sophia's friend she would have to accept his offer of help.

The man made a visible effort to collect himself and cleared his throat. "Truthfully, miss, I was wondering if there is work I could do in exchange for something to eat?"

So he was not known to her aunt. She opened her mouth to refuse, but his stomach rumbled, and she bit back her words. She hadn't the heart to turn away a hungry man. At least he hadn't complimented her to win his way, as the wealthy, elite men in Buffalo were wont to do. She ignored her unease and handed him the basket. "Follow me." Not a very gracious response perhaps, but she was heartily sick of men.

The hems of her long skirts whispered against the wood as she climbed the steps, crossed the wide porch and entered the back door. The smell of the beef stew she had simmering over the fire filled the kitchen. The man's stomach rumbled again. "Set the basket there on the worktable, then hang your jacket on one of those pegs and have a seat." She swept her hand toward the smaller dining table against the wall. "I'll bring you some food."

"You're most kind."

The man removed his knit hat, winced and shoved it into his pocket, shrugged out of his plaid wool jacket and lowered himself into a chair. There was something careful about his movements. Was he injured? Is that why he was not working? Spring was such a busy time of the year for loggers.

She pushed aside her contemplations, took a knife, fork and dish from the hutch, crossed to the fireplace, ladled a large serving of stew onto the dish from the iron pot hanging from the crane and walked to the table.

The man glanced up at her, raised his hand and rubbed the stubble on his chin. He looked uncomfortable about it. But most loggers let their beards grow until they came to town. She placed the dish in front of him.

"Thank you."

Her nod set the wisps of black curls around her face aflutter. She brushed them back off her forehead. "There is more stew should you wish it. I'll get you some bread and butter."

The logger offered quiet thanks for the food, and then there was the click of the fork against the dish. His prayer took away some of her unease, but still there was something odd about the situation. The man was begging food, yet the blue wool shirt he wore looked new, as did his jacket, pants and boots. Well, no matter. He would soon be gone.

She uncovered a loaf of bread and cut off two thick slices, grabbed the crock of butter from the basket he'd carried in for her, returned to the table and gasped.

The man jerked his head up, winced.

"You've a nasty wound on your head, Mr...."

"Ryder." He lowered his fork to his plate and stood. "My apologies, miss. I thought there was only a lump, not a visible wound or I would not have subjected you to—"

She banged the bread plate down on the table and looked straight into his astonished gaze. "I am *not* a delicate flower that must be pampered and coddled, Mr. Ryder! I have seen wounds worse than yours. I was merely surprised by it. Now please sit down and eat your meal. That wound needs care. I will tend to it when you are finished."

"You're very kind, miss, but I can't permit—"

She jutted her chin up a notch and stared at him.

A puzzled look flickered in his blue eyes. He gave a small nod. "Very well." He sat, took a bite of the stew, then lifted a piece of the bread from the plate and dipped his knife in the butter.

Heat spread across her cheeks. Perhaps she had reacted too strongly, but she was so *tired* of men seeing only her beauty and none of her worth. She'd come back to Pinewood to escape that—at least for a little while.

Her long skirts flared out at her pivot, swishing over the tops of her shoes as she strode to the stove. She poured warm water from the iron teakettle into a large bowl, moved to the dry sink and draped a few clean cloths from the bottom shelf over her arm, snatched a small, covered crock from a shelf and walked back to the table.

The man crossed his knife and fork on his empty dish. "My compliments, miss. That stew is the best I have ever eaten."

"There's nothing like hunger to refine the palate." He had praised her *cooking*. She smiled, set the crock and bowl on the table and glanced at him. He was staring at her with that *look* she so hated. Her hands tightened on the bowl of water. If he told her she was beautiful, she would—

"Callie dear, I've been thinking about—" Her Aunt Sophia swept into the room, stopped and stared. "And who are you, sir?"

The logger rose and made her a polite bow. "Mr. Ezra Ryder, at your service, madam."

Her aunt's delicately arched brows rose, her gaze

shifted to Callie. She gave a small shrug. "Mr. Ryder asked if there was work he could do in exchange for a meal, Aunt Sophia." She dropped one of the cloths into the bowl of warm water. "Is there something you needed? I was about to tend a wound on Mr. Ryder's head."

"Nothing that can't wait, dear. Please be seated, Mr. Ryder." Sophia came to the table, glanced at the man's wound then took the chair opposite him.

She recognized the expression in Sophia's eyes from her days of youthful escapades with her friends. A smile tugged at her lips. Her aunt would soon know all about the logger. She squeezed the excess water out of the cloth and held it on the lump at the crown of Ezra Ryder's head to loosen the dried blood.

"How did you injure yourself, Mr. Ryder?"

Her smile grew. Sophia's inquisition had begun.

"I was ambushed by two men intent upon relieving me of my…wages."

Why had he hesitated? She frowned and moved the position of the wet cloth.

"Here in *Pinewood?*"

"No. I was attacked in Dunkirk on my way here."

"Greed makes men do evil things." The words left a bitter taste in Callie's mouth. Her father was numbered among the greedy. Why else would he plan to sell her hand in marriage to the highest bidder? Her stomach knotted. She looked down, rinsed out the cloth then applied it to the wound again.

"Sadly, that's true, Callie. And what brings you to Pinewood, Mr. Ryder? Are you seeking employment as a logger? Or a sawyer or teamster?"

"I came to visit a distant cousin…Johnny Taylor. But I was told by the clerk in the mercantile that Johnny and a man by the name of Arnold Dixon quit their jobs and headed west a few days ago."

Johnny Taylor and Arnold Dixon. Thomas Hunter's friends. The men who had so frightened Willa. Was Ezra Ryder of the same ilk? She frowned, turned the cloth over and again held it on Ezra Ryder's bowed head. "What a shame your cousin didn't know to expect you, and you made your journey in vain."

"Yes, indeed." The sympathy in Sophia's voice belied the sharpened look in her eyes. "Were you close with your cousin, Mr. Ryder?"

"No, not at all. I know him only from when we were young boys, and my uncle brought his family to visit us on the farm. My visit here was to renew our acquaintance."

There was something underlying the ring of truth in Ezra Ryder's deep voice—something he wasn't telling. Her shoulders tensed. She detested lies and subterfuge. And disdained the men that indulged in them. In her experience, they were many. She dabbed the softened blood from his hair, dropped the cloth in the water, dried her hands on the long white apron that covered her blue wool dress and opened the small crock.

"So you are without funds, and without a place to stay?"

"Thanks to those thieves, and my cousin's leaving town, yes. That is why I inquired if there is work I can do in exchange for my meal…and perhaps a place to sleep?"

"I see." Sophia glanced around. "I'm sure there is something…"

"The stables need a thorough cleaning." A cheeky suggestion. It was not her place to interfere in her aunt's business, but she didn't want the man given work around the kitchen. It was her sanctuary. She clamped her jaw to keep from saying more, and smoothed the salve over the exposed gash.

"An excellent suggestion, Callie." Sophia gave her a warm smile, then lowered her gaze to Ezra Ryder. "My groom suffers from rheumatism and can no longer care for the stables as he once did. You may clean them as payment. But you must do so as Joseph directs."

"I understand, madam."

There was politeness and acquiescence in Ezra Ryder's voice, but not a hint of subservience. Sophia ran her gaze over his neatly trimmed hair. The man had recently been to an excellent barber. She frowned, held back the questions crowding into her mind and put the cover back on the crock and placed it on the table.

"Very well. There is a cot you may sleep on in the equipment room. You'll find a mattress tick you can stuff with fresh hay in the tin cupboard, and— Yes, Mary?"

The maid in the doorway gave an apologetic smile. "Begging your pardon, Mrs. Sheffield, but there's a gentleman out front that wants a room."

"Thank you, Mary. I'll come right along." Her aunt rose.

Ezra Ryder stood and made her a small bow. "Thank you for your kindness, Mrs. Sheffield."

Sophia nodded and stepped toward the doorway,

paused and looked over her shoulder. "Callie, Ezra will need blankets. You'll find some in the chest in my bedroom."

Something akin to shock flashed in Ezra Ryder's eyes at the subtle message of his servile position contained in her aunt's use of his given name. It was followed by a flicker of amusement. A strange reaction for a man come begging. He glanced her way, caught her studying him.

"I'll get the blankets." She hurried through the door that led to her aunt's private quarters, snatched three blankets from the chest at the foot of the bed and returned to the kitchen. He had donned his jacket.

"Here are the blankets—" She glanced up at him and his first name stuck in her throat. There was something about the man that commanded respect. "The Allegheny has flooded the fields out back and is only a few feet from the stables, but these should be sufficient to ward off the damp and the cold." She handed him the wool blankets and stepped back.

He nodded, fastened his gaze on hers and smiled. "Thank you for your suggestion to your aunt that I might help in the stables. I'm grateful for the opportunity to earn bed and board. And thank you for tending my wound. It already feels better."

She turned from the look of admiration in his eyes and began clearing the table. "The salve is made by the Senecas. It's very effective. I'll apply more in the morning."

"I don't want to trouble you, Miss... I'm sorry, I don't know your name."

"It's Conner. And it's no trouble to dab salve on a wound." She glanced up and again found that look of admiration in his eyes. "Try not to roll onto your back while you're sleeping, or you'll irritate that wound."

A smile curved his lips and crinkled the corners of his blue eyes. "I shall do my best, Miss Conner."

She stared at his smile, then leaned down and picked up the dishes she'd stacked. There was definitely something amiss. The man was too self-assured, too confident for someone in his situation. "Breakfast is at daybreak. Come along with Joseph. It would be well to eat before you go on your way." The reminder of his temporary stay helped. There was something unsettling about Ezra Ryder.

He nodded, opened the door and stepped outside.

She listened to his uneven footfalls cross the porch and thump down the steps then shook her head and carried the dishes to the sink cupboard. Mr. Ryder was a handsome man with impeccable manners and a very charming smile. He was, also, a man with a secret. She had no idea what he was hiding or why, but she was certain he had not been completely honest. How she hated deceit! The social circle in Buffalo was rife with it.

She turned to the worktable, unloaded the basket and began the pudding she had planned for the hotel guests' dessert tomorrow. She should never have mentioned the deteriorating condition of the stables. The sooner Mr. Ryder left the better.

Ezra scowled at the pain that shot down his leg. The boots of the men who had ambushed and robbed him last night had left their imprint in the bruise on his shoulder and on his right leg. The protest in his thigh when it took his weight coming down the porch steps confirmed that.

He paused and rubbed the ache to loosen the stiffened muscle, then flexed his sore fingers and smiled grimly at the memory of his fist connecting with one of his attacker's jaws before something solid slammed against the back of his head and darkness took him.

One good thing. He'd already followed Johnny's suggestion and purchased and changed into the rough clothes he'd wear for his visit here in Pinewood before he'd taken the stage from Buffalo. His city clothes and shoes would never have held up to the long walk he'd been forced to make from Dunkirk in the inclement weather. Thank goodness for the kindness of the teamster who had offered him a ride on his supply wagon or he'd still be slogging his way down the muddy, rutted road to Pinewood.

He scrubbed at the back of his neck to try and ease the dull throb in his head and started down the path to the barn. He would not forget Will Gladeon's good deed. When he'd found a way to contact his bank in New York City, the teamster would be amply rewarded. As would Mrs. Sheffield and Callie Conner.

He frowned and kicked a stone out of his way. He would have to be cautious around Callie Conner. The young woman was stunningly beautiful, but she was also prickly and wary. He hadn't been able to see her face with her standing behind him, but he'd felt her stiffen a few times while he was telling his tale. And the way she had looked at him when she handed him the blankets...

His frown deepened to a scowl. There was no doubt

Miss Conner was suspicious of him. Evidently it would take more than Johnny's suggested change of clothes to convince people he was a logger. He'd have to be careful. He had to stay in this village until he'd figured out a plan to get home to New York City, and the last thing he wanted was for people to discover he was a wealthy man.

The thought of the people of Pinewood learning the truth about his financial state soured his stomach. Still, there was no reason for that to happen. His trip here to Pinewood for a respite from the constant stream of people back home who pretended to favor him because of his money and position could still work. All he need do was allay the wary Miss Conner's distrust.

What a shame your cousin didn't know to expect you...

The thought he'd been holding at bay ever since Callie Conner had spoken those words crashed into his mind. Johnny *had* known. And that answered a lot of questions. Like how the thieves had chosen *him* to rob when he was dressed like a logger and others on the stage looked far more prosperous. Or why Johnny would quit his job and head west when he had expected his visit. Johnny and his cohort. Two men. Two *thieves?*

He sucked air into his tightened chest and limped forward. Johnny had told him to bring enough funds to carry him through his visit and pay for his return trip home as there was no bank in Pinewood. He had brought more than enough money to pay for two trips west. And Johnny had known the stage would make an overnight stop in Dunkirk.

He clenched his hands and set his jaw. Everyone

wanted his money. Even family. And evidently some were willing to kill him to get it. His only protection was his anonymity. He couldn't trust anyone.

Chapter Two

"I've finished the bread dough for tomorrow's baking, Aunt Sophia. I'm going over and visit with Willa and Matthew for a little while." Callie smiled and swirled her burnoose around her shoulders.

"That's a lovely idea, dear." Sophia rested her hand on her account book and lifted her head. "You're working too hard."

"I'm enjoying every minute of it. I never get to cook or bake at home." She caught her breath, then gave a little laugh to cover her verbal slip. "You know how it is in the social whirl. There are always visits to make and parties to attend. Why, I don't even own an apron!" She gave another little laugh, lifted her hand in farewell and headed toward the front entrance.

"Remember me to Willa and Matthew, dear."

"I shall." She let herself out onto the large porch and hurried through the pool of light created by the lamps on either side of the door to the steps.

A gust of wind flipped the sides of her burnoose backward and fluttered the curls at her crown. She pulled the attached hood forward and yanked the edges of the short cape back in place against the chill of the damp air. Cold, wet drops splatted against the back of her hands as she lifted her hems and picked her way across the muddy ruts of Main Street. She angled a look from beneath her hood toward the night sky. "Please, almighty God, not another storm. The floodwater is almost to the barn."

The wind whipped her words away. Raindrops pelted her face. She ducked her head and ran up the walk to the parsonage, trotted up the steps to the shelter of the front porch and rapped on the door. Yellow light glowed in the window beside her, disappeared as someone crossed in front of the lamp inside. The door opened. She smiled at the silhouette against the light.

"Callie! What a lovely surprise. Matthew has gone to pay a sick call, and I was wishing for some company. Come in," Willa said, then stepped back, a welcoming smile curving her lips and brightening her blue-green eyes.

"Thank you, *Mrs. Calvert.*" She laughed, scrubbed the soles of her shoes on the braided rug in front of the door and stepped into the warmth of the small entrance hall. "It still seems so strange to think of you as a married woman, Willa. And a *mother.*" She hung her burnoose on a peg by the door and pushed the curls back off her forehead.

"I know. It's hard for *me* to believe at times it happened so quickly. But when Matthew grinned at me…" Willa laughed and led her to the chairs by the fireplace in the sitting room. "Well, let's just say my resolve to never marry—"

"—disappeared like the mist over the river when the sun comes up." She finished Willa's sentence as they'd done for each other since they were old enough to talk, and both of them dissolved into giggles.

"Exactly." Willa gave her a quick hug. "It's so good to have you back in Pinewood, Callie."

"It's good to be back. It's…comforting." She stretched her chilled hands out to the warmth of the fire. "I thank God every day that Rose went to live with her daughter the day after I arrived. It made everything work out perfectly. Aunt Sophia has never questioned my stepping in to temporarily fill her need for a cook at the hotel."

"You mean you haven't yet told Sophia the reason for your unexpected visit? You've been back for over a week."

Guilt tweaked her conscience. She gave a reluctant nod. "That's why I came over tonight. I need your advice, Willa. Aunt Sophia mentioned today that she will have to start seeking a cook to replace Rose, and that will take away my excuse for prolonging my stay and—"

"—Sophia will start wondering why you don't go home."

"Exactly." She turned and sank into the chair opposite Willa. "If I stay overlong she will become suspicious." A wry smile curved her lips. "And you know Aunt Sophia when she is after information."

"I do indeed." Willa's eyes crinkled. "Remember when we came home with our skirt hems all wet and she suspected we'd gone floating downriver on Daniel's homemade raft?"

"And we *denied* it."

The coconspirators in childhood crimes burst into laughter.

"It's funny now—" Willa wiped tears from her eyes and shook her head "—but, when Sophia plunked us down on that porch settle and—"

"—we sat there with our skirts dripping water and shaking our heads no, too scared to even talk."

"Scared? I was terrified! Sophia was relentless—until we confessed and promised to never do it again."

"I know. I've never been able to withstand Aunt Sophia's questioning. Not to this day." Her laughter faded. She looked down and smoothed a fold from her long skirt. "And that makes things…difficult."

"Not if you tell her the truth, Callie."

Her stomach tensed. She shook her head. "It's not that easy, Willa. I want so much to stay here and live with Aunt Sophia, but I can't tell her I ran from home to escape Mother's and Father's plans to marry me off to a wealthy man. Mother is her *sister*. And their relationship is already strained since we moved from Pinewood."

Willa's smooth brow furrowed. "I thought Sophia knew that your parents' reason for moving to Buffalo was so you could make an…advantageous marriage."

"Yes." She nodded and let out a long sigh. "That's why their relationship suffered. Aunt Sophia knew how I felt about Mother's and Father's plan. How can I tell her that they will not listen to my pleas, but continue to parade me on the social circuit like some bauble for purchase! She would be *so* upset with Mother. Oh, why couldn't God have made me *average* or even *plain?*"

"Are you questioning God's wisdom, Callie?"

"No. I know His wisdom is perfect. It's my submission that is faulty." She surged to her feet, strode across the room and stared at the rain making tiny rivers down the small window panes. "It would be so much *easier* if I were plain. Father never would have moved us from Pinewood, Mother and Aunt Sophia would not be estranged and I could have a normal life."

She drew in a breath and spun back around. "Those rich men in Buffalo don't care about me, about who I am, Willa. They only want me because I will look pretty on their arm at their social gatherings. I'm no more to them than…than their expensive watch fobs, or their perfectly matched horses that pull their fancy carriages. I'm only another way for one of them to gain ascendancy over the others. They don't love me—they want to *own* me. And they're bidding against one another for my hand— to Mother and Father's glee."

The tension in her stomach turned into painful spasms. She pressed her hand against her abdomen and raised her chin. "Those men are greedy, arrogant, shallow and pompous. And they are duplicitous liars, the lot of them. You know it's true, Willa. You met a few of them when your heart was broken, and you came to visit. Well, I'll not have any of them! I want a husband who loves *me,* not one who wants to own my beauty."

The starch left her spine. She moved back to the chair, sat and took a slow, deep breath to ease the discomfort in her stomach. "I cannot bear the thought of being wed to one of those men, Willa. But how do I stand against Mother's and Father's wishes? All of their aspirations for increased wealth and prestige rest on me. I have no wish to disobey or disappoint them, but I despise the shallowness of the life I will lead if I marry any of the men who are bidding for my hand—especially Mr. Strand. And I'm afraid he is the one who will win Father's blessing. What am I to do?"

Willa rose and came to her. She yielded to the warm comfort of her friend's arms about her, blinking back the tears that stung her eyes.

"I think you must tell Sophia the truth, Callie. Tell her that there are men vying for your hand, and that you came to stay with her to gain time to decide what you will do. And then trust the Lord. He will provide your answer."

Ezra folded the end of the ticking to hold in the clean hay, flopped the stuffed mattress down on the taut roping of the narrow cot and spread one of the blankets over it. He unfolded the other two to use for covers and looked around his sleeping quarters.

The small room boasted wood plank walls with one small, dirty window instead of the painted plaster and large, draped mullioned windows in his bedroom at home. And the furnishings! A cot with a straw tick and wool blankets instead of a four-poster bed with a feather mattress and linens. A dusty old grain chest instead of a polished, mahogany highboy. Harness and halters and bridles hanging from pegs on the wall instead of paintings and a bookshelf. And a bare puncheon floor instead of waxed wood and an Oriental carpet. And no fireplace. No source of heat at all.

He shook his head, sat on the wood edge of the cot

and removed his boots. He was too sore from his beating last night and too weary from the work he'd done this evening to be concerned about the lack of luxury. And the cot was a vast improvement over the pile of hay he'd found himself in when he'd come to after his assault by those thieves—no, by Johnny Taylor and his friend. He'd been thinking about it all evening, and he had no doubt it was Johnny. It was the only thing that made sense.

The shock of his cousin's betrayal struck him again. To rob him was one thing, but to knock him unconscious and leave him half buried in a haystack to die...

He scowled and rubbed the back of his neck. Had Johnny told anyone else of his wealth? Was he in danger? It didn't seem likely, since Johnny had wanted his money himself. Still, he'd have to figure a way to get in touch with Tom Mooreland and have his business manager send funds to pay for his return trip to New York City. Perhaps Mrs. Sheffield would advance him postage money and add the expense to his room and board. He'd found the post office inside the mercantile when he'd gone to ask the proprietor where to find Johnny.

The incongruity of his position brought a grim smile to his lips. He owned a bank and an insurance company along with various other enterprises, was one of the wealthiest and most highly respected businessmen in New York City, and he hadn't money enough to post a letter. Ridiculous!

He stretched his muscles, grimaced at the pain in his shoulder and thigh, and took a deep sniff of the air. The smell of the hay and grain and leather and horses reminded him of his parents' farm in Poughkeepsie. It had taken a lot of hard work to keep the place going, but he'd always found time to spend with the horses. He'd missed them when he'd started working for Mr. Pierson at the brokerage. Perhaps he could talk Mrs. Sheffield into keeping him on until his money arrived. At least he'd have food to eat and a place to sleep. One of his strengths as a businessman was his ability to make fair, but advantageous deals. It was worth a try.

He snuffed the stable lantern, stripped down to his long underwear, tossed his clothes on the chest, slipped beneath the covers and stretched out on his right side. The hay crackled and yielded beneath his weight. He folded his arm beneath his head for a pillow, careful not to wipe the salve from his wound.

Callie Conner. He'd never seen a woman possessed of such beauty. Her skin was flawless, her features delicate and refined. And those incredible violet-colored eyes! But it wasn't only her face. Her voice was soft and melodious, her movements lithe and graceful. Best of all, there was no coquetry, no coyness, about her. Far from it. The woman seemed completely unaffected by her beauty. He couldn't say the same for himself. She'd drawn his gaze the way flowers draw bees. He'd had to remind himself not to stare.

He frowned and adjusted his position to ease the ache in his thigh, listened to the drumming of the rain against the wood shingles on the roof. Why was someone as beautiful as Callie Conner content to be a cook in her aunt's hotel? It certainly wasn't because she lacked spirit. Those beautiful, violet eyes had thrown sparks when he'd tried to refuse her care of his wound. That baffled him.

He'd only been trying to protect her sensibilities. Why should that make her angry?

He broke a stem of hay that was poking him in the ribs and closed his eyes. Why was Callie not out front greeting guests in her aunt's hotel? One look and men would vie for the chance to court her. Wealthy men. He should know. She had certainly drawn his interest. And not only because of her beauty, but because she was different than the young society women he knew—all of whom were eager to marry his money. Or was she different? Was the beautiful Miss Conner as unaffected as she seemed, or was it simply that she hadn't yet had the opportunity to marry a wealthy man?

He opened his eyes and stared at the shadowed darkness. He'd made this visit to Pinewood to free himself from those sort of doubts, to spend a few weeks among people who did not know him so he would not have to weigh every word and action to determine if someone liked him, or was merely trying to curry his favor in order to secure a loan from his bank or gain a position of note in one of his companies. Why should he let the robbery and Johnny's treachery ruin the plan?

He tugged the blanket closer around his neck to stop the cold air sneaking beneath it from chilling his back and closed his eyes. It would be pleasant to get to know the prickly Miss Callie Conner better. Much more pleasant than dodging the sycophants back home. If he could talk Mrs. Sheffield into keeping him on as a stable hand to pay for his room and board, he'd hold off on writing that letter to Tom.

Chapter Three

Her eyes burned from her sleepless night. Callie tied her apron on, stepped to the fireplace and lifted the large bowl of risen bread dough off the warm hearth. She squeezed her eyes shut to bring moisture into them, dumped the dough out onto the floured worktable and gave it a punch to deflate it. Hopefully, Sophia wouldn't notice the faint circles under her eyes.

She separated the dough, shaped and slapped it into the pans she had waiting and covered them with a towel. Sophia would welcome her into her home permanently if she asked, but, in spite of Willa's reassurances last night, it was not that simple. The words she'd overheard her father speak to her mother three years ago haunted her.

"My dear Mrs. Conner, we have produced an exceptionally beautiful daughter, and the young men in Pinewood are noticing. I believe it is time we moved to Buffalo and introduced Callie to the social circuit. One of those wealthy men will pay handsomely for her hand and our financial future will be secure."

She sighed, shook down the ashes in the stove and

added kindling and wood to the embers to heat the oven. Were her parents in financial stress? It didn't seem so, but how could she know? She had learned from over-hearing bits and pieces of conversations between the wealthy businessmen who traveled in the social circuit that things were not always as they appeared. And then there was the rift between her mother and Sophia to con-sider. She did not want to cause greater estrangement between the sisters.

She adjusted the damper on the stove, walked to the door, put on her cape and stepped out onto the porch. Moisture dripped from the eave, but it had stopped rain-ing. She crossed to the rail and looked up at the still dark sky. "Most gracious and loving God, I do not wish to be selfish in my actions or disobedient to You or to my parents, yet my heart—" She closed her eyes to hold back a rush of tears. Her heart was not to be trusted. It wanted its own desires. She took a breath and forced out the words she dreaded to say. "May Your will be done, dear God. Amen."

She sighed and opened her eyes. There was a dull gleam of yellow light visible at the small window of the equipment room in the barn. Ezra Ryder was awake. Joe would be bringing him for breakfast soon.

She laid her problems aside and headed for the kitchen to make batter for griddle cakes.

Ezra fingered the three-day growth of beard on his face, scowled and ran his thumb along the edge of the hoof trimmer. If he could get hold of some soap—

"Kinda desperate, are ya?"

He turned and gave Joseph a wry grin. "You might say that."

The elderly man nodded and limped toward the end wall. "There's somethin' over here that'll serve yer need."

Something to help him shave? He frowned and trailed after the groom.

"Lift that stuff aside."

He stared down at a scarred chest piled with stable paraphernalia. Clearly, Joseph had misunderstood his intent for that hoof trimmer. What was the man thinking? Well, his was not to reason why. He was here at the largess of Mrs. Sheffield, and Joseph was his boss. He eyed the gnawed corner of the chest lid, slapped at the pile of burlap bags on top of an old, torn buggy seat to scare off any mice, then lifted the seat to the floor.

Joseph opened the chest, leaned his stooped body over and began rummaging through the contents. "Now where— Ha! There it is!" He hauled a wood case out of the chest and closed the lid. "One of Mrs. Sheffield's guests left this a couple years back. I put it in here to keep, but he never come for it. I reckon you might as well have the use of it." A chuckle rumbled out of the groom's sunken chest. "It'll save ya cuttin' yer face up tryin' to shave off them whiskers with that hoof trimmer you was eyein'."

Ezra smiled and took the polished case into his hands. "It would have been an awkward, bloody affair all right, but to be rid of this itching on my face would have been worth it."

He balanced the case on his flattened palm and flipped the latch. The lid opened a crack, and a faint

scent escaped. He sniffed. *Witch hazel?* He shoved the
top up and gaped at the items in the case. A shaving
cup, brush and soap, straight razor, strop and mirror,
the corked bottle of witch hazel, small towels, scissors, a
comb and a pair of silver-backed hairbrushes that rivaled
the ones on his washstand at home, all tucked neatly
away in their own compartment. His mouth slanted into
a wide grin. Queer how circumstances changed your
perspective. It felt like he held the riches of the world.
"Thank you, Joseph."

"Joe's good enough." The elderly man headed for
the stalls ranged along the side wall. "I heat water for
washin' on the old brick forge in my room at the other
end of the barn. There's still some in the pot. You'd best
hurry with your shavin', it's 'bout time for breakfast."

Callie jerked her gaze from Ezra Ryder back to the
worktable and wielded the knife she held in a crisscross
pattern, dicing the apples she'd peeled and cored. He'd
caught her staring. Foolish of her, but *gracious* the man
was handsome without those dark, stubbly whiskers hiding half of his face. And he was younger than she'd
thought.

She stole another look at him through her lowered
lashes. He had a sort of stubborn-looking chin, but a
nice mouth. And truly lovely eyes. The corners crinkled a little, like he was ready to smile. Heat spread
across her cheekbones. Just what was she doing, admir-
ing Ezra Ryder's good looks? She hated it when people
did that to her.

She buttered a deep bowl, tossed in enough of the

chopped apples to make a thick layer, sprinkled them with sugar and a dusting of cinnamon, then added a layer of the diced bread.

"There any more coffee, Callie?"

She laughed, dusted the bread crumbs from her hands, and turned to lift the coffeepot from the back of the stove. "One of these mornings I'm going to surprise you and say no, Joe."

She grinned at his answering chuckle, and poured the hot coffee into his cup. "Would you like more coffee, Mr. Ryder?"

"Mr. Ryder?" Joseph dropped a lump of sugar into his cup and fixed a quizzical look on her. "Why've you gone all niminy-piminy for? We don't use last names 'mongst us workers, and he's workin' here. His name's Ezra." He returned to stirring his coffee.

She glanced at Ezra Ryder. His dark brows were raised and his blue eyes were bright with awareness. He shot a look toward Joseph then returned his gaze to her. "I would appreciate another cup of your excellent coffee…Callie."

"As you wish…Ezra." Heat shot into her cheeks. She poured his coffee, spun on her heel and hurried to the stove, set the coffeepot on the side to cool and glanced back at the table. Ezra was gazing at her with an odd, unreadable expression on his face.

She finished layering the remaining apples and bread crumbs into the bowl, put the cover on, then slipped the bowl into the oven. The temptation to look at him again tugged at her. She fought it down and busied herself cleaning off the worktable.

"Good breakfast, Callie. See ya at supper." Joe's chair scraped on the floor. She glanced toward the table, watched him pull on his battered felt hat and limp toward the door.

Ezra drained his cup and rose.

"Wait, Mr.—Ezra. Your wound needs more salve." She lifted the small crock down off the shelf, grabbed a cloth and carried them to the table. "You'll have to sit down."

She avoided his gaze, opened the crock and stepped behind him. "The swelling has gone down some, and the gash is already healing over. It looks much better this morning." She spread some salve on it, wiped her fingers on the cloth and closed the crock.

Muted shouts came from outside.

"What's that?" Ezra surged to his feet and grabbed his jacket.

"They've started rafting." She pivoted, grabbed her cloak and turned to the door. He reached around her and opened it. She rushed out onto the porch and hurried over to the steps. "Look!" She pointed to a pair of rafts of lashed-together logs floating down the flood-swollen Allegheny, then looked at him. His face was a study in amazement.

"I've never seen such a thing. Those rafts are huge!" He shrugged into his jacket, took her cloak from her and held it open.

"It's quite a sight. I've missed seeing them since we moved away." She stepped beneath the cloak, felt the warmth of his fingers on her neck as he draped it around her shoulders. Smooth fingers, not rough or dry or callused.

"You don't live in Pinewood?"

"No. We moved a few years ago. I'm visiting Aunt Sophia."

"I see." He stepped up beside her and peered out over the rippling water. "What are those shanties in the middle of the rafts?"

"They're for cooking and sleeping. See the smoke coming out of the chimney stacks?" She brushed back a curling tendril being stirred by a rising breeze and cast a measuring look at him. "Daniel says people pay to go along on the trip. They take advantage of the opportunity to ride the rafts to Pittsburgh and then head west."

"Brave souls."

Brave souls? What a strange comment from a logger.

He glanced up toward the brightening sky and moved to the top of the steps. "I must get to work and earn my bed and board. Thank you for breakfast." He dipped his head in a polite bow, walked down the steps and headed for the barn.

His limp wasn't as pronounced this morning. She stood staring after him a moment, then turned and went inside to clean up the breakfast dishes and check on the pudding she'd put to bake in the oven for dinner. She was certain now that Ezra Ryder was a liar. All loggers and lumbermen knew about rafting the winter's stockpile of logs down river to market when the spring floods came. Why didn't he?

"Mmm, that roasting chicken smells delicious, Callie. And what is that you're peeling? Rutabaga?"

"Yes." Why didn't Ezra leave? She drew her gaze

from the window and smiled at her aunt. "I thought I would cream them with some carrots for supper."

"That sounds tasty. What's so interesting outside?"

"Nothing really. It's turned into a lovely spring day." She cut a thick slice from the rutabaga and diced it into a pot full of water.

Sophia strolled to the window and looked out. "Ezra is watering one of the horses. I must say I'm surprised. I expected he would eat his free meal, sleep the night in the barn, have breakfast this morning and be on his way. That's what most of the itinerant workers who come begging for food do."

She diced the rest of the rutabaga into the pot and picked up another one to peel. "I don't believe Ezra Ryder is an itinerant worker, Aunt Sophia."

Her aunt's brows rose. "Whatever are you talking about, Callie?"

She frowned, chopped the peeled rutabaga in half, then cut it into thick slices. "Don't you find something… odd about him?"

"*Odd?* In what way?" Her aunt donned an apron, joined her at the worktable and began slicing the cleaned carrots.

"Well, in little things." She glanced out the window. Ezra and the horse were gone. She went back to dicing the rutabaga. "For instance…his clothes are all new, and of good quality."

Sophia nodded. "Yes, I noticed that. But logging is a rough business, and if he had finished a long job perhaps his clothes were worn, and he bought new ones."

She shrugged her shoulders. "Perhaps. His boots are

new, also. And he hesitated when he said the men robbed him of his *wages*."

Sophia met her gaze. "You don't believe he was robbed?"

"Oh, yes." Her hands stilled. "There was anger in his voice when he spoke of it. And his wound bears witness. But I don't believe he was robbed of *wages*." She picked up the last slice of rutabaga and diced it.

"Then what?"

"I don't know." She furrowed her brow and stared into the distance. "Perhaps of his possessions...or money from some source other than logging or like occupations."

"But there would be no reason for him to lie about that."

"I suppose not." She added wood to the fire in the stove, then set the pot of rutabaga on to cook. "But Ezra is hiding something." She thought back to that moment on the porch when he had helped her into her cloak and his hands had brushed against her neck. "He is not a laborer, as he allows us to believe."

"And why do you accuse him of shamming, Callie? What would be his purpose?"

"I don't know, Aunt Sophia. I only know it's so. His face is not tanned from the weather. His hands are smooth, not rough or callused. His speech is educated, and he has impeccable manners. Ezra Ryder is not who he pretends to be."

"You may be right, though I still cannot think of why he would go to such elaborate measures to get a free meal. Nor does it matter to me. But *you* do. And I have taken advantage of your generous nature for too long. Why, you've been so busy cooking and baking for my guests, you haven't even had time to visit your friends."

Her heart sank. *Please, Lord. I'm not ready to face going home.* "I don't mind, Aunt Sophia. I enjoy cooking."

"Even so, you should have time to enjoy your friends before you must leave for home." Sophia added the carrots she'd sliced to the pot of rutabaga and removed her apron. "I'm going to Olville tomorrow and place a notice for a cook with Mr. Percy at *The Citizen*."

Who was Daniel? Callie's brother? Her suitor? Ezra frowned and threw the last shovelful of manure and soiled bedding onto the wagon at the end of the open stall. Whoever Daniel was, he must be a logger. And someone who rated high in Callie Conner's opinion, if the fondness in her voice when she spoke of him was any indication. He scraped the shovel along the planks in the stall gathering the last of the detritus into a pile, scooped it up and tossed it into the wagon. Perhaps Joe would know about Daniel? But if he asked, Joe would know of his interest in Callie.

His interest in Callie.

He braced his folded arm on the shovel handle and stared into the distance. It was true. He was drawn to Callie in a way he'd never experienced with other women. There was something different about her. Something real and honest. But what chance would an itinerant stable hand have of gaining Callie Conner's respect, let alone regard? Perhaps he should ask Mrs. Sheffield for the money to mail a letter to Thomas. He could repay her with interest once his funds came, and then he could take a room in the hotel and— No.

He set his jaw, tossed the shovel in the wagon then led the horse pulling it forward until the box was in front of the next stall. "Whoa. Good girl." He patted the solid shoulder of Mrs. Sheffield's horse, then climbed the ladder to the loft and forked fresh bedding down into the stall he'd just cleaned. He did not want Callie Conner to know about his wealth. He'd had enough of women pretending to care for him because he was rich. He would simply have to take his chances.

He climbed down, put fresh hay in the rack, then untied the guest's horse from the snub post in the center of the barn and led him to the watering trough. At least he could be the best stable hand Mrs. Sheffield had ever had.

The horse lifted his head, snorted. "Had enough, boy?" He led him into the clean stall. "There you are, fellow, fresh hay to eat." The horse stretched his head forward, pulled a mouthful of hay from the rack and started munching. He trailed his hand over the arched neck, patted the sturdy shoulder, then stepped out of the stall, closed the door and moved on to the next. If he hurried with mucking out the stalls, he'd have time to groom the horses before supper.

He went to open the barn door wider and let in more light, glanced toward the hotel and frowned. Callie was standing on the porch laughing with some tall, handsome, well-dressed man. Daniel? No. Daniel was a logger. And, from the looks of things, he had no hold on Callie Conner's affections. It seemed Miss Conner might be interested in wealthy men after all.

Chapter Four

Callie shrugged into her plain, green wool dress and fastened the fabric-covered buttons that marched single-file from the high collar band to the waist. A quick shake settled the full skirt over her petticoats and straightened the hem. Two small tugs pulled the long sleeves down to her wrists. Now, for her hair. She sighed, looked into the mirror over the washstand and undid the bow at the nape of her neck. The ribbon came free in her hand, and her thick, curly hair spread across her back and shoulders like a frothy, black cloud.

She frowned, grabbed her brush and turned from the mirror. An image of the smooth, thick roll of dark chestnut hair that graced the nape of Willa's neck rose in her mind. She'd always envied Willa her well-behaved hair. She bent forward, brushed her silky curls toward the crown of her head, grabbed the green ribbon that matched her dress, then paused and listened to the muted sounds coming from the kitchen. Why was Sophia up so early? To prepare for her trip to Olville? A spasm hit her stomach.

She straightened and hurried to her door, her unrestrained curls bouncing on her shoulders and down her back. "Aunt Sophia, I need to—Ezra!" What was the man doing in the kitchen?

He pivoted. Stared. The pile of stovewood in his arms slipped and tumbled to the floor.

Her hair! She whirled back into her bedroom and slammed the door, her cheeks burning.

"Mercy..."

The word came through the door, gruff and sort of strangled sounding. Then came a sound of movement, followed by wood thudding against wood.

She closed her eyes and took a deep breath to calm her racing pulse, then walked to the washstand to finish her toilette. The reflection in the mirror of her long, flowing curls brought the heat surging back into her cheeks. Ezra Ryder had seen her looking like that.

She snatched up her brush and swept her hair toward her crown, wound the green ribbon around the thick mass and tied it off, capturing as many of the rebellious ends as possible. As always, several strands escaped.

She leaned toward the small, framed mirror, caught up the errant strands and jabbed them into the curly pile atop her head. That was better.

A quick twist of her wrist turned down the wick and snuffed the lamp. She tiptoed to the door and pressed her ear against one of the panels. Silence. Had he gone? No matter. There was work to be done. She squared her shoulders, pulled the door open and strode out into the kitchen.

Empty.

Thank goodness! She collapsed against the worktable and blew her breath out in a sharp gust.

The back door opened.

She whipped around, watched in dismay as Ezra, his arms again loaded with stovewood, backed into the room, held the door from slamming with his booted foot, then turned toward the woodbox. Their gazes met. She stiffened, waited for his comment on her abandoned appearance at their earlier encounter.

He dipped his head. "Good morning, Callie. I'm sorry if I startled you earlier, but I noticed the woodbox was almost empty when I finished supper last night and thought I'd fill it." He emptied the load in his arms into the box, straightened and smiled. "I wanted to be sure there was wood enough for you to make breakfast. And some of that good coffee."

She gave a stiff nod.

"Well, I'll get out of your way." He stepped up beside her and picked up an old, dented lantern sitting on the worktable. The circle of golden light around them wavered. He nodded and headed for the back door.

He wasn't going to say anything about her appearance? No comment about her long, curling tresses? No flowery compliments about her beauty? The tension in her shoulders eased. "If you've no pressing work to do, I can have coffee ready in a few minutes. It's the least I can do in return for your bringing in the firewood."

He stopped, and turned. "That's not necessary—but there's no work pressing enough to make me miss a good cup of coffee."

It was impossible not to respond to his grin. Her lips

tugged upward. "Then if you will light the lamps, I'll start the coffee." She turned to the stove and reached for the door to the firebox, felt the heat radiating off it and glanced at the dampers. They'd been opened a bit. "You started the fire?"

"Yes. I hope that's all right?"

He was close behind her—too close. In her experience that meant he would try to steal a kiss. She braced herself, gripped a cooking fork and glanced over her shoulder. He was standing with his back toward her, lifting down one of the lamps that hung over the worktable. The tension flowed from her. "Of course. Thank you."

She frowned, grabbed the coffeepot, lifted the tin of ground java off the shelf and inched to the side. She hadn't thought about how close they would be while he was lighting the lamps. She scooped some of the coffee into the pot, replaced the tin on the shelf, then moved to the sink cupboard and ladled in water from the bucket.

He adjusted the wick on the first lamp to a steady flame, hung it back on its hook over the worktable and moved to lift down the second lamp.

He certainly had broad shoulders for a lean man. She eyed the narrow space between his body and the stove, changed direction and walked around the other end of the table.

"Bringing in firewood and starting the fire brought back memories. It made me feel right at home." He gave a soft, low chuckle that made her want to share the memories. "When we lived on the farm, I did those chores for my mother before I headed out to the barn to help my father."

She set the coffeepot on the front stove plate where it would heat rapidly, and let her mind form a dream of such a life.

Light swayed side to side on the wall in front of her, shadows danced, then steadied. He'd hung the second lamp. She heard him step toward the dining table and let out a quiet breath of relief. He'd be out of the way now. She could start breakfast.

She turned toward the worktable, collided with his solid body and bounced backward toward the stove. He shot out his hands, grabbed her upper arms and yanked her back toward him.

"Sorry. I should have warned you I was behind you. I was after the lamp on the shelf. You didn't burn yourself?"

She gazed up into his blue eyes warm with concern and shook her head. "No. You caught me in time." Heat from his hands passed through her sleeves and warmed her skin, spread out into a shiver. She held herself from leaning forward to breathe in the blend of fresh air, hay, horses and witch hazel that clung to him.

"You're trembling."

His eyes darkened. His gaze dropped to her mouth, jerked back up to her eyes. His brows knit together. His hands lifted from her arms and cold replaced the warmth. She shivered and stepped back.

"I think you were more shaken than you realize. Perhaps you should sit down and rest a moment."

She shook her head, avoided his eyes. "I'm fine. And I've work to do. The guests will be wanting their breakfasts. Some of them like to leave at first light."

Speaking of the commonplace settled her shaken nerves. She checked on the coffee, stepped to the pantry and gathered the dry ingredients for griddle cakes, placed them on the table and walked to the door. She draped her cloak around her shoulders, snatched the basket off its peg and stepped out onto the porch.

The sky was brightening in the east. Dawn was on the way. She'd have to hurry. She moved down the steps and headed for the buttery to get eggs and milk and bacon. Her steps lagged by the door. She glanced down the pathway where Ezra had come striding to her to ask for food and her mood went as gray as the sky in the west.

Why did he let them think he was a logger? What was he hiding? Mr. Ezra Ryder was most certainly a liar. She'd best not forget that just because he had a disarming smile and told charming tales of living on a farm.

Ezra turned at the sound of quick, light footsteps, spotted the tall, slender woman hurrying through the stream of sunlight coming in the barn door and stepped out of the stall. "Good morning, Mrs. Sheffield. May I be of service?"

Surprise swept across Sophia Sheffield's face. "You're still here, Ezra?"

He dipped his head in polite acknowledgment. "The stalls are cleaned, but I have not yet finished cleaning the barn."

"Well, gracious, I didn't mean you had to set the whole barn to rights in exchange for a meal and a night's sleep."

"We made a deal, Mrs. Sheffield. And I am a man of my word." Would it work? Would she allow him to stay?

"Hmm." Sophia gave a small nod and stepped to the stall on her left, peered inside and moved on to the next.

He thought of his head groom at home, tamped down his amusement and stood quietly and waited. It was odd being on the other end of such a decision—made one want to squirm. He'd be a little more patient and understanding of job applicants from now on.

"Where is Joseph?"

"He went to the apothecary to get some ointment. His back is troubling him."

"I see." Sophia turned to face him. "You've made an excellent job of cleaning these stalls, Ezra. You said you were raised on a farm?"

"Yes."

"And did you handle the horses?"

He smiled and nodded. "I did indeed, madam. My father always said I had a gift for handling them."

She nodded, gave him a speculative look. "Would you be interested in staying on to help Joseph? I would pay you a fair wage in addition to your meals. And you would keep your sleeping quarters in the equipment room."

He hid his elation with a small bow. "I would be most appreciative of the opportunity, Mrs. Sheffield."

"Then you will help Joseph with the horses as well as cleaning the stalls, but mind you, my guests' horses must be fed and cared for as their owners dictate."

"I understand."

"Very well. You may start your employment by hitching Star to the shay and bringing it to the back door. Come to the kitchen when it's ready." She turned and walked away, the dust motes disturbed by the hems of her long skirts dancing in the sunlight as she neared the open doors.

He listened to her soft footfalls hurrying toward the hotel and let his smile free. He'd done it. His hard work had earned him employment with Sophia Sheffield and, more importantly, the opportunity to get to know Callie Conner. The way she had looked this morning... He yanked his thoughts from the memory, spun on his heel and headed for Star's stall.

Callie stiffened at the opening of the door. It was too soon for Sophia to return from her trip to the post office, and Joe never came to the kitchen except for meals. It had to be Ezra. Presumptuous of him to enter without knocking. Warmth climbed into her cheeks at the memory of him holding her so close earlier. If he thought...

She turned from stirring the stew simmering over the fire, the spoon she'd been using held like a weapon in front of her. "Aunt Sophia!" She glanced at the basket on Sophia's arm. It was empty. "You're back early. Is something wrong?"

Her aunt placed the basket on the table, removed her bonnet and looked across the kitchen at her. "I chanced to meet Doctor Palmer on my way to the mercantile. Charlotte Deering had her baby early. She had a rough time of it."

Concern shot through her. "Is Charlotte all right? And the baby?"

"Thankfully, yes." Sophia draped her shawl over a chair and smoothed back her hair. "Doctor Palmer decided to check on her last night on his way home from a call at the Hoffmans. She'd been in labor all day and was weak and exhausted. The baby was in the wrong position. She never could have birthed it on her own. He said it was a near thing, but he was able to save them both—though the baby is only a little scrap of a thing."

"Thank the good Lord Doctor Palmer chanced to stop by."

"Yes. He says Charlotte has to stay in bed until she mends or she could bleed to death, and that she has no one to do for her or her little ones. Charley's gone downriver with the rafts."

Tears stung her eyes at the thought of the young woman's plight. "Perhaps we could bring Charlotte and the children here and I could care for her. She could have my bed and—" Shock turned her mute when Sophia shook her head. Her aunt was the most generous person she'd ever known. Why would she refuse?

"I offered to bring Charlotte and the children here, but Doctor Palmer said it would not be safe to move her. So, I told him I would send meals and see the chores are taken care of meanwhile. But we must hurry. Charlotte is alone with those small children. What have you on hand?"

She should have known. She smiled as Sophia joined her and glanced down at the pot of food hanging over the fire.

"That's venison stew. And there's bread and apple butter. And I'm sure the children would like some doughnuts." She pointed to the crusty, brown rounds draining on the slotted rack resting atop the dishpan she used to mix the dough for bread.

"*Wonderful*. The stew should help Charlotte regain her strength. And those little ones— Yes, Cora?"

"There's two gentlemen want rooms, Mrs. Sheffield. And Mr. Betz is wanting to leave. He's got Mr. Totten holding the trolley out front for him." The maid scuttled back to her work.

"Oh, bother!" Sophia scowled and headed for the hallway that led to the front of the hotel. "Gather the food into a basket, Callie—and don't forget oatmeal and a bit of sugar. Sweetened oatmeal water might keep the baby alive until Charlotte is able to nurse him. Oh, and take extra broth from the stew. Get as much of it into Charlotte as you can."

"*Me?*"

Sophia paused at the door, turned to look at her. "Why, yes. *I* cannot leave the hotel. Now, hurry, dear. Ezra will be bringing the shay for you any moment. Tell him I said he's to wait and bring you home. He can occupy himself doing any heavy chores. And don't hurry, dear. Wait until you have those children in bed for the night before leaving. I'll manage supper. It won't be the first time."

"But—" she stopped, shook her head and picked up a large, wicker basket off the floor at the end of the fireplace.

"What is it, dear?"

"Nothing really. It's only that I thought Ezra would be gone by now."

"Oh. He did an excellent job on the stalls. I've asked him to stay."

Chapter Five

Callie clutched the hastily assembled bundle in her arms and hurried down the path. If she were quick enough, she could climb into the shay before Ezra could secure the basket on the shelf in back and come around to assist her. Since it was certain he would. The man's manners were faultless. But, after this morning, she was leery of letting him hand her into the vehicle. Not that he'd done anything wrong. Far from it.

She laid the bundle on the seat, gripped the dashboard, placed her booted foot on the small iron rung and stepped up. Ezra's actions had been innocent enough—even heroic, saving her from a possible burn. And he had made no attempt to take advantage of the situation—as her wealthy suitors would have done. For that she was grateful. Still, the thought of her hand in his was unsettling. The man made her nervous. Which was odd, since she had no such reaction to the wealthy men courting her. Indeed, she had become quite adept at escaping their advances without causing offense. Her father had cautioned that she was not to offend the suitors he permitted to call. After all, it might lower their bid for her hand.

The bitter thought stole the luster from the sunny day. She frowned, shook out her long skirts, settled herself and lifted the bundle onto her lap. The shay trembled as the weight of the basket hit the shelf and the attached straps were tugged tight around it. Ezra's boots crunched on the gravel. A flutter rippled through her stomach. She stole a sidelong glance as he stepped to the hitching post. There was no sign of a limp. And the swelling on his head was gone—though the scab of the healing gash was visible at his crown. What was the truth about Ezra Ryder? He was no more a logger than she. Why did he lie? He turned toward the shay, the freed reins held in his hand, and she jerked her gaze from him. Heat crept into her cheeks. And of what concern were Ezra Ryder's doings to her? She had troubles enough of her own to ponder. She straightened in the seat and pulled her burnoose close about her.

The vehicle dipped left as Ezra stepped up, ducked beneath the hood and took his seat. His shoulder brushed against hers. She scooted as far right as possible in the narrow space and looked straight ahead, wishing that Sophia had ordered the carriage brought around instead of the smaller shay.

"Ready?"

She glanced over and met Ezra's smiling gaze. Another flutter tickled her stomach. She must have been feeling more confined since her arrival than she realized if the prospect of a simple ride to the country brought such a reaction. She pressed the bundle hard against her abdomen to stop the sensation and nodded. "Yes."

He made a clicking sound and shook the reins. Star moved forward and the shay rolled along the graveled way to the entrance to Main Street and stopped. "You'll have to direct me, Callie. All I know of Pinewood is the wooden walkway between Cargrave's Mercantile and your aunt's hotel."

She looked away from his smile. There was something of the little boy in it that made her want to trust him, and she'd trust a liar as far as a pig could fly. "We go left, then turn right onto Oak Street." She gestured across the road a short way up Main Street from the hotel. "It's there, beyond the gazebo."

A wagon loaded with bundles of thick, wood shingles rumbled by, headed toward Olville. She held herself immobile as Ezra flicked the reins and urged Star out onto Main Street in the wagon's wake.

Olville. In the concern and bustle over Charlotte, she'd forgotten about Sophia's trip. Relief stole the tension from her body. Sophia would not be going to Olville today, and the *Citizen* was only printed on Fridays. She was safe for another week.

Star's hooves thudded against the drying mud of the roadbed. The shay swayed around the corner onto Oak Street, rumbled past the gazebo in the park on the corner. She shifted her gaze to the left side of the street, spotted the Hall home ahead and smiled. She'd spent a lot of time in that house when she was young. She and Willa and Sadie coming to play with Ellen—or to get Ellen to come off on an adventure with them. Her smile turned into a sigh. So much had changed. Sadie had moved to Rochester. She now lived in Buffalo. And Ellen was in Buffalo, too, staying with her Aunt Berdena. But they had little in common now, only their memories. Ellen was after a rich husband and loved every minute of the social whirl, coveting the attentions of the wealthy men drawn by her blonde beauty. She was welcome to them. Including Jacob Strand. *Especially* Jacob Strand. The man was beyond—

"There's a bell hanging on the porch of that small building. Is that a schoolhouse?"

She started, drawn out of her thoughts by Ezra's question. "Yes, it is. My friend, Willa, was the schoolmarm until a few months ago."

He looked her way. "She lost her position?"

"She got married." Amusement rippled through her. Willa, who had trusted neither men nor God and vowed she would never marry, was the first of the four of them to do so. Matthew Calvert had come to pastor Pinewood Church, and his love and lopsided grin had brought the wall of defense around her friend's heart crashing down as surely as the walls of Jericho had tumbled at a shout. Now, Willa was Matthew's wife and mother to his charges—the young son and daughter of his late brother.

Envy rose, fastened a choking grip on her heart. She was happy for Willa, truly she was. But, oh how she wished she could marry a man like Matthew. An honest man who would love her for herself. Not one of the rich men who took one look at her and professed undying love. Liars! They didn't even *know* her. If they did, they would know she was not impressed by their wealth or their arrogant boastings and would not be *bought*. Pain shot up her arm. She glanced down. Her fingers were buried in the bundle of old sheeting. She took a slow breath and relaxed her grip, dipped her head toward the dirt road that wound up the hill on their left. "We'll turn here."

Ezra looked from the spidery shadows on the dirt road to the bare limbs of the huge trees that cast them. What a beautiful, shaded lane this would be in the summer. Too bad he wouldn't be around to enjoy a ride with Callie then.

He lowered his gaze, shifted it to the right. The rough ride over the rain-gouged gullies in the road had shaken Callie's hood back a bit, exposing her exquisite profile. He had a sudden urge to make her look at him, talk to him. She'd been quiet since they'd left the village. "It's a nice day. The sun is quite cheering, though there's still a chill to the air."

"Yes." She glanced his way, then tugged her hood forward.

He frowned and shifted his gaze back to the road. Polite and brief. Clearly, Callie did not care to engage in conversation with him. Why? Was it her initial suspicion of him? Or had she sensed his intent this morning when he'd thought about kissing her? His tenacious side reared, formed a list of questions she would have to answer with more than a yes or no. He wasn't a successful businessman because he backed away from a tough opponent. And the first step to making a fair and beneficial deal was to get your adversary to talk with you.

He tugged gently on the right rein turning Star into the sharp curve ahead. "This road is getting pretty bad. How much farther do we have to go?"

"I don't— Oh!"

Callie bumped hard against him as they rounded the curve and the front wheels dropped into a wide washout running diagonally across the road. He shot his arm out to brace her as Star lunged forward and the shay rocked up and over the other edge.

"Whoa, Star!" The shay shuddered to a halt. He dropped the reins and twisted toward Callie, their faces almost touching in the small enclosed area beneath the hood. His heart jolted against his ribs. "Are you all right?" He searched her face, looked into her eyes. So close…

She gave a little nod, and the death grip she had on his arm released. He sucked in air, drew back and worked to get his pulse under control as she straightened and slid as far as possible toward her side of the seat. She turned her head toward him. Her gaze fastened on his, but shifted away before he could read her expression.

"Once again, I must thank you, Ezra. That is the second time today you have saved me from possible harm."

"No thanks are needed." Her violet-blue gaze touched his again, then slid away.

"Nonetheless, I appreciate your thoughtfulness, and your…concern for my well-being."

Her soft voice held an undercurrent he could not decipher. He rose and backed out of the shay, away from temptation. "I'll just check for any damage, and then we'll be on our way." He glanced at the wheels, ducked down to look over the undercarriage, then walked to her side and did the same.

She leaned out and turned her face toward him. "It's a good thing you strapped the basket down tight. There would be a frightful mess if the lid had come off the pot of stew."

His lips quirked. It had taken an almost accident, but at last she had addressed him voluntarily. "Not to mention the waste of your excellent cooking." He ran his hand along a spoke of the wheel to keep himself from stepping forward and kissing her.

"Is anything broken?"

"It doesn't appear so. I believe it's safe to go on."

"It shouldn't be far. Aunt Sophia said the Deering farm is the first one on this road."

Her voice held a different tone. He straightened and looked at her. She smiled. A genuine, friendly smile that was unbelievably sweet—not at all like the heretofore cool and polite curve of the lips she'd given him. And her eyes, her incredibly beautiful violet-blue eyes, had lost their guarded look. There was a warmth, a *trust* in their steady gaze. It was tentative to be sure, but it was there. What had changed? No matter. The change was something to build on. He'd figure out the reason for it later. He brushed his hands free of dirt and gave her a wry grin. "I'll try not to wreck the shay and spill the stew before we get there."

He'd not heard her laugh before. It was like music. *Lord, I don't know what the future holds. But, whatever it is, please, let me never disappoint this woman.*

He walked back around to his side, climbed in and

urged Star forward, keeping a tight rein on the growing wish to take the sweetness that was Callie Conner into his arms.

Ezra carried the cot and blankets into the barn, went back into the equipment room and brought out the tonsorial case and his jacket. He snatched the broom from where it stood propped in the corner and went back inside and destroyed the cobwebs clinging to the beams in the ceiling. The thought of a spider dropping down on him while he slept held little appeal. And he wasn't going anywhere. Not after today.

Callie was so *beautiful*. So *unspoiled*. Could it be true? The woman affected him like no other he'd ever met.

He yanked the dusty, scarred chest into the center of the small room, manhandled the tin cupboard out of the corner and swept down the walls, including the halters and harness equipment hanging from pegs. They'd been sorely neglected. He'd start oiling them when he'd finished cleaning the barn. He stomped a scurrying spider and started sweeping the floor. Dust swirled in the dull light of the lantern.

He'd never in his life seen a sight that could equal the beauty of Callie Conner standing in that doorway this morning with her violet eyes shaded by her long, black lashes, her delicate features warmed by the golden light of the lantern and her hair— Whoo! Her *hair*.

He puffed out a breath and swept with new vigor. He'd been so stunned by the sight of her with those black, silky curls around her face and tumbling over her shoulders he'd dropped that whole armload of firewood. Shocked himself. And her, too. She'd whirled into that other room and slammed that door faster than a blink.

He coughed, shot the pile of debris he'd swept up out into the barn area and hurried out the door to catch a breath of dust-free air. Callie Conner was an enigma. Every other woman he knew would have taken advantage of that moment. And the moment later on, too, when he'd caught her to keep her from burning herself on the stove. He'd been so tempted by her.

The women he knew would have encouraged him to kiss them. Of course, they knew he was wealthy. It was so good to not have that problem. To not have to wonder if it was you or your money a person was interested in. Not that Callie had shown any interest.

He dunked a grooming cloth into the watering trough and strode back into the equipment room. A few quick swipes and moonlight streamed through the small window to mix with the lantern's glow. He ran the cloth over the dusty chest, shoved it back against the wall and did the same to the tin cupboard.

Perhaps that's why Callie hadn't encouraged him. Perhaps she thought he was just a poor, itinerant worker with nothing to offer her. She had certainly seemed friendly toward that well-dressed man he'd seen her with on the porch. She hadn't smiled at him like that. Until later on. After their near accident in the shay. He'd been sorely tempted to kiss her then, too, with their faces so close, and her holding on to his arm. If she had shown any encouragement at all he'd have given in and pulled her into his arms. But she had slipped away from him to her side of the seat.

Perhaps she hadn't encouraged him to kiss her because she was promised to someone.

An odd mixture of anger, helplessness and frustration struck him at that thought. He threw the wet rag over a nail in the wall, grabbed up the tonsorial case and put it beside the lantern sitting on a thick plank shelf that had held old horseshoes. He manhandled a short, thick log into the room, upended it beneath the shelf, plunked a bucket on top and felt some better after the physical exertion. Another cloth draped over the bucket's handle completed his personal grooming area.

Or maybe Callie was exactly what she seemed—a woman totally unaffected by her beauty, and free of guile.

The way she'd been with those children today. And the sight of her cuddling that tiny infant...

The frustration swarmed back. He pivoted on his heel, strode to the cot and carried it back into the cleaned equipment room. One thing was certain, he was not going to leave the Sheffield house until he found out the truth about Callie and his growing attraction to her. And now, thanks to Sophia Sheffield, he would be able to maintain his disguise as a laborer. She had given him the perfect excuse to stay.

It was useless. The longing in her heart wouldn't let her sleep. She never should have held Charlotte Deering's tiny newborn. But she'd been unable to resist. Callie tossed back the covers, grabbed her dressing gown from the foot of the bed and pushed her feet into her slippers. She needed something warm and comforting—like the strong arms of a husband who loved her. But she'd have to settle for a cup of tea.

She shrugged into the dressing gown, fastened the ties and walked out into the kitchen. Moonlight streamed in the windows, made a dark shadow of the open doorway to Sophia's private quarters. She tiptoed over and pulled her aunt's door closed, stopping before the latch clicked into place and woke her. She was too vulnerable to hide her feelings in a chatty conversation.

A twist of the damper in the pipe and another to open the bottom draft brought the embers in the stove to life. She grabbed the lifter, quietly set aside the front plate, then reached for some wood. There were only a few pieces in the bottom of the box.

The image of Ezra standing in the kitchen with his arms full of stove wood snapped into her mind. Would he bring more in the morning? Or would he decide to move on in spite of her aunt's offer of steady work? Who knew what to expect of Ezra Ryder, except for good manners?

She added three small sticks of wood to the glowing embers, ladled water into the iron teakettle and set it over the fire. Caring for the Deering children today had awakened the longing in her heart for a family of her own. And holding that tiny newborn... Tears flooded her eyes. It was going to be a long night.

The silk of her dressing gown whispered softly in the silence as she placed the china teapot on the worktable and crossed to the shelves on the wall. She reached for the tin of tea, paused and stepped closer to the window. A small square of yellow lantern light glowed through the silver of the moonlit night. The equipment room window. Ezra was awake. What was he doing at this late hour?

She frowned, took down the tea and walked back to spoon some into the teapot. He'd worked hard today. Whatever else Ezra was lying about, there was no gainsaying the fact that he knew what was needed on a farm. She'd caught glimpses of him out the window, tossing hay to the cows and carrying buckets out to the pigpen. And then he'd found a hen's nest...

She put down the spoon and rested her hands on the table, remembering the way he'd come to the house and lifted Lily into his arms, took little Asa by the hand and went back out to show them the baby chicks. And the way he'd coaxed them into eating supper by telling them silly stories about animals until they forgot to be upset about their mama not getting out of bed.

Did Ezra have children of his own? Is that why he'd been so relaxed and natural with the Deering children? The men she knew were uncomfortable around two- and three-year-old toddlers. She placed the lid on the tea tin, carried it back to the shelf and peered out the window. The barn loomed in the darkness, the moonlight casting an argent sheen on the gambrel roof. There was no lantern light glowing in the small window. He'd gone to bed. Did he have a wife somewhere wishing he was home with her?

The thought sickened her. She didn't want to believe it. But it was certain the man was hiding something. Why not a family? Perhaps that's why he hadn't taken advantage of the opportunity to kiss her this morning. Or in the shay.

It was the first time in her life she'd wanted a man to kiss her…

Oh, how *foolish* was she, letting a liar reach her heart. She knew better than that. And it would stop right now. The silk dressing gown billowed out around her as she turned from the window and went to pour the water for her tea.

Chapter Six

Knuckles beat a sharp tattoo against wood.

Callie jumped, the knife in her hand slicing through the smoked ham to strike the bone.

"Gracious! Who would that be at this early hour?" Sophia put a towel-wrapped loaf of bread into the basket they were readying and hurried to the door.

"Why, Casper Karcher! You about startled the life out of us. What brings you knocking on my door? Come in." Sophia stepped back and opened the door wide.

Callie smiled as her aunt's old friend stepped across the threshold. "I've fresh coffee brewing, Mr. Karcher. Would you care for a cup?"

The lanky man looked her way and shook his head. "It smells good, Callie, but I've no time for socializing. I've got a wagonload of grain to get to Olville." He turned back to her aunt. "I stopped to tell you there's no more call for you to concern yourself with Charley's family. Joanna heard about the baby being early and all, so I took Agnes over. She'll stay and do for Charlotte and the little ones until there's no more need. And Seth will see to the chores."

"How kind of your children. Thank you for stopping to let me know, Casper."

"Didn't want Callie going out there for naught." The man's homely face was transformed by a smile. "Sorry about the scare, Sophie." His smile widened into a grin. "Hiding behind that bush in the schoolyard and jumping out at you always made you scream. Guess you haven't changed much."

"Apparently, neither have you, Casper."

He chuckled at her aunt's rejoinder and turned away.

"Remember me to Joanna!" Sophia shut the door and looked over at her. "Well, that's good news. Agnes is a very competent young woman. She will take good care of Charlotte and the children."

"Yes." She looked down at the sliced ham she'd intended for Lily and Asa's lunch and fought to push back the cloud of disappointment settling over her. That's what she got for allowing herself to pretend. To dream. But, she'd thought she'd have another few days.

"Is there something wrong, dear?"

She tensed as Sophia came close. She couldn't deny it outright, her aunt was far too discerning for that. "Not really. It's only that I enjoyed Charlotte's children yesterday." She forced a smile. "I seldom see children, and I was looking forward to being with them again today."

Sophia looked at her.

Oh, dear. She shouldn't have said that.

"You have no friends with children?"

"A few. But they employ wet nurses and nannies." It

wouldn't do for them to miss their teas and parties and soirees. Her stomach clenched in a painful spasm. That would be *her* life if she married into that elite circle as her mother and father wished.

"Hmm." Sophia removed the bread from the basket.

Please let that satisfy her. She tightened her grip on the knife she held and sliced ham to avoid Sophia's gaze.

"Mr. Anderson and Mr. Gerben left yesterday afternoon. I've only three guests at present."

What? She glanced up. "I beg your pardon?"

Sophia's head dipped toward the table. "That seems like quite a bit of ham."

She looked down at the pile of slices she'd amassed. Another mistake. There was far too much to fry for breakfast. "What I don't use this morning, I will combine with potatoes and onions to bake for supper."

"Hmm. The guests should enjoy that. Perhaps some slaw, also." Her aunt set the emptied basket on the floor at the end of the fireplace. "Have we any cabbages?"

So casual. So…*disarming.* "Yes. Mr. Hoffman brought us three large ones when he delivered the milk and cheese." She rubbed her palms against her apron and moved toward the door. "I need to get eggs for breakfast." *And get outside before you continue questioning me about that slip of the tongue.* She reached for her cape.

"You should have your own."

Too late. Perhaps humor would divert her. "Eggs?"

"Children."

"I believe one needs a husband to accomplish that."

She gave a little laugh and stepped toward the door, careful to keep her back toward her aunt.

"And that is another thing you should have, a husband. Since you were a little girl, all you've wanted was to be married and have a family. Why aren't you married or betrothed, Callie? And don't give me some nonsense about not being asked. I'm not blind. You are a sweet, intelligent and exceptionally beautiful young woman, gifted in the art of keeping a home. Yet you are still alone. Even most less attractive, less talented young women are married by your age. You'll soon be twenty."

Her aunt's skirts rustled, the hems brushed against the floor and the soft pad of her slippers drew near. She blew out a slow breath and turned to face her.

"I know you're troubled and unhappy, Callie. You've been hiding in this kitchen since you arrived." Sophia rested a hand on her arm. "Why don't you tell me what's wrong, dear? Is it your mother and father, because I—"

"No!" She clenched the cape in her hands as the lie burst from her mouth. *Forgive me, Lord.* "I mean, not exactly." She groped through her memory for the explanation Willa had suggested the other night. "The truth is…there are men vying for my hand. I came to stay with you to gain time to decide what to do."

"You mean, which man you will choose?"

"I—" She stopped, took a breath. Unless God intervened that is exactly what she would have to do. *I've given it You, Almighty God. Have Your way.* "Yes."

She stood quietly under Sophia's measuring gaze. She dare not look away, or close her eyes, or burst into tears, or do any of the things the pressure in her chest demanded she do.

Sophia's lips pursed. She gave a series of small, almost imperceptible nods, reached out and took the cape from her. "Sit down, Callie."

She stared down at her empty hands and made one more try. "The eggs…"

"We've time for a chat." Sophia hung the cape back on a peg and gestured toward the table. "The guests won't begin stirring until dawn breaks."

She did as she was bid, braced herself as Sophia pulled a chair beside her, sat and took hold of her hand.

"Now, tell me…exactly what do you mean by 'vying,' dear? Do you mean these gentlemen are competing in courtship of you, for your heart? Or do you mean they are contending against each other with your father, who will sell his blessing on your marriage to the highest bidder?"

She tried her best, but the tears would not be stopped. They welled in her eyes. She blinked, and stared down at their joined hands.

"So Ellen was right."

"Ellen?" She jerked her gaze to Sophia's face.

"I ran into Frieda when I went for the mail yesterday. She asked how you were—said she'd been concerned about your state of mind ever since she received Ellen's letter telling her how you'd run off without accepting any of the gentlemen who had received your father's permission to pay court to you."

She surged to her feet. "I should have *known* Ellen

would write to her mother about me. And that Mrs. Hall would tell you."

"They do like to gossip, dear. And, to be fair, Ellen is concerned about you."

"Ha! She only wants to know when I will return so she can make her plans accordingly. There is no other woman on the Buffalo social circuit who can match Ellen's beauty and she's thrilled to have the attentions of all those wealthy men to herself. She's after a rich husband, and does not bother to hide the fact. At least not from me. Well, Ellen is welcome to the whole, arrogant, self-serving, duplicitous lot of them!" She stopped and stared at Sophia, horrified by what she'd blurted.

"I hope you have made your feelings clear to Penelope and Edward."

The sound of her mother's and father's names cooled her anger as effectively as a fire being doused by a bucket of the cold flood waters of the Allegheny. She folded her lips over her teeth, spun on her heel and walked to the stove. "I need some tea. Would you care for a cup, Aunt Sophia?"

"You haven't told them you don't wish to marry any of these men?"

She took the tin of tea off the shelf and reached for the china teapot. Sophia wasn't going to give up. She chose her words. "I've tried. Father feels he knows what is best."

"For you? Or for his purse?"

She gasped and whirled about, caution forgotten. "You *know* of their financial straits?"

Her aunt's face went taut. "I know Edward was running through his inheritance like a fire through dry brush before he moved you all to Buffalo." Sophia's eyes narrowed on her. "How did you learn about it? I know Penelope is besotted with the man, but surely she wouldn't tell—"

"No! No, Aunt Sophia, you mustn't think that of Mother. I overheard Father telling her that if they moved to Buffalo and introduced me to the social circuit, a wealthy man would pay handsomely for my hand and their financial future would be secure." Her voice broke. She sat the teapot on the worktable, and swallowed to ease the tightness in her throat.

"And you've been carrying that burden ever since. No wonder you're troubled and unhappy."

Sophia rose, marched toward her and gripped her upper arms. She stood frozen, awed by the sight of her aunt's eyes flashing with violet sparks.

"Now you listen to me, Callie Rose Conner. The Lord did not see fit to bless me with children of my own, but He brought you into my life, and I'll not see your life ruined by the selfish desires and wasteful habits of your father and mother."

Sophia's hands tightened on her arms, gave her a little shake. "You will *not* marry a man to fill your father's purse. That is senseless. Edward will only run through the money the same as he has his inheritance, and, no doubt, in shorter time. And then what? You will be married to a man you don't love and living a lifestyle you have no taste for—and your parents will be no better off than before."

"But, Father and Mother need—"

"No, Callie, that way lies folly. You cannot save your parents from themselves—and I'll not let you sacrifice yourself trying. You will live here with me until you meet a man you wish to marry. And should your parents find themselves in need, they are welcome to come live with me as well. Penelope is my sister and I'll not see her in want. As for her wastrel husband—I'm quite sure he would enjoy strutting among my guests as if he owns Sheffield House."

"Oh, Aunt Sophia—" Her throat closed. She threw her arms about Sophia's neck, buried her head against her shoulder and burst into tears. Sophia's arms closed around her.

"Hush, dear. There's no reason to cry."

"But, I thought—" she gulped back tears "—I thought I'd have to—"

"I know, Callie. But that's over. Everything will be fine."

Bootheels thudded on the porch floor.

She jerked erect. "Breakfast! I forgot all about it." She swiped the tears from her eyes.

Sophia leaned forward, kissed her cheek, then gave her a little push in the direction of her bedroom. "You go freshen your face, dear. I'll deal with Joseph and Ezra."

She ran toward her room, whirled about in the doorway and choked out the words clogging her throat. "I love you, Aunt Sophia."

"I love you, too, dear. Now, go!" Sophia made a shooing motion with her hands as the back door opened.

She darted into her bedroom and shut the door, the beauty of her aunt's smile glowing through a deluge of unstoppable tears.

* * *

The sun hung high in the blue expanse overhead, but the western sky promised rain. Not that it mattered. Nothing could dampen her spirits today. Callie drew her gaze from the dark clouds rolling and piling one against the other in the distance, lifted her skirt hems and dashed out onto Main Street, darted between two wagons and hopped up onto the board walkway on the other side.

Not very decorous behavior for a young lady of her age, but she felt so light since her conversation with Sophia that morning, it was a wonder her feet were even touching the ground. Standing and waiting for the lumbering wagons to pass was unthinkable. She hurried around the parsonage to the back porch and ran up the steps.

"Woof!"

"Hello, Happy." She leaned down and scratched behind the dog's ears. "Aren't you the smart dog, getting up on the porch before the rain comes?" His tail wagged his agreement. She laughed and patted his shoulder, then straightened, tapped her knuckles against the door and entered.

The gray-haired woman at the worktable glanced up from her work and smiled. "Hello, Callie. She's in the sitting room."

"Thanks, Bertha." She hung her burnoose on a peg by the door, sniffed the air and glanced at the dough the woman was rolling out. "Rose water cookies. Yum."

The older woman laughed. "I'll bring you some with tea, soon's the first batch comes out of the oven."

"Lovely!" She smiled and rushed down the hall into the sitting room. "You were right, Willa!"

Willa spun about and rose from her chair at the secretary desk in the corner, her eyes wide, her mouth agape. "Callie! What—"

"I'm *staying,* Willa. I'm going to live with Aunt Sophia." She crossed the room and enfolded her stunned friend in a quick hug, whirled away and came to an abrupt, teetering halt on the tips of her toes. "Oh!" She caught her balance, ignored the heat stealing into her cheeks and smiled at her friend's husband standing in the doorway. "Hello, Reverend."

"Good afternoon, Callie. Forgive my intrusion, but I heard the excitement and came to investigate."

She stared at the man's smile and realized, all over again, why Willa had lost her heart to him. "Please come in and share my good news, Reverend."

"Good news?"

"Callie is going to be staying in Pinewood." Willa turned to her. "I'm so glad you told Sophia the truth." Willa's blue-green eyes searched hers. "You did tell Sophia?"

She shook her head. "Ellen wrote Mrs. Hall about my leaving home without accepting any of the men Father had granted permission to court me, and Mrs. Hall told Aunt Sophia."

"Oh, my. I didn't think of Ellen doing that." Willa sighed and motioned to the chairs by the fireplace. "I must say, I'm not surprised."

"Nor I. But, odd as it sounds, I'm grateful to Ellen." She leaned down and stroked the yellow cat curled on the hearth soaking up the warmth of the fire. "Hello, Tickles."

She smiled at his contented purr and straightened, glanced at Matthew, standing beside Willa's chair, and sobered. "I believe this is one of those times when the Lord works in mysterious ways. My heart was in conflict with my parents' wishes for me to marry a man, for whom I had no personal regard, for his wealth."

She sat, looked over at her friend and smiled. "The other night, Willa told me to trust the Lord. I had struggled against that." She returned her gaze to Matthew. "I was afraid of what He would require of me."

"You're not alone in that, Callie. Many people fear what God will ask of them if they give up control and trust Him to have His way in their lives. But God understands our fears. And He wants only what is best for us."

Matthew's eyes and his soft voice held no condemnation. Something deep inside her eased. She nodded, smiled as Tickles rose and stretched and leapt up into her lap. "I finally came to the place where I gave the situation into God's hands, but I'm afraid it was more out of desperation than trust." The cat purred, his back arching beneath her stroking hand.

"God understands that, too. And He honors that first step of faith."

A smile rose from deep inside, curved her lips. "I believe that's true. For now this has happened. Everything has worked out for the best. Sophia has invited me to live with her—and my parents as well, should they have the need. I will not have to marry for gain, and—"

Lightning snapped, sent a white brightness flickering through the room. Thunder clapped. Rain spattered against the windows, turned into liquid fists beating upon the small panes of glass. "Oh, my, I must be going." She lifted Tickles to the floor and rose.

"I'll get the umbrella and walk you home." Matthew hurried from the room.

Willa rose and linked arms with her. "I'm so happy you'll be living with Sophia, Callie." A smile warmed her friend's face. "It will be like old times, being close to each other. I wish Sadie—"

A loud clap of thunder made them both jump. They laughed and hurried to the kitchen, everything but the need for haste forgotten. She smiled at the housekeeper. "Tea will have to wait for another time, Bertha."

The door burst open. She jumped back as Happy darted inside, followed by little Sally, who threw herself against Willa and buried her face in her long skirt.

Envy, as sharp and jagged as a lightning bolt, jabbed her heart as Willa went to her knees, took her stepdaughter into her arms and stroked her hair in a mother's comforting caress. "It's all right, Sally, you're home now."

Thunder boomed.

Joshua bolted through the door, slammed it behind him. "Made it!" He shook like a dog, drops of water flying off his blond curls onto her dress. He stopped, frowned, then grinned up at her. "Sorry, Miss Callie."

She grinned back. "That's all right, Joshua. I'll have more than a few drops on me by the time I reach home." She took her burnoose off the peg and swirled it around her shoulders.

"I see school was dismissed early—as per the rules

for a storm." Matthew strode into the kitchen, a smile on his face.

She hurried to fasten her cape, then paused and stared at that smile, watched it grow warmer when he stopped beside Willa.

"Want to go for a carriage ride, Mrs. Calvert?"

Pink crept across her friend's cheeks. Love shone in their eyes. She turned from the intimate moment to finish fastening her cape. *Please, Almighty God, if it be Your will—*

"You're safe, small stuff."

She looked back. Matthew was crouched by Sally. He kissed the top of her head, rose and tousled Joshua's curls. "Thanks for taking care of your sister, Josh." A crooked grin slanted his mouth. "Bertha's baking cookies."

An identical grin tilted the boy's mouth. "I smell 'em. C'mon, Happy." He trotted over to Bertha, his dog at his side. Sally lifted her head from Willa's shoulder, sniffed, and hurried after her brother. Tickles strutted into the room.

Her heart clenched at another sharp jab of envy. This was what she wanted. Not an empty life of parties and social pursuits, polite conversations between husbands and wives, and nannies caring for one's children. And now, thanks to Sophia, maybe someday she would have her heart's desires.

"Are you ready?"

Matthew's deep voice drew her from her thoughts. She nodded, gave Willa a quick hug and followed him out the door onto the porch.

Lightning crackled and flashed white light across the darkened sky. Thunder crashed and rumbled. Rain sheeted down from the roiling, black clouds.

"Looks like this is going to be a nasty one. We'd best hurry."

She nodded, pulled her hood up and stepped close. They hurried down the steps and out to the street, the umbrella Matthew held over her quivering and bucking in swirling gusts of wind. He tilted it forward and the driving rain stopped pelting her face. Raindrops slapped at the taut silk in fury, the din drowning out all other sound. Beneath the umbrella's edge she saw a horse's hooves flash by, splashing muddy water. She lifted her hems in front, despaired for her slippers and the back hems of her petticoats and dress.

Matthew grasped her elbow, guided her across the rain-filled ruts of Main Street. The hotel shielded them from the worst of the storm as they hurried around to the back porch. He tightened his grip, helping her up the water-slick steps. Rain drummed on the roof, drowning out the sound of their footsteps as they crossed to the door.

"Thank you for bringing me home." She looked at the rain-soaked front of Matthew's coat and at his hat, dripping rainwater from the brim, and frowned. She leaned close to be heard. "Please come in, Reverend. I'll fix you a good hot cup of tea and—"

He shook his head, sending drops of water flying. "I'd best get back to Willa. I like to be with her in a storm." Something warmed his eyes, then was gone. A memory? Perhaps, judging from the smile playing at his lips.

She tamped down another spurt of envy. "Then you'd best hurry. And tell Willa I said she is to coddle you with a good hot cup of tea in front of that nice warm fire."

His smile widened. "I shall give her your message, but I'll make that tea a cup of strong, black coffee."

Matthew's laugh drew an answering smile from her. He touched the brim of his hat, turned and hurried away.

She watched until he disappeared around the corner of the building. What had happened between Matthew and Willa in a storm? Would she ever have such memories? An image of Ezra leaning over her in the shay flashed into her head.

Lightning sizzled a yellow streak against the growing darkness. She frowned, removed her burnoose, gave it a few shakes to free it of raindrops and went inside.

Hooves thudded against the planks of the barn. Ezra laid the harness he was oiling on the chest, wiped his hands on a clean rag and hurried out into the stable area.

"Good afternoon, sir."

"There's nothing good about it. A man could drown in that rain." The man on the horse looked around, then climbed from the saddle and handed him the reins. "Water Duster, then rub him down and give him feed as well as hay. Put him there in that front corner stall. I don't want him close to the other horses. He gets fractious, especially during a storm. I expect you to keep him calm."

The man slapped rain from his hat, placed it back on his well-groomed head, and brushed at the soaked sleeves of his garrick coat. "Filthy weather." He untied a leather case from behind the saddle, tugged his coat collar up around the back of his neck and strode through the open barn door toward the hotel.

"He's a pleasant one."

He glanced toward Joe's room at the other end of the barn and smiled at the head groom standing in the doorway, turned into a shadow by the lantern light behind him. Joe had befriended him thinking him nothing but a poor drifter, and it felt good. "I guess he doesn't like getting wet." He smiled at Joe's chuckle and gave a gentle tug on the reins. "Come along, Duster. Let's get you that drink of water."

Lightning cracked, flickering light through the dark interior of the barn. Thunder crashed and grumbled. The horse snorted and jerked his head up, the whites of his eyes shining in the glimmering light. He lunged toward the door, hopped on his front legs as the reins drew taut. His hooves landed with a dull thud against the floor. His shoulder muscles bunched.

"Whoa, boy. You're all right." Ezra took a shorter grip on the reins, held the bay's head down and stepped close. "That's better." He stroked the trembling flesh on the tense, arched neck, watched the ears twitching back and forth. "It's only lightning and thunder—it's not going to hurt you. You're all right." He kept his voice low, soothing.

The bay blew, tossed his head and whickered.

"That's right, you can trust me. Now, let's get you into that stall, and I'll bring you a bucket of water." He held the reins close, gave another easy tug.

The horse snorted, then stepped forward. He led him

into the stall, tied the reins to the manger and slipped out of his shirt. "This should help, fella." He draped the shirt over the horse's head, tied the sleeves around its neck and patted the sturdy shoulder, feeling the tense muscles relax. "Good boy."

Lightning glittered through the windows. Duster stood quiet, blinded by the thick, blue wool of the shirt. Thunder grumbled. The bay snorted, pawed at the clean bedding on the stall floor, then quieted.

He hummed a tuneless accompaniment to the drumming rain, removed Duster's saddle and blanket, rubbed his back and girth with a clean feed sack, then moved forward and scooped grain into a feed bucket nailed to the wall. The horse's nostrils twitched. He stretched his muzzle forward and sniffed the offering, blew, then pulled his head back. "All right, it's there when you're ready, fella. I'll give you a good brushing when I get back." He removed the bridle and stepped out of the stall, latched the door and snatched up a bucket.

"Good job, calming that horse." Joe tugged the barn door he'd closed open wide enough to let him go through.

The wind was blowing the rain sideways. He looked at the elderly groom, and gave him a wry grin. "I don't suppose you'd like to get the water?"

The old man chuckled and handed him an old horse blanket. "This'll help keep your undershirt dry. I'll go watch the horse."

"Thanks." He grinned, threw the blanket across his shoulders to dangle down his back, and stepped to the door.

Lightning streaked across the sky, illuminating two

people hurrying up the porch steps of the hotel. Callie and—he squinted through the rain—that man. The one he'd seen her with before. Only this time he was holding Callie by the elbow. The smile she gave him was the same. His stomach tensed, his hand tightened on the bucket handle. Who was that man? And what was he to Callie?

He watched as the man lifted an umbrella over his head, trotted down the steps and hurried away. Callie stood looking after him, a bemused expression on her face, then removed her cape, shook it and went inside.

He frowned, ducked his head and ran to the trough to fill the bucket. Tomorrow he would try and find out who that man was. If you wanted to make a deal, you had to find out who was standing in your way. This situation was no different. Except he'd never before felt as if a horse had kicked him in the stomach.

Chapter Seven

He was doing it again. Ezra jerked his gaze back to his plate. He couldn't stop looking at Callie. Ever since he'd taken his place at the table this morning, he would draw his gaze from her to the others or to his plate or his cup, and then, there he was, looking at her again. It was always difficult to keep from drinking in her beauty, but today there was a sort of happy glow about her that hadn't been there before. It was mesmerizing. And disturbing.

And she was *humming*. The soft, liquid notes seemed to flow out of her straight to his stomach. He was beginning to feel as if he'd been kicked by that horse again. He stabbed a piece of sausage, brought it to his mouth. What had happened to make her so happy? Had it to do with that man she was with yesterday? The sausage turned sour. He frowned, swallowed the meat and lifted his cup. Empty.

"Is something wrong, Ezra?"

He glanced across the table at his employer. There was a cautious, questioning look in Sophia Sheffield's eyes, the kind men had when they felt something unsettling in a deal they'd made. Had Sophia sensed his interest in Callie? Foolish question. How could she not, with him sitting there acting like a besotted schoolboy? He dredged up a smile and set his cup on the table. "I've no coffee."

"I'll get you more." There was no answering smile.

"I'll bring it, Aunt Sophia." He glanced over at Callie, admired the natural grace of her movements as she laid down the fork she was using to turn sausages in a frying pan and reached for the coffeepot at the back of the stove.

"No. I'll get it, dear. You're busy with breakfast for my guests."

He looked back at Sophia, found her gaze steady on him. She rose and walked to the stove, blocking his view of Callie. On purpose? He frowned and took a bite of fried apples. His employer's friendly manner had fled. Obviously, Sophia Sheffield's kindness to an itinerant laborer did not extend to his becoming enamored of her niece. He discarded his plan to get information about the man from her.

There had to be a way to find out who the fellow was and, more importantly, what he was to Callie, without giving himself away any more than he already had. He held back a frown and took a bite of his potatoes, sorting through other possibilities. This afternoon he was going to the mercantile to add a new shirt to the necessary things he'd bought on account now that he had employment. Perhaps he'd see the man in the store and could ask someone about him. Or perhaps the man would be in church tomorrow—with Callie.

That thought turned the potatoes as sour to his tongue as the sausage. He lifted his coffee and took a swallow, all but scalding his mouth and throat. Blast! He'd forgotten Sophia had just refilled his cup. He sucked air through his gritted teeth, then coughed.

Joe slanted a wry look at him. "Hot, was it?"

He managed a grin. "Hot and strong—just as I like it."

Joe chuckled, then turned toward Sophia Sheffield. "Got some bad news. That patch young Daniel put on the barn roof last summer has held up right well to the snow and ice and rain, but we've sprung another leak down at the far end. Rain's dribbling in around the base of the cupola, too. Drops hit me square on the top of the head last night. I reckon a good daub of pitch will take care of it 'til the weather clears and the shingles can be replaced."

Sophia shook her head. "You're not to climb up on that roof with your rheumatism paining you so, Joseph. It's not safe. Daniel's at the lumbering camp, of course, but I'll hire someone—"

"I'll do it." His offer drew Sophia's attention. She swept her gaze over his face, then looked down at his hands. A tiny frown creased her forehead. He glanced down at the healing blisters, his reward for chopping firewood at the Deering farm the other day, and realization struck. It took more than clothes to look like a logger or laborer, and his hands, probably a few other things, had given him away. That was why Sophia and Callie were wary of him. They didn't believe his story—though he had told the truth as far as he went.

"Have you ever repaired a roof, Ezra?"

Sophia looked doubtful. From the corner of his eye he saw Callie hand a platter of potatoes and sausages to the maid to carry to the dining room, then turn their way. The doubt and distrust in her eyes made up his mind. He'd have to go a little deeper into his story. He focused on Sophia and nodded. "My father had a lame leg. Once I was old enough, whenever there was a need, he'd tell me what to do and send me up to the roof to make repairs."

"But you've not done such work since you were young?"

It was a statement, posed as a question. He stole another sidelong look at Callie. She was standing so still she seemed not to be breathing. He took heart that his answer mattered. "That's right. My father died shortly after my twelfth birthday, and the farm was sold to satisfy debt."

He crossed his fork and knife on his empty plate, buying time. How much should he tell? "We moved to the city, and it fell to me to support my mother, sister and brother. I found employment with an insurance broker delivering messages and carrying moneys to the bank. The broker had problems with his eyes and he taught me how to keep the accounts. I've worked in the insurance business ever since."

He stopped, and hoped that was enough truth to erase Callie's mistrust, because he wasn't going to tell her he now *owned* the insurance company. And two banks. And a shipping line—

Callie's skirts rustled. He looked up as she came and stood at the end of the table. "If you're a businessman, Ezra, why were you dressed as a logger when you came?

And why did you let us believe it?" There was a challenge in her voice.

He sifted through the facts, chose what to share. "My cousin suggested I would better fit in with his cohorts if I dressed as a logger for my visit. And after I was set upon by those thieves I had no choice—they took everything but the clothes on my back." He studied her face, read tentative acceptance in her eyes and continued.

"The driver of a supply wagon gave me a ride on the road from Dunkirk, and when we arrived in Pinewood, I found my cousin had left town. I had nowhere to go, and in my wounded condition I needed a place to rest out of the weather. I saw your barn and thought perhaps I could sleep inside." He held his gaze steady on hers. "I was headed there when I saw you holding that basket of food." The doubt left her eyes, and he knew she was remembering their first meeting.

He looked at Sophia and smiled. "And now, I'm a stable hand."

"And a good one you are. Got a way with horses."

He jerked his gaze to Joe, grateful for the unexpected diversion.

The elderly groom thumped him on the back and shoved away from the table, looking over at Sophia Sheffield. "Businessman or not, I never seen the likes of the way Ezra calmed that skittish horse during that storm last night. Sweet-talked him right into that stall while the lightning was flashing and the thunder was rumbling. He knows his way around a barn, too—sees what needs doing, and sets about getting it done. Right now, that's leaks in the roof."

Joe's hand clamped on his shoulder. "Finish up, Ezra. We've got to get that pitch daubed on while the sun's shining. There's no telling when it'll decide to rain again."

"I'm finished." He rose, glancing at Sophia.

She nodded. "Be careful on that roof, Ezra."

"Yes, do be careful. We don't want to have to nurse you through another injury."

His pulse jolted. He shifted his gaze back to Callie. There was warmth in her smile. It looked as if his chances of getting to know her better had just improved. Now if he could only find out about that man…

An account book lay open on the secretary desk in front of her aunt, sunlight from the window lighting its pages. A tiny frown pulled down Sophia's naturally arched eyebrows.

Callie's heart sank at the concerned look on her aunt's face. Was Sophia in financial straits as well? Was nothing ever what it seemed? Her secure feeling evaporated like morning dew. She took a firm grip on the tea tray in her hands and turned to go.

"Callie?" The velvet of Sophia's gown whispered softly as she rose and came to her sitting room door. "Tea? How lovely. Come in, dear."

She forced a smile and shook her head. "I didn't realize you were busy and thought we might chat. I'll come back later."

"Not at all. I'm doing nothing pressing, only checking my accounts." Sophia took the tray from her hands and carried it to the small stretcher table flanked by two Windsor chairs. "I had to secure a loan in order to make extensive repairs after that fire two years ago, and I hope to pay off the remaining debt this year. I want to replace that troublesome barn roof next spring." Sophia gave a delicate sniff. "Mmm, ginger cookies. They smell delicious."

"They should. You're the one that taught me to make them." She gazed about the room and her laughter died. This was her true childhood home. "I learned so much from you, Aunt Sophia. Mother was so often away with Father…"

She shook off the memory and ran her hand over the curved back of the settee that sat at a right angle to the fireplace. A smile warmed her heart and curved her lips at the sight of the needlework frame in front of it. "Do you remember the sampler you were making that I ruined by 'helping'? How old was I? Six or—"

"You were five. And you did not ruin the piece. It hangs over my bed." China chinked as Sophia set their places and poured tea into the cups.

"So, you were able to save the sampler?" She moved to the stone fireplace, lifted one of the pair of chalk pigeons that stood on the mantel and felt a rush of triumph. She'd not been allowed to touch them as a child.

"Callie Rose Conner, I treasure that sampler."

She tossed an astonished glance over her shoulder. "With my oversized, childish stitches in it?" Her mother would not have kept such a disgraceful piece in her house.

"*Because* your oversized, childish stitches are in it." Sophia sat and picked up a cookie, then took a bite. "Mmm, these are good. You have surpassed your teacher, dear."

She blinked and turned to look out the window to hide a sudden onslaught of tears. How foolish to be so moved over her aunt saving her childish gift of help.

"Something interesting outside, dear?"

"Ezra is preparing to climb off the barn roof. Oh, my!" She spun away from the window.

"What is it? Did he fall?" Sophia surged to her feet and hurried toward her.

"No, but he *might*. He's dangling over the roof edge, feeling for the ladder rung with his feet. And he has a *bucket* in his hand. If he loses his grip, or misses that rung—" She pressed her hands against her stomach, feeling sick.

Sophia peered out the window. "It's all right, dear. He's safely on the ladder."

The tension fled, leaving her knees weak. She blew out a breath and took her seat at the table, thankful for the hot tea that would calm her stomach. She took a swallow.

Sophia resumed her seat, and gave her a searching look. "That was quite a strong reaction. Do you care for Ezra, Callie?"

"Well, of course I care about him."

"That's not what I asked, dear."

She looked into her aunt's eyes and discarded any further evasions—they wouldn't work. But what should she answer? She was unwilling to admit, even to herself, the strong draw Ezra Ryder had on her emotions. To acknowledge it would be to give it power. "I believe I could, should I permit myself."

"I see. You have reservations about him, then." Sophia lifted the plate and offered her a cookie. "Is it that he is a mere laborer with no wealth or social position?"

"Certainly not! That is the last thing I care about."

"Then what is it that causes you to hold your affections in check?"

She waved away the cookies, rose and went to the window. The ladder was gone. "That is what I came to speak to you about." She turned back to face her aunt. "Do you think Ezra was telling us the truth this morning?"

"Yes…but I feel his story is incomplete."

Her hope sank like a rock in still water. She'd been wishing that Sophia would tell her her suspicion was nonsense. "So you, too, sense that he is hiding something—not being honest with us?"

Sophia nodded, a thoughtful expression on her face. "I believe he is hiding something, yes. But I also believe he is being honest in what he tells us."

"Subterfuge. I detest that, Aunt Sophia. It colors every conversation of the elites in Buffalo." She wrapped her arms about her torso and turned back to stare out the window. "They are underhanded in their dealings with one another. There is always some hidden purpose for the things they say and do. They are either trying to gain more wealth, or to increase their social standing by buying the grandest house or the fanciest carriage or—"

"—the most beautiful wife?"

"Yes. And I'd rather be a spinster than marry a deceiver. I cannot abide a liar." *And I refuse to fall in love with one.*

* * *

Bells tinkled a warning. Ezra stopped as two women emerged from a millinery shop and threw curious glances his way. He touched the rolled brim of his knit hat and stepped aside to allow them space to pass.

The older woman dipped her head in response. A small smile curved the younger woman's lips. She gave him a coy glance over her shoulder as she turned and followed her mother into the dressmaker's shop next door.

He looked down at his blue wool shirt, coarse twill pants and heavy loggers boots and smiled. There was no sign of wealth to be read in his appearance. That young woman had been interested in *him*. And the friendly nods and smiles he'd received from the people he'd passed on the wood walkway were genuine as well. Their smiles weren't given in the hope of currying favor with a rich man. Nobody knew. To them he was only another laborer.

He whistled a few notes as he strode to Cargrave's Mercantile, then sobered and looked up and down the opposite side of the road in the hope of spotting the man he'd seen with Callie. He'd had no luck thus far.

He frowned, stepped into the recessed entrance and opened the door. Bells jangled. He nodded to those who looked his way, stepped to the dry goods section and eyed the shirts piled on a shelf. Wool shirts, in blue and green and red. He may not be able to purchase a suit that would compete favorably with that man's attire, but he could manage a new shirt. He was heartily sick of the one he was wearing, and, since last night, it smelled of horse.

He reached for a green shirt, then paused as he caught

sight of two other shirts farther along. He fingered the cotton, rather coarse to his touch, but a vast improvement over the wool, especially with warm weather coming. He chose the light gray one over the brown and held the shirt against his shoulders. It was broad enough.

The bells tinkled. He glanced toward the door. A handsome man dressed in a brown suit, a brocade waist-coat, and a spotless white cravat entered. It was him.

"Good afternoon, Reverend."

The chorus erupted around him. *Reverend? Callie's friend was a man of the cloth?* He frowned, and carried the shirt to the counter.

"Good afternoon, everyone." The man glanced his way, gave a polite, friendly nod, then strode to the window in the center of the wall of glass boxes that formed the post office.

"This all for today?"

He pulled his gaze back to the clerk. He could get some writing supplies and send that letter requesting funds home, but he wasn't one to back away from a deal just because the going was tougher than he expected. "Yes, that's all. Put it on my account, please."

He set his jaw, picked up his shirt and walked out of the store, not even casting a sidelong glance at the man. He'd seen enough to know he was in a hard battle for Callie's affections. But it was a battle he meant to win.

Chapter Eight

How was she to concentrate on today's sermon? The man was so...so *there*. She simply found it impossible to ignore him the way she could other men. Callie held back a frown and smiled and nodded to those already seated as she followed her aunt, escorted by Ezra, down the center aisle. What was Sophia thinking asking Ezra to sit with them in her private pew? It had been bad enough when they'd met him on the porch on their way inside. Simply knowing he would be in the building had discomforted her. And, now—

She stiffened as her aunt stopped. Ezra opened the pew door and bowed. Oh, no. Manners dictated he be the last to enter, and she was *not* going to sit beside him. She stepped forward. "Allow me, Aunt Sophia. I know you like sitting near the aisle." The twilled silk of her gown whispered softly as she gathered her full skirt, stepped into the box and sidestepped along the wood seat before her aunt could reply.

"That's far enough, dear. We have plenty of room. The box will seat six."

She stopped and glanced back. Her gaze skipped over her aunt, who had seated herself, and landed full on Ezra. He was looking her way, no doubt waiting for her to sit so he could take his seat.

Gracious, but the man was handsome! Their gazes met. Warmth surged into her face. She dipped her head forward, sank onto the velvet cushion padding the pew and wished she'd worn a bonnet that would hide her reddened cheeks instead of the wide, flower-trimmed ribbon band hat she preferred. And just why was she blushing anyway? Because she found the man's appearance pleasing? She had admired other men's good looks with no such reaction. But it wasn't only that Ezra's features were handsome. He—

There was a clearing of throats, a sound of movement. She lifted her head, rose quickly to her feet as David Dibble stepped to the front of the center aisle. The organ struck a chord for the opening hymn. And she hadn't even heard the opening prayer. She took a breath to compose herself as David Dibble's strong voice led the singing.

"Oh, Lord, our God and Savior true…"

Sophia's soprano rang out pure and clear beside her. She stared straight ahead and added her own soft alto to the singing.

"Our Deliverer in ages past…"

Ezra's tenor, quiet but rich, floated her way from the other end of the box. She stole a quick, sidelong peek at him. He looked so different from when he'd arrived, pale and with his face taut with pain. She'd thought his looks arresting then, but now he'd taken on color from his outside work making his bright blue eyes look even bluer—like pieces of the sky. And with the glow of health adding vigor and strength to his features... Her singing faltered, then faded.

She skimmed her gaze upward, over his dark, straight brows and tanned forehead to his brown, wavy hair. It had grown and wanted to curl, in spite of whatever he'd used to slick it back this morning. She glanced at the nape of his neck where crisp, dark hair brushed against the collar of his light gray shirt and her fingers tingled with the remembered thickness, the springy touch of his hair when she'd tended his wound. It had been—

She started, looked down at the hand tugging at her arm and turned a questioning gaze on her aunt. Her *seated* aunt. The soft, rustling sounds of people making themselves comfortable caught her attention. A quick glance around showed she was the only one not sitting— except for Ezra. His manners had kept him standing.

She dropped like a stone onto the pew and busied herself smoothing her long skirt, acutely aware of the quizzical look in Sophia's eyes and of Ezra seating himself at the other end of the box. She slipped the drawstring of her reticule off her wrist, fussed with her soft, kid gloves to keep from meeting Sophia's gaze.

"I take my text this morning from Proverbs, chapter six, verse sixteen. 'These six *things* doth the Lord hate: yea, seven *are* an abomination unto him.'"

Thank goodness the preaching had started. She looked up and focused her attention on Matthew, determined to corral her wandering thoughts and listen to every word of the message he was about to deliver.

"I am going to speak on these abominations over the coming seven weeks." Matthew's gaze scanned the congregation, touched hers. His lips curved in a small smile before his gaze moved on. "The first abomination is the basis for my address this morning. You'll find it at the beginning of verse seventeen—'a proud look.' Why would God hate that?"

She stiffened, clenched the reticule in her lap to keep from blurting a response to the rhetorical question.

"The 'proud look' I'm speaking about is one of inordinate self-esteem, of a conceit of superiority. It is the opposite of humility."

What a perfect description of Jacob Strand and the other men her father had given permission to court her. To have them treat her less like a person and more like a fancy piece of jewelry to buy and wear on their arm was enraging. But she had escaped here to Pinewood. And thanks to Sophia, she would not have to return home and accept one of those suitors against her will.

Gratitude filled her heart. She turned her head and smiled at her aunt, her senses achingly aware of Ezra sitting straight and tall on Sophia's other side. He was not like Jacob Strand and the others. He had a strong, confident air about him, but nothing of arrogance. Only a sort of sureness and niceness that made one want to trust him.

Her stomach clenched. She looked down at her lap, feeling sick. If only he weren't hiding something. But he was. The Lord hated that, too. And so did she.

The narrow dirt path looked little used. It tended north, all but hidden by the flood-flattened grasses of the field behind the hotel, then disappeared into the band of trees that followed the Allegheny's watery course.

Ezra glanced up at the sun hovering above the western rim of the surrounding forested foothills. There was time to explore a short distance before dusk settled in. The ground, still spongy in spots, gave beneath his boots as he crossed the open area, firmed as he neared the trees and stepped onto a sun-dappled trail littered with twigs and bits of bark and old leaves pulled from the undergrowth by the retreating flood. The river whispered along the bank on his left, chuckled around a low hanging branch that dangled in the water, the sibilant flow at odds with his roiling thoughts.

The reverend was married. He'd learned that much today. So why had the man been with Callie on those two occasions? Were they old friends? Or something more? No. That wasn't possible. He was adept at judging character, and Callie Conner was a true lady, not a "something more" woman. So where did that leave him?

He scowled, tore a piece of loose bark off the trunk of a tree and pitched it into the water. It broke the surface and disappeared, then bobbed up and floated away. That was the way he felt, like he was floating. And he didn't like it. He was accustomed to being in control.

He brushed the bark dust from his hands, ducked beneath a limb and walked on. He'd never been so strongly attracted to a woman the way he was to Callie. And he'd never been in such an uncomfortable position. He always dealt from a place of truth, but he couldn't tell her the truth yet. Not until he found out if she shared his feelings—and if those shared feelings developed into something deeper. If Callie cared for him, it had to be for himself alone, not for his money. And there was only one way to know. He had to woo her as Ezra Ryder: itinerant laborer. He had to risk her rejection, risk his pride.

He stopped and scowled. Was that what had been stopping him from paying court to Callie? Had he been fooling himself by thinking it was the other man? In all the business deals he'd made over the years, he'd risked only money and possessions. With Callie he would risk his pride. His heart. Was he willing?

He kicked a stone out of his way, rounded a bend in the trail and found his answer.

She was standing perfectly still, looking toward the trees. The lowering sun's rays defined the valleys and crests of the riotous pile of black curls at her crown, warmed the alabaster flesh at the nape of her neck, gilded the red wool of her modest gown. There was a softness, a vulnerability in her posture he'd never seen. And he knew. A sureness settled in his heart that could not be denied. He loved her. And he would risk himself and all he possessed to win her.

"What holds you so rapt, Callie Conner?"

"Oh!" She whirled his direction. There was a flash of white among the trees, the snap of twigs. She whirled back. "She's gone. You've frightened her off."

"Her?"

"A doe. She was about to cross the trail to the water. The deer come here at dusk to drink before they bed down." She glanced over her shoulder at him, moved forward a short distance and stopped, facing the trees. "Their track is here." She gave a graceful little wave.

He took it as an invitation and walked up to stand beside her. It was a struggle to tear his gaze from her face. She was looking at the ground, lost in her discourse about the deer, and none of the reserved air she usually wore masked the gentleness, the warm beauty of her spirit. It shone in her eyes, softened the line of her mouth. His mouth went dry. He jerked his gaze from her face to the rutted track.

"The deer have used this path for years." She gave a joyful little laugh that drew his gaze back to her. "Sadie and Willa and I came here often to watch them. Sometimes Ellen would come along." She glanced up into his eyes, and the breath froze in his lungs. "Daniel showed us the track and taught us to sit quiet and still until the deer came. That's why Ellen didn't come very often. She's not a patient person."

A tiny, vertical line formed between her arched brows. Her beautiful violet-blue eyes clouded. Anger, at whatever caused her distress, shot through him. He clasped his hands behind his back and cleared his throat. "I take it Sadie, Willa, Ellen and Daniel are childhood friends?"

"Oh, yes. We were very close. And then Father moved us to Buffalo." She turned away, and wandered up the trail.

It was plain she hadn't liked moving from Pinewood. He fell into step beside her, eager to keep her talking, to learn all he could about her. "It's hard to leave your home and your friends, especially when you're young and have no say in the matter."

"Yes. But even had we stayed, things would have changed. Sadie moved to Rochester." Sadness, and something he couldn't define, tinged her voice. "And Ellen is in Buffalo…"

"And Willa and Daniel?" Especially Daniel.

Her smile returned. "They are here in Pinewood. Daniel works for Mr. Townsend—" she gave him another sidelong glance "—that's Sadie's grandfather. Daniel is a teamster at one of his logging camps. And Willa—" She gave a rippling laugh, full of delight. "Willa is Reverend Calvert's wife. It's lovely, her living in the parsonage where I can simply dash over across the street for a visit—though I've learned to go prepared for weather. I was caught there by that thunderstorm the other night and the reverend had to escort me home under their umbrella. He's very kind and thoughtful."

He could have burst into song. He'd been sure there was an innocent explanation for Callie's being with the reverend, but to have it confirmed… He stepped to the side of the path, broke off a budding sprig of pussy willow and offered it to her with a bow. "I wish this were a rose." He straightened, and smiled.

"A kind thought, sir. But I prefer the pussy willow."

She looked down and reached for the sprig. Their hands touched. She went as still as she'd been when he'd come upon her standing in the path. Her fingers trembled against his. His pulse leapt. He stepped closer.

"Callie…" Her name was a hoarse whisper, a question.

She shook her head, and stepped back. "Thank you for the willow twig." The words were mere breath. She turned and started back toward the hotel.

He fought his thudding heart into submission and fell

into step beside her. She edged away a bit, putting more space between them, which was probably for the best. He clasped his hands behind him and shortened his strides to match her shorter steps, and heard her take a breath.

"You told Aunt Sophia it had fallen on you to support your family when you moved from the farm to the city. I envy you. I've always wanted a brother or sister." She slanted a glance his direction, then quickly lowered it again. "Your family must be eager for your return."

He looked down at the budding sprig she was slowly twirling between her index fingers and thumbs. He clasped his hands tighter and shook his head. "No one awaits me. Mother passed from this life three years ago, and my sister is married and lives in Philadelphia." He glanced up at the darkening sky as they left the band of trees and walked out into the open field. "As for my brother, he is in Europe seeking his fortune." A costly enterprise that he was paying for. "Mind the mud."

She nodded, lifted her hems and stepped around the dark, wet spot of ground in front of her. "I'm sorry for your loss, Ezra. It's difficult to lose a loved one." Another sidelong glance came his way. "You must miss your brother and sister."

"No longer. I've grown accustomed to their being gone."

His pulse quickened as they approached the hotel. He would take her elbow and help her up to the porch, bid her good-night at the door.

She stopped at the base of the steps, still holding her hems, and looked up at him. The soft, fading light of dusk made dark shadows of the long, thick lashes that hid her beautiful eyes.

"Good evening, Ezra."

The finality of her tone made her meaning clear— he was to come no farther. She climbed the steps and crossed the porch, the red wool of her modest gown whispering softly.

He waited until she was safe inside, then blew out a long breath and headed for the barn. He was accustomed to young women welcoming his slightest attention, not turning their backs on him. Courting Callie Conner could prove to be more costly to his pride than he imagined.

Callie cracked opened her bedroom door and peered out into the empty kitchen. Sophia's doorway was dark. She'd finally retired.

She tiptoed to her aunt's rooms and listened. Soft, regular breathing announced Sophia's sound sleep. She hurried back to her bedroom, grabbed the handle of the lantern and walked quietly to the back door. The hinge creaked. She froze, listened. There was no stirring.

She slipped outside, eased the door closed, then hurried across the porch and down the steps. It had to be somewhere along the path. The golden circle of light swept back and forth across the ground as she swung the lantern, searching.

It was lying at the edge of the dark, wet patch of mud. She must have dropped it when she took hold of her skirts to lift the hems. She bent and picked up the sprig of pussy willow, her breath catching at the memory of Ezra picking it for her.

She glanced toward the glint of gray that was her aunt's bedroom window, lowered the wick and snuffed her lamp. She would make her way back to the hotel in the dark. Should Sophia awake and look out her window, she didn't want to have to explain why she had come outside. Indeed, she couldn't. Who could explain the treachery of one's heart?

Chapter Nine

She'd caught them in time. They were a little darker and crisper around the edges than she normally cooked them, but not burned. Callie shoved the pan of fried potatoes to the back of the stove to keep warm and glanced down at the pancakes. The little bubbles at their edges were bursting. She flipped the rounds of batter over to cook the other side and checked the bacon sizzling on the other griddle, then pushed a curl back off her forehead with her free hand.

If only he would stop *looking* at her. She could feel his gaze, and it played havoc with her concentration. She never burned food. But she had come close with those potatoes.

"Is there anything that needs my attention this morning?"

She stared at the stove, holding back a sigh. *Please let there be nothing for them to discuss with Aunt Sophia. Please.* She eyed the steaming coffeepot beside the pan of potatoes. She would make less tomorrow. Joe always left when the coffee was gone and Ezra went with him.

"The sorrel mare that belongs to the man who came in last night has a loose shoe. I discovered it this morning when I was leading her out to the watering trough. You might want to tell your guest so he can plan on having the shoe fixed before he's ready to leave."

Ezra's deep voice eroded her self-control. She slid her gaze toward the table. He was looking at her over the top of his coffee cup. She yanked her traitorous gaze back to the stove, raised her hand to brush another dangling curl off her forehead and stopped midway. If she kept fidgeting, he'd know his presence unsettled her. She had to stay calm.

Calm? She wanted to stomp her foot and demand that he get out of her kitchen. Or run to her bedroom and hide. Oh, why did he have to chance upon her on the deer trail yesterday? She'd been doing fine until then. Now she kept remembering the look in his eyes when he'd picked that sprig of pussy willow and handed it to her, the way he'd said her name as if she were something precious. *Her.* Not her appearance. He'd never once mentioned her beauty. Her throat tightened.

She took a deep breath and closed her eyes. *Please, Lord, You know he's a deceiver. Please keep me strong. Don't let me care for him. And please, help me make it through breakfast without betraying my—*

A sharp odor stung her nostrils—the odor of char.

"The bacon's burning, Callie."

She snapped her eyes open at Joe's warning, glanced down at the sizzling, blackened slices, shoved the griddle to the cooler area at the side of the stove and scooped the burned bacon onto a plate. She coughed and waved her hand through the smoke from the hissing, popping grease.

"Never seen you burn food before, Callie."

"It's my first time, Joe, but I'm sure I'll get better at it." Her attempt at humor fell flat to her ears, but the elderly groom chuckled and went back to eating. She picked up the turner and slipped the scorching pancakes off the griddle onto the plate with the burned bacon, refused to look Ezra's way though her nerves tingled with awareness of his gaze fastened on her.

Sophia appeared at her side, grasped her hand and gently removed the turner. "Did you burn yourself, Callie? Do you want me to take over?"

She shook her head, rubbed her palms on the apron covering her long skirt. "Thank you, Aunt Sophia, but I'm fine. My fingers sting a little, but it serves me right for—" *mooning over a sprig of pussy willow.* She caught her breath, groping for something she could say. "—for building castles in the air."

Sophia studied her face then looked toward the table, returned her gaze to her.

Why didn't Sophia *say* something? She looked away from the conjecture forming in her aunt's eyes, grabbed a towel, pulled the griddle back to the front of the stove and forked on more bacon thankful for the heat of the stove that excused the flush burning her cheeks.

"All right, dear. As you wish." Sophia handed her the turner, gave her hand a pat and walked back to the table.

What did that little pat mean? She let out her held breath, spread a little grease onto the other griddle and spooned on batter. No more burned food. She must stay focused on her cooking and not allow herself to be distracted by Ezra's presence. The man was a liar. She must keep reminding herself of the fact no matter if it sat like a leaden weight in her chest. It was proving to be her only defense.

The hotel guest took the reins, mounted the sorrel and thrust his fingers into his waistcoat pocket. "A reward for your diligence."

Sunlight glinted on a small, silver coin the man flipped in his direction. Ezra snagged it in midair and watched the man ride away before he opened his hand and grinned at the sight of the half dime resting on his palm. How his life had changed.

He chuckled, tossed the coin in the air, caught it and turned to go into the barn. He needed the money now, but when he returned to his true life, he'd give all of the small rewards he'd earned to Joe—and more besides. Much more. Joe was a true friend. The first he'd had since before he'd amassed his fortune.

He stopped, opened his hand and stared down at the coin. It would have been a boon to him once, as it now was to Joe. A sense of unease settled over him. How would Joe react when he told him the truth? Would the disparity in their financial standings make a difference in their friendship? Would Joe trust him after he learned he'd been living a lie? A man was known by—

"A word with you, Ezra."

How long had Sophia Sheffield been behind him watching him lost in thought? "Of course, Mrs. Sheffield, how may I help you?" He turned and walked toward her.

"I've been meaning to ask your opinion of the barn roof." Sophia tilted her head, lifted her hand and shaded her eyes against the sunlight. "Did you see anything dire while you were up there the other day, or do you think the roof will hold up until next spring?"

"I saw a dozen or so badly cracked shingles which may give trouble. There—" he pointed to the thick wood shakes he was talking about "—and there. I spread pitch on as many as I could easily reach, but I didn't want to walk around any more than needed. The shingles are sun-baked and would crack easily beneath my weight."

"I see. Do you think the pitch will keep out the rain?" Sophia sounded worried. He looked down, read deep concern on her face. "Normal rains, yes. I can't say how successful it will be against another thunderstorm—especially one with strong winds like we had the other day. And I don't know how the damaged shingles in that area will hold up to the snow and ice of winter."

"No, of course not. My questions are foolish—a search for reassurance." She turned her head and peered up at him from beneath her open hand shading her eyes. "I have another I don't want Joe to overhear. Come with me."

Something in her voice had changed. He turned and followed her back toward the hotel, wishing he'd been able to read her expression. Was this about Joe? Did she want him to replace her elderly, rheumatic groom? He discarded the idea. While the work was becoming too much for Joe, Sophia Sheffield was kindness itself—

such an action would be out of character for her. Unless finances forced her hand. He frowned, glanced over his shoulder at the barn. Is that why she'd asked about the roof lasting another year? Was she struggling financially?

"This is far enough. We cannot be seen from the hotel here." Sophia stopped in the shadow of the buttery and motioned him to her side.

He stopped, and waited. Speculation would gain him nothing. He had to know the problem before he could work out a way to help.

"I am no longer a young woman, Ezra. And over the years I have learned not to let my emotions become entangled with my common sense—which is my way of saying I am not easily duped."

Duped? What had that to do with Joe or the roof? He hastened to readjust his thinking. "You have left me foundering, Mrs. Sheffield."

She fastened a sober, stern, but not unkind look on him. "I am neither dead nor blind, young man, and I would have to be one or the other not to know that you are attracted to my niece. *And* to not know that you are hiding something."

The shock of her pronouncement struck him clear to his toes, set every sense vibrating with warning. He stayed mute, waited for her to go on. To be successful you had to learn your opponent's strengths—and how much they knew about you. Had Sophia somehow learned who he was?

"You are not telling the complete story about yourself, Ezra Ryder—" her eyes narrowed on him "—if that is your true name."

"It is." She didn't know, it was only suspicion. The jangling warning eased to caution.

She stared at him a long moment, then gave a small nod. "Having judged by your actions since your arrival that you are a basically honorable and upright young man, I will accept your word on that—and I am going to assume you have a good reason to keep whatever your secret is hidden for the time being. However, this you must tell me—straight out and true—are your intentions toward my niece honorable?"

"They are." He met her probing gaze without flinching, carefully choosing his words. "I confess Callie is drawing my affections. I hope she will agree to spend time in my company so we might learn to know one another better and discover whether we wish to enter into a formal courtship—with your permission, of course."

Sophia stood studying him, her lips pursed, her gaze intent. "And this thing you are hiding—will it cause Callie hurt, now or ever?"

Her voice was suddenly stony, inflexible. He looked at the older woman's set face and knew he dare not try to evade the issue. He had to acknowledge her suspicion as valid. Nothing but the truth would satisfy. "I promise you it will not."

Sophia took a deep breath, keeping her gaze riveted on his. "And will you also promise me if Callie accepts your suit and grows to return your affections, you will tell her what this secret is before you ask for her hand?"

"I shall tell Callie, and you also. You have my word."

Their gazes remained locked. At last Sophia sighed and nodded. "I'm no fool, Ezra, and I believe you. Nonetheless, heed my words—Callie is the daughter I never had, and I will be watching. I am kind by nature, and fair and just by design, but I can be a formidable foe when the occasion warrants. I'll not have my niece hurt by you or any man. Take that as a warning—do not dare to hurt her." She stepped from the shadow, her back straight, her head high as she walked toward the hotel.

He stood by the buttery and watched until she went inside, then turned and headed for the barn, a frown tugging at his brows. If Sophia thought he was hiding something and realized he was attracted to Callie, why would she simply not order him off the property? Why would she not tell Callie he was hiding some truth about himself and put an end to his hopes of courting her? People did not do things without a reason. What was Sophia's? Dare he hope, that for whatever reason, he had an ally in his quest for Callie's affections—albeit a reluctant one?

"You're home!" Sadie's grandmother stepped out of the mercantile, rushed down the wood walkway and enfolded her in a warm hug. Callie kissed the elderly woman's soft, warm cheek and straightened.

"It's so lovely to have you back home in Pinewood, Ellen." The short, plump woman stepped back and beamed a smile at her. "You must come pay me a visit. We'll have a nice, long chat."

"It's Callie, Rachel. Callie Conner."

The elderly woman shot her husband a perturbed look.

"Well, of course it is, Manning. Why ever would you say such a thing?"

"You called her Ellen."

"I did?" The woman looked back at her, the green eyes, so like Sadie's, clouded with distress. "I'm sorry, Callie, dear. I can't imagine why I would do such a thing. I know perfectly well who you are."

"Of course you do, Mrs. Townsend. It's easy to misspeak." She leaned down and gave the woman another hug. "I'm cooking at the hotel and that keeps me quite busy, but I'll come for a visit as soon as I can."

"Lovely!" Rachel Townsend's green eyes warmed with pleasure. "And you must come too, Willa, dear. It will be like it used to be when you both came to visit… except Sadie is gone." The woman's ample body seemed to shrink, and she placed her pudgy hands on their arms. "Do come soon, Callie…Willa."

She glanced at Willa, and received a nod. "We shall, Mrs. Townsend. We'll come as soon as we can."

She watched Manning Townsend escort his wife down the three steps from the walkway to the road and hand her into their buggy, then smiled and waved as they drove off. "I'm glad we chanced to meet them, Willa. Grandmother Townsend is as sweet as ever." She watched the Townsends' buggy rumble across the Stony Creek bridge then turned and resumed their interrupted stroll down the walkway toward Cargrave's Mercantile.

"Yes, she is." Willa glanced over at her. "But I'm becoming concerned about Grandmother Townsend, Callie. She seems to be easily confused lately. She called you Ellen."

"Well, that's understandable, Willa. I haven't been in Pinewood for a long time."

"Perhaps, but Ellen was here until a short time ago, and there have been other instances." Willa slanted a look at her. "Matthew and I were favorably impressed with Mr. Ryder when Sophia introduced him to us after church on Sunday. He's very polite and well-spoken. Handsome, too. Why didn't you tell me about him?"

She tried her best not to react to his name. "Why would I? I've had more important things to discuss than Sophia's new employee. Oh, my! Look at that yellow bonnet." She stopped in front of the window of the millinery shop. "It's like a piece of sunshine sitting there."

"Why, Callie Conner—" Willa stopped, and gaped at her. "You're *attracted* to Mr. Ryder."

She huffed out a laugh, tried to look astonished. "Whatever gave you that notion?"

"Your attempt to change the subject." Amusement replaced the shock on Willa's face.

She feigned a look of surprise. "Why ever would you say that?"

Willa's blue-green eyes sparkled at her. "Don't even try to dissemble, Callie. It won't work. I know you too well. You hate bonnets—you *never* wear yellow—and you're doing that thing you do with your eyelids when you're uncomfortable and want to distance yourself from a conversation."

"*What* thing?" She jerked her gaze to her reflection in the window, but couldn't see anything odd about her eyelids. Willa's smiling face appeared close beside hers.

"You can't see it when you are looking at yourself, but you lower them halfway down—as if you want to hide."

The whisper tickled her ear. "I'm sure I don't know what you are talking about. Why should I want to hide?"

"*That* is what I'm wondering."

She shook her head in seeming incredulity. "Simply because I dislike *wearing* bonnets doesn't mean I can't admire one, Willa. Even a yellow one." She turned away from their reflections and started down the walkway to hide her face. Willa was right—she *did* know her too well.

"That's true." Willa fell into step and gave her a sweet smile. "So tell me, when did Sophia hire Mr. Ryder?"

She sighed, stepped into the recessed entrance of the mercantile and shot a look permitted by lifelong friendship over her shoulder. "Did anyone ever tell you you are a most persistent person, Willa? You really should work to temper your tenacity. At times it can be most… unattractive."

"Such as now—when I am asking about Mr. Ryder?"

"Did I mention you are also incorrigible?" She lifted her chin at Willa's delighted laugh and shoved open the door, woefully aware that the tinkling bells only announced a delay, not an end to the conversation.

Chapter Ten

The sun shone full on the wagonload of seasoned oak bolts thrown helter-skelter one upon another by the man who had delivered them.

Ezra eyed the shrinking shadow where he worked, put down the ax and rolled the sleeves of his blue wool shirt up to his elbows. Splitting stovewood wasn't hard, but it was hot work. Too bad he couldn't shuck his shirt the way he had done as a young boy on the farm.

He crooked his elbow, swiped the sheen of moisture off his forehead, picked up the ax and took a low, underhanded swing at the end of the nearest bolt lying on the ground, its butt hard up against the pile. The short length of log split. He set one half on the large, upended log used for a chopping block, took a firm grip on the ax and swung from the shoulder in a smooth, continuous rhythm. The stove-sized pieces split from the thick chunk in rapid succession and toppled from the log to litter the ground at its base. He repeated the procedure with the other half of the bolt, then stopped and rolled his shoulders. He'd forgotten how good it felt to have his muscles flexing and stretching with physical labor.

"Well, there's no doubt you have chopped wood before, Ezra. That's as neat a job as I've ever seen."

He turned toward the porch, and grinned up at Sophia Sheffield. "Not to boast, but wait until I get back into practice."

"Ah, a *modest* man." She laughed and offered him the glass she held in her hand. "I thought a cool drink of water might be in order."

"Just the thing, thank you." He stepped to the porch, took the glass in his free hand, and looked toward the kitchen door.

"She's busy roasting chickens and baking biscuits for supper."

He drank the water, and gave her a wry smile and handed the glass back up over the railing. "Am I that obvious?"

"I'm afraid so." She took the glass and turned. "I'll let you get back to your work."

"Mrs. Sheffield?"

She turned back. "Yes?"

He grounded the ax, crossed his hands on the butt of the handle and looked up at her. "I do not mean to meddle into your affairs nor to set myself forward in any way—but I've been thinking about what you said about the barn roof the other day and I wondered if, perhaps, you were a bit concerned about your finances?"

She stiffened, and he held up his hand to stop her from speaking. "I am not seeking to pry, madam, but, as I've told you, I worked in an insurance brokerage, and I have some knowledge of business." He looked full into her eyes, letting her read his sincerity. "I also have experience of dining in restaurants in the city, and I declare to you, I have never eaten finer meals than I have had since I came here."

A small frown creased her brow, etched tiny lines at the corners of her violet eyes. "Callie is an excellent cook. She's a very talented young woman. What has that to do with my finances?"

Clearly, Sophia was not fully in his camp when it came to Callie. She was withholding judgment, but it was obvious he still had to earn her trust. He nodded, and held her gaze. "It's not Callie I wish to discuss."

Her brows rose, her eyes took on a curious, suspicious cast. He had her full attention, even if it was less amenable than he would have liked. He leaned closer to the railing. "Mrs. Sheffield, have you ever considered opening your dining room to the public? I believe it would become an excellent, added source of revenue for you."

She gaped down at him, slowly shook her head. "Why, no. I've never thought of such a thing."

He allowed a moment for the idea to take hold, watched the surprise, the initial look of resistance fade from her face, and pressed his point. "There is no place, at present, in the village where a young man can take a young woman he is courting, or for a husband to take his wife, or for friends to meet for tea."

"Tea…"

He smiled at the speculative, receptive tone in her voice. Sophia's quick mind was latching on to the possibilities. "Your dining room sits empty except for your guests at meal times, so you would have no expense other than an increased food budget. And, perhaps, eventually, a few more tables with chairs."

Sophia nodded, and pursed her lips. "I would need more kitchen help, of course—but I've been intending to hire another cook as the number of guests always increases when the weather turns better for travel. Callie can teach the new one...perhaps Agnes..." She gave her head a little shake, leaned down and held out her hand to him. "I'll ponder it a bit more, but right now I can see no reason not to take your excellent suggestion. Thank you, Ezra."

"My pleasure, Mrs. Sheffield." He took her hand in his and made her a small bow.

"An insurance brokerage, you say?"

The unexpected comment froze him for a moment. Sophia Sheffield was quick indeed. He dipped his head.

She stared down at him, then slipped her hand out of his. "I shall accept that for now, Ezra—and look forward to the day you tell us the rest of your story." She turned and walked to the kitchen door. It squeaked open, and closed.

Us. Sophia had just given tacit approval to his wooing Callie. He grinned and turned back to the log chopping block. He leaned his ax against it, loaded his arms with the split stovewood and carried it to the dwindled stack at end of the porch. His whistled tune blended with the solid *thunk* of the pieces as he added them to the pile.

"What do you think, dear?"

Callie smiled, ran her fingertip along the molding

on the mantel. "I think Agnes is a wonderful choice for the new cook, Aunt Sophia. I hope she accepts. And that the Karchers will agree to her staying here through the week."

Sophia laughed, reached into her sewing box. "I've no doubt of that. I'm certain Joanna and Agnes are already thinking of the eligible bachelors that come to stay here in the hotel."

"And I think you are remarkably calm." Callie strode from the fireplace to the settee, and watched Sophia grasp the protruding end of a strand of crimson needlepoint wool and pull it through the eye of her needle. "Does the idea of turning the hotel dining room into a restaurant not excite you?"

"Does it you?"

"Gracious, yes! I couldn't wait until supper was over and the guests settled in so we had time to discuss it. My mind has been swarming with ideas since you told me. It's like a beehive in here." She laughed, tapped her temple and dropped onto the settee beside Sophia, then immediately rose and walked to the window, glanced toward the barn at the small equipment room window glowing with lantern light and wished she could share the news with Ezra.

"What ideas?"

"Well…" She tugged her errant thoughts back to the subject at hand. "You shall have to have a new sign made."

"Perhaps."

"Oh, no, you *must*." She turned back to face Sophia, looked up, lifted her hand above her head and drew it slowly through the air as if reading. "The Sheffield House Inn and Restaurant. My! That sounds impressive."

"And a bit grand for Pinewood."

She loved Sophia's laughter. It brought the happy memories of her childhood to the fore. "Not at all. Your friends will all be proud and happy for you." She lowered her hand, and tugged the braid of ribbon that encircled her waist back into place. "That's what's so lovely about living in a small village—your friends truly wish you well."

"It's not that way among your friends in the city?" Sophia paused in her stitching, looked up from her work on the needlepoint frame. Suspicion shadowed her eyes.

"Not among the elite society." She gave a small shrug to brush it off as unimportant, moving back toward the fireplace. "Tell me, what made you think of starting a restaurant?"

"I didn't." Sophia took a stitch and pulled the wool thread taut. "It was Ezra's idea."

"Ezra's?"

"Yes. Didn't I mention that?"

"No. No, you didn't." She ran her hand over one of the chalk pigeons on the mantel and fought the urge to go look out the window again. "It seems an odd thing for him to suggest. Why would he even think of it?"

Sophia slanted a look up at her. "Because of you. He said he'd never eaten finer meals than those you've prepared—not even in the restaurants in the city."

Pleasure spread, warming her like a comfortable blanket. "He said that?" Her gaze drifted back toward the window.

"Yes."

She turned her back to the temptation and faced the settee. "And that gave you the idea of starting your own restaurant?"

"No, dear. The entire thing was Ezra's idea." Sophia stuck her needle into the linen backing, rested her hands in her lap and looked up at her. "The other day I asked Ezra's opinion on the barn roof lasting until next spring. He realized I was a bit concerned over the finances involved in replacing it and so he came up with the idea of the restaurant as a way for me to make additional profit. He's a very intelligent and thoughtful young man."

Intelligent and thoughtful and kind and handsome and— "He's also a deceiver and a liar." She took a breath and turned so Sophia could not see her face and read in her eyes how much it hurt for her to name him so.

"No, Callie." Her aunt's voice firm, resolute, turned her back around. "Ezra has not lied."

The hope she worked so hard to suppress struggled to surface—she held it down. Her aunt was an astute woman and she trusted Sophia's instincts implicitly—but she was wrong this time. It seemed not even an older woman was immune to Ezra's charm. "You like him, don't you?"

Sophia smiled. "As do you. Although in a different way."

Heat crawled across her cheeks. She smoothed her palms down her skirt. "I confess I find him…attractive and charming—but that does not excuse his duplicitous behavior."

Sophia pursed her lips and nodded. "I find your opinion interesting, but a bit bewildering, Callie. Tell me, why do you persist in calling Ezra a liar when everything he's told us about himself is true?"

"Because he's let us *believe* lies about him. And that—"

"Why did you come to visit me, Callie?"

She stopped and stared at Sophia, confused by the abrupt change of subject. "Why…because I love you and missed you and wanted to see you."

Sophia rose, came to stand before her. "And because you wanted to escape the men courting you."

It was a flat, undeniable statement of fact.

"Yes." *Oh, Lord, please don't let her be hurt that I—*

"And did you tell me why you had come running to me, Callie? Or did you let me *believe* it was because you missed me?"

Tears stung her eyes. "Oh, Aunt Sophia, that *was* the reason. Simply not—not all of it. I couldn't tell you—" She stopped, sucked in a breath and caught her lower lip between her teeth. Sophia's soft hands cupped her face.

"Why don't you consider that Ezra, too, might have good and sufficient reasons for not telling us everything about himself, Callie? Grant him the right to his privacy, dear. Whatever he is withholding may not concern us at all."

Her aunt's words freed the hope. It burst from its restraint along with doubt and joy and a dozen other emotions that tangled into a knot she would have to unsnarl. "I hadn't thought about it that way."

Sophia smiled and hugged her close. "Perhaps it's time you did, dear."

* * *

Sleep evaded her. The silk hem of Callie's dressing gown brushed against the braided rug as she paced the small bedroom, her thoughts and emotions swinging between hope and fear of hope, doubt and disgust with herself for still doubting. There was no question but that Sophia was right.

She sighed, lifted her hands and massaged her aching temples with her fingertips. How could she have not have seen that she was guilty of the same deception of which she accused Ezra? How could she be so...so *self-righteous* and unfair?

An owl hooted. She glanced toward the window, heard the whir of the owl's powerful wings, saw the flash of its shadow as it passed between the streaming moonlight and dark glass intent on its prey.

"Run and hide, little mouse or rabbit or whatever you are. Hide and keep yourself safe."

Her soft words faded into the silence, echoed in her spirit. *Hide and keep yourself safe.*

She frowned, then lifted a ribbon off the washstand and captured her long, wild curls inside its length, trapped them there with a bow at the nape of her neck. She'd become adept at hiding and keeping herself safe ever since those first few times when she'd believed the men who'd said they loved her but meant they loved that she was more beautiful than their associates' lady friends or wives.

She whirled from the nightstand, from her reflection in the mirror and resumed her pacing. The truth that she was nothing more to those men than a pawn in their games of one-upmanship had hurt even though it was only her pride and not her heart involved. With Ezra, it was different. Those few moments when he'd pulled her close to keep her from burning herself on the stove had taught her that. If she allowed him in, she would never be able to keep her heart safe.

She stopped, frozen in place by the truth. She had been using her unflattering assessment of Ezra as a shield. It was, indeed, her defense against risking her heart. But no longer.

Resolve settled in her spirit. She glanced toward the bedroom door. The woodbox in the kitchen was almost empty. Ezra would fill it in the morning, and this time she would not hide in the bedroom until he left as she had done since that first morning. This time she would be waiting, with coffee brewing on the stove. She eyed her gowns dangling from pegs on the wall, made her selection. The violet one. It matched her eyes.

She walked to the bed, removed her dressing gown and slipped beneath the covers. Ezra had never told her she was pretty. Perhaps tomorrow morning he would.

Her stomach fluttered. She pressed her hands against it, glanced at the pussy willow twig on her nightstand, smiled and closed her eyes.

Chapter Eleven

Ezra leaned back, bracing the pile of stovewood in his arms against his chest and used his chin to help balance it as he groped for the door handle.

The door squeaked open.

"Good morning."

He almost dropped the pile of wood. Again. He stared at Callie standing in the doorway, a soft smile on her full lips. His pulse thundered. No woman should be that beautiful—it completely undermined a man's strength and self-control. He took a firmer grip on the wood, felt the sharp edges press into his flesh through the sleeves of his shirt. It helped. He returned her smile. Her *warm* smile. His pulse kicked up again. He cleared his throat. "You're up early."

"A bit." She pulled the door wider.

He stepped over the threshold, sniffed.

She laughed and closed the door. "The coffee's ready."

"Smells good." So did the faint floral scent that assailed his senses as he passed her. He stepped to the woodbox, dumped the load in, brushed bits of dirt and bark off his arms and made a manly effort to get ahold of himself. Her sweet welcome had surprised him. He filled his lungs, expelled the air and turned.

She held a steaming cup out to him. "Hot and strong. I believe that's right?"

"Perfect." And he wasn't talking about the coffee. He looked at the soft curve of Callie's smile, at the warmth in her dark violet-blue eyes. Something had changed. The reserve with which she treated him was gone. There was an openness about her. The vulnerability he had inadvertently seen on the river path Sunday evening was in her posture, the sweetness of her spirit in her eyes. It drew him like a magnet, yet gave him pause.

Lord, let me be equal to her trust. Let my growing regard for her protect her always.

He reached for the cup, and couldn't resist letting his fingertips brush against hers. Rose tinged her cheeks. Her long, thick black lashes swept down. She slipped her hand off the cup and stepped back, ran her palms down her skirt. She wore no apron. Was that for his sake? The thunder in his pulse started again.

"Aunt Sophia told me about your suggestion that she start a public dining room." She stepped to the worktable, lifted her apron from a peg on the end, slipped it on and reached behind her back to tie the strings.

He jerked his gaze to the cup he held and gripped it with both hands.

"I think it's a wonderful idea."

Was that what the warmth of her greeting was about—gratitude? His ego deflated along with his hope. His pulse slowed to its normal, steady rhythm. He blew across the top of the coffee, took a tentative sip. No sense in scalding his mouth again. He leaned back against the other end of the worktable and stared down at the dark brown brew. "It seemed sensible. The dining room sits empty, except for guests at meals." He looked over at her, then yanked his gaze back. It was too intimate standing there drinking coffee while she began her preparations for breakfast. He straightened, moved to the other side of the table. "It will mean more work for you."

"I don't mind. I enjoy cooking and baking. And I know Aunt Sophia was concerned about…expenses."

A tiny frown line appeared between her brows. He took another swallow of coffee to give himself something to do. "Like the barn roof?"

"Yes." She leaned down, filled a bowl with potatoes and put it on the table, then looked up at him. "Thank you for giving me a way to help ease Aunt Sophia's worry. She's done so much for me. It's wonderful to be able to do something for her."

He looked down into her eyes, at the gratitude that warmed them to a deeper violet and wished it were something more. Time to leave. He drained his cup and set it on the table. "The woodbox isn't full. I'll bring in another load."

The door squeaked. A smiling, bearded face topped by a thick shock of brown hair thrust through the narrow opening. "I hear there's someone named Callie Conner here."

He heard Callie's gasp, saw her spin and run toward the door.

"Daniel, oh, Daniel!"

The happiness in her voice plunged like a knife into his chest.

The young man charged inside, caught Callie up in his arms and spun her around, his deep laugh melding with her soft, rippling peal of joy.

Something dark and ugly, foreign and uninvited rose in Ezra. He'd wondered about Daniel. Now he had his answer. And he didn't like his reaction to it. It really *was* time to leave Pinewood. He looked at Callie's arms wound tight around Daniel's neck, strode across the kitchen and grabbed the door that had slammed against the wall.

"What's going on in here?"

He looked toward the door to Sophia's private quarters. The older woman stood shoving a comb into the twist of graying black hair on her crown. He forced a smile. "A reunion, from the looks of it. And I was just about to get out of their way." *For good.* He dipped his head, stepped outside and pulled the door closed behind him.

Daniel stopped whirling and lowered her to the floor. "Who's that fellow?"

She followed his glance to the door, stepped back and tugged her twisted dress back into place, then pushed at the curls that had come loose to hang down her neck. "His name is Ezra Ryder. He's Aunt Sophia's new stable hand."

"From that look he gave me, I'd say he'd like to be more than that to you."

Her cheeks warmed. "Stop teasing."

"Who's teasing?" Daniel's grin flew straight to the spot in her heart reserved for him. "I don't think that fellow—Ezra, is it?—is a man to make light of. Why, he could be outside laying in wait for me this very moment."

"What an outrageous thing to say." She laughed and turned toward the stove. "You have not changed a bit in the years I've been gone. Come have a cup of coffee."

He followed her as far as the worktable, leaned down to rest his elbows on it, tapped the empty cup with the bit of black coffee in the bottom and grinned up at her. "Looks like I'm not the first fellow to have coffee with you this morning. Guess it's no wonder this Ezra thinks I'm competition for your affections. Too bad he's not right." He waggled his eyebrows. "Look at you, Callie Conner, all grown up and beautiful as the violets God used when He made your eyes."

She crinkled her nose at him. "You're not going to repeat that old story you used to tell me about how God lifted my eyelids when I was born and squeezed violet juice into my eyes, are you?"

"Why not? It's true."

"It makes my stomach squeamish."

He chuckled. "That's why I said it."

She shook her head and handed him his coffee. "It used to be milk you drank while leaning on this table, and Aunt Sophia you watched work. You've grown up, too. And, may I say, you have grown into a very handsome man, Daniel." She tilted her head, grinned. "At least I *think* you're handsome under that beard."

"Oh, to be sure I am!" He waggled his eyebrows again. "You make certain you tell that to Ellen when you go home. I want her to know what she's missing, being courted by all those rich men in Buffalo."

He was laughing, but there was something in his eyes... She sobered, and gazed at him.

He looked down, swirled the coffee in his cup and took a swallow.

She studied him a moment, then shrugged the strangeness off as her imagination. "I'm not going back to Buffalo, Daniel. I'm staying here in Pinewood with Aunt Sophia." She picked up a potato and her paring knife. "I have to work while we visit. I'm the cook for the hotel now, and it'll soon be time for breakfast."

"I heard about the cooking part." He looked up and returned her smile. "The rest of it is news to me. Good news, Callie. Sophia must be happy to have you here with her."

"Sophia is *very* happy to have her here."

He winced, just the way he had when they were young, and he'd been overheard saying something wrong.

She grinned.

He mouthed "traitor" and turned.

"I meant no disrespect, Mrs. Sheffield." A self-deprecating smile twisted his lips. "I didn't know you were in the room."

"I noticed." Sophia laughed and began putting dishes on the table. "Will you stay for breakfast, Daniel?"

"The way that fella Ezra looked at me, I don't think that's a good idea. I remember your rules, Mrs. Sheffield—no fighting in the kitchen."

"Daniel!"

He chuckled, looked back at her and shrugged his shoulders in mock innocence as he mouthed "revenge."

"What's this about Ezra and you fighting?"

"Nothing, Aunt Sophia." She shot him a look. "Daniel is only teasing. He'll stay for breakfast."

"Nope. I can't, Callie. I'm headed right back to camp. I only came to town to pick up some medicine from Doc Palmer. The 'spring complaint' is making its way through the men. I've escaped it. Probably because I spend most of my time with the horses now that I'm a teamster."

"Aunt Sophia wrote me about your promotion, Daniel. And of how proud your mother is of you. Willa wrote me about it, also. And about the injury to your shoulder when that falling tree hit you." She frowned, glanced at his shoulder. "Have you any lasting problems with your arm, or are you fully recovered?"

"I'm good as ever." He drained his cup and set it down beside the empty one. "I'm glad you're in Pinewood to stay, Callie. The next time I have a free weekend, I'll come over and we'll go for a walk along the deer path— see if they still come along that track to water before they bed down."

"They do. I—" She stopped, tongue-tied by a sudden image of Ezra handing her the sprig of pussy willow. She glanced up. Sophia was looking at her. Daniel was waiting for her to finish. She dropped the peeled potato in a bowl of water and picked up another. "I went walking there last Sunday at dusk—just as you taught me." The childhood memories surfaced. She looked at Daniel and smiled. "I saw a doe."

He nodded. "It's nice to know some things don't change."

That odd note was back in his voice.

He touched an imaginary hat brim and strode to the door. "Good morning, ladies. I hope to see you soon."

"Goodbye, Daniel." She stared at the closed door, frowned and turned to her aunt. "There's something wrong with Daniel, Aunt Sophia. Have you heard anything?"

"No, I haven't, dear." Sophia put on an apron and picked up a knife to help her. "But I agree. There *is* something wrong. Daniel hides it well, but he's an unhappy young man."

Yes. She recognized the shadow of unhappiness in his eyes, the underlying sadness behind his smiles and laughter. It had been in her own eyes and voice until now.

She glanced at the dawning light outside the window, smiled and went back to work, a knot of anticipation in her stomach. It wouldn't be long until Joe and Ezra would come in for breakfast.

It had eaten at him all day. Did he have a chance of winning Callie's affections or not? Ezra checked his reflection in the mirror, poured a slash of witch hazel in his palm, rubbed his hands together and patted it on his newly shaved face. His emotions had risen and fallen all day, like those rafts he'd seen floating on the floodswollen Allegheny when he first came to Pinewood. Up and down—up and down—carried along on a tide he had no control over.

He frowned, grabbed the hairbrushes and swiped at

his still-damp hair. The warm welcome Callie had given him this morning had set his hopes rising—until he'd realized it was only an expression of her gratitude for helping Sophia. That had sunk his hope. But the way she'd reacted to his touch couldn't be explained by gratitude and his emotions had soared again, only to fall to a new low when Daniel arrived.

Daniel. The happiness on Callie's face when she'd seen him—the way she had called his name and run to him... Could childhood friendship account for that?

He'd made up his mind to write to Mooreland and tell him to send funds to pay for his trip home, but then at dinner, and again at supper Callie had been so...so attentive...no...responsive—he groped for the right word, gave up and settled for different—toward him. And now, his plans were in place, and he was going to find out if he had a chance of winning her or not.

He scowled, adjusted the collar of his new, gray cotton shirt and closed the tonsorial case. He strode from the equipment room into the barn and headed for the doors, his boot heels thudding against the planks. He walked around the shay, parked in the middle of the barn floor waiting, stepped to Star's stall and stroked the muzzle she thrust at him over top of the door. "Be patient, girl. I'll be right back."

He hurried out through the doors and onto the path, then looked toward the hotel. Sophia Sheffield was as good as her word. She and Callie were sitting on the matching porch settles. Callie glanced his way, lifted her hand and did something with her hair.

He quickened his steps lest she go inside, stopped at

the bottom of the steps and dipped his head in a polite bow. "Enjoying the pleasant evening, ladies?"

"Yes, indeed."

He smiled at Sophia, then fastened his gaze on Callie. "Joe told me the Senecas are holding a festival dance tonight, Callie. I've never seen one and thought I would attend. I would be honored if you would accompany me."

Her eyes widened. "Why, I—"

Clearly, his invitation had startled her. He kept his gaze fastened on hers.

"I'm sorry, but I must decline, Ezra. Agnes is coming and—"

"I'll help Agnes settle in, Callie." Sophia smiled, waved her hand in dismissal. "You go and enjoy yourself. You've done nothing but work since you came."

"Well…" Callie glanced at him, then looked back at Sophia. "If you can get along without me…"

His pulse leaped.

She turned toward him, a shyness he'd never before seen in her smile. "Thank you, Ezra. I'll be most pleased to accept your invitation. I haven't attended an Indian dance since we moved away, and—oh, no…" Her smile faded. "It won't be possible. The Indian village is too far away to—"

"You may take the shay."

Yes, Sophia was as good as her word. He looked at her and smiled. "You're most kind, Mrs. Sheffield. I'll go get Star hitched."

"And I'll change into something warmer, in case the evening turns chilly."

He started down the path. The porch door squeaked open, then closed.

"Ezra."

He stopped at the quiet hail, turned and looked up at Sophia now standing at the top of the steps. "I'm trusting you, young man. See that you treat her well."

"You have my word, Mrs. Sheffield." He turned and hurried down the path to get the shay.

Callie hadn't said no! Of course, it didn't mean she wanted to spend time with him. It could be that she simply wanted to visit the Senecas and see them dance. But, either way, it was a first step. And before they returned home he would know if she would welcome his suit, or if she had already given her heart to Daniel.

Chapter Twelve

The glow of the setting sun warmed the valley, gilded the misty green and gold haze of the budding trees and towering, dark green pines on the surrounding hills. Ezra relaxed his grip on the reins, let Star set her own pace and glanced over at Callie so close beside him in the small shay. His gut tightened. He dragged his gaze from her profile and concentrated his attention on the narrow, brown ribbon of road wending its way through the velvet growth of spring grass. "I'm not sure where the Senecas are encamped. Joe only told me to take this road."

"Their village is on the other side of that rise ahead." She turned her head to face him. "You'll see their long houses when we start down the other side. And their fires will be visible, also."

He looked into her eyes, and got lost in their violet depths. "You said you watched the festival dances before you moved away—did your parents bring you?"

"No." She looked down, smoothing the hem of her jacket against her skirt. "I'm afraid my father holds the Senecas in low regard. It was Sadie's grandparents who brought us." A smile touched her lips. "Their buggy was too small, so Grandfather Townsend would pile hay in his farm wagon and we'd all climb in—Sadie, Willa, Daniel and Ellen and I. It was great fun." Her eyes glowed with the memory.

"Daniel?" His opportunity to find out about her relationship with the man had come sooner than he'd expected. "Is that the fellow who showed you the deer track? The man who came to visit you this morning?"

A smile lit her face. "Yes, that's Daniel. He hasn't changed at all since we've grown, and I was so afraid that he would." A small shake of her head set the pile of black curls at her crown bouncing. "He's a terrible tease, but I don't mind. Daniel's the brother I never had. We girls followed him everywhere." She laughed and the rippling sound shot straight to his heart. "He was our hero."

Wonderful word, *our. Brother* was more so. And *was*—that was the best word of them all. *Lord, let me be her hero now. Let me be the one to make her eyes shine with happiness.* "Our? As in Willa and Sadie and Ellen and you?"

"Yes. Well, not so much Ellen." She gave him a sidelong look that invited him to understand. "Ellen was always a bit resentful of Daniel's teasing, which, of course, made him tease her all the more."

"Of course. It was like that with my sister and me." A grin tugged at his lips.

"I can tell by your face that it was. And did you get her in trouble? Daniel used to lead us on such adventures…"

He looked at the warm, teasing glint in her eyes, and

lost himself in imagining how it would feel to be admired by her.

"...when we were ten and Daniel was twelve. We followed him onto a log that had fallen across the creek and Ellen lost her balance and fell in. Daniel heard her cry, turned and dove off the log right into those swift-flowing floodwaters. I was so frightened! I thought they would both drown, but Daniel saved her. I still don't know how he managed to get her to the bank and haul her out onto the ground."

"He *was* a hero."

"Yes." Her eyes flashed. "You would think Ellen would be grateful! But—" She stopped and leaned forward as they topped the rise. "There are the long houses. Follow that trail on the left. Grandfather Townsend always parked the wagon there by that stand of trees and we walked to the celebration dance area."

He reined Star onto the path she'd indicated, halted her beside the trees and jumped to the ground, tied the reins on a low growing bush and turned. Callie hadn't hurried to alight as she had on their previous ride—she was fussing with her jacket. An excuse to wait for him to assist her? His pulse quickened. He stepped to the other side of the shay and offered her his hand.

Her gaze met his, then skittered away. She twisted on the seat, placed her foot on the iron rung and laid her hand on his. A beat pulsed in his ears. It took him a moment to realize it was a drum and not the sound of his own pounding heart. "It seems we've arrived in time."

"Yes. They start dancing when the sun sinks behind the hill."

He watched her shake out the long skirt of her dress, tug the hem of the jacket into place at her small waist, and wished she would look up at him—was thankful she didn't. They were so close he could— He stepped back and cleared his throat. "Which way do we go?"

"This way, through the trees to a path that follows the creek to the clearing where they dance."

Her voice was soft, hushed as the quiet that surrounded them. She turned and started through the budding trees, graceful as a doe, more beautiful than any flower he'd ever seen. He followed her through the shadowed copse to a creek with white ripples curling around rocks then smoothing out to disappear in the dark, whispering water.

"Mind the twigs." He stepped to her side, took her elbow and helped her over a tangle of fallen branches onto the dirt path.

"A moment..." She stopped, twisted around a bit and tugged at her skirt. "My hem is caught."

"Allow me." He stepped behind her, stooped and took hold of her skirt, the fabric soft against his fingers as he freed it from the hard stub of a broken branch. "Got it." He looked up and their gazes met. His heart bucked like an untamed stallion at the soft warmth in her eyes. He rose, holding her gaze with his. Her cheeks turned pink, she looked down and started walking.

The drums beat. Voices chanted. Ahead, shadow figures danced around a fire with flames leaping up into the growing darkness. A sense of expectation hovered, and filled him with the knowledge of the night's silent awakening. He moved beside her acutely aware of their surroundings and of everything about her—her beautiful face above the graceful column of her slender neck, the way the curls atop her head bounced slightly with her steps, the quiet brush of her hems against the ground. He looked down at her delicate hand, pale against the darkness of her long skirt and remembered the smooth softness of it in his. His fingers twitched.

She stopped and turned toward him. "We always watched from these trees along the creek. It seemed less…intrusive—though the Senecas have always welcomed us." Her gaze lifted, touched his and retreated beneath the downward sweep of her long lashes.

He took a firm hold of his emotions and surveyed the area. "I see a likely place." He took her elbow and guided her to a spot between the thick boles of two trees, the strike of his boot heels against the hardened earth an offense to the soft, rhythmic thud of the Seneca dancers' moccasin-clad feet. He stopped and released her arm… waiting. She didn't move away. He stood drinking in her beauty, the tantalizing hint of floral scent that clung to her, then looked at the dancers and reminded himself of his purpose—to learn if she was attracted to him while knowing nothing of his wealth. His pulse pounded with hope. It seemed she was—unless he had misread her blush and the look in her eyes.

A quiet rustle of fabric drew his attention. He tensed, then turned his head. Two young Seneca girls walked out of the woods, crossing in front of them.

"Sgééno." Callie spoke quietly, and smiled.

"Sgééno." The girls returned her smile, glanced at him, then hurried off toward the fire.

"You speak their language?" He stared down at her, shaking his head. "I don't know which I am most—shocked or impressed."

Laughter danced in her eyes. "You needn't be either. I only know their greeting. I came here only a few times when I was very young. After that, Father forbade me." The shadow he'd seen darken her eyes when she'd mentioned her father earlier swept away the laughter. She turned back to face the dancers. "Daniel can talk with them. He came here often."

Daniel again. Had the childhood feelings for him she'd spoken of before changed into something romantic since she'd grown? Perhaps that look in her eyes earlier had only been flirtation. Women were masters at coy looks, though he'd never have thought it of Callie. Of course, he'd been fooled before. He stepped forward, bent and picked up a small branch and tossed it aside, stopped in position to see her face. "He seems to be a very talented man, your Daniel."

"He's not *my* Daniel, but I wish he were someone's."

She sighed, and slanted a look up at him. He found nothing flirtatious in her expression, only sincere concern.

"Daniel will be a wonderful husband and father, and I want him to be happy. And he's not, in spite of his promotion at the logging camp." She frowned, that tiny vertical line appearing between her brows. "I could tell that this morning."

What job would make Daniel a good husband in her eyes? A bookkeeper perhaps? Something better than a stable hand. "He's won a promotion?"

"Yes. He's a teamster now." A smile curved her soft, full lips. "You have that in common with him—you both love horses."

A *teamster?* Surely that was tantamount to a stable hand?

She didn't care about wealth! And she'd made it obvious she had no romantic notions about Daniel. He returned her smile. "From all you've said, I believe I shall like Daniel when I meet him."

"I'm certain you will. And that he will like you as well." Her hand lifted, her fingers toyed with the top button of her jacket. "You two may become fast friends— should you decide to stay in Pinewood."

Her long lashes lowered, hid her gaze, but too late. He'd seen the look of hope, the flash of interest in them. And it was there in the soft way she spoke the question as a statement. His heart thudded. He tucked his arms behind his back, clasped his hands and held tight, but nothing could stop his heart from reaching out to her. "Nothing could move me from Pinewood, Callie." She looked up, and he let his eyes say all he dare not yet put into words. "Not even the horses Daniel cares for could drag me away."

She didn't say I'm glad—but her eyes did. She gave a small nod and turned to watch the dancers.

His pulse surged as before, picked up the accelerated beat of the drums and moccasined feet of the dancers. He leaned against the bole of the tree beside him and folded his arms across his chest to control the urge to draw her into an embrace. He must go slow and treat her with the respect and honor she deserved. But every doubt he'd held was gone. Callie Conner was the woman he'd been searching for—a woman who would love him for himself, not for his means. And she was the only woman who had ever stolen his breath with a glance and made his heart race with a smile.

The chanting grew louder. The dancing took on new fervor. It held no interest for him. He watched the flickering light of the fire's dancing flames play over Callie's beautiful face and slender form and knew his heart had made its decision—he loved her.

Determination to win her affections rose. *Callie Conner, prepare to be courted to a fare-thee-well, because I will never give up until you are mine.* He pushed away from the tree and stepped to her side. She glanced up. The firelight flared, bathing them with its warmth. He caught her gaze with his and smiled.

Moonglow lit the valley, turned the haze of the budding trees ashen and silvered the feathery silhouettes of the towering pines on the surrounding hills. Night sounds blended with the rumble of the wheels and the plod of Star's hooves on the narrow, gray ribbon of road that bisected Pinewood. Callie looked at the outline of the Sheffield House looming ahead and wished she could stop Star, make the evening last a little longer. The Senecas' dance had ended far too soon.

She stole a sidelong glance at Ezra and her pulse quickened. There was something different about him tonight. There had always been a sort of confidence about him, but now there was a sureness that drew her. She looked at his hands holding the reins, so strong and capable. Her breath caught in her throat. She would soon feel the warmth and strength of his fingers curled around hers again.

The horse turned into the way, the wheels crunching against the gravel. The shay rolled forward, then swayed to a halt. Ezra reached forward to hang the reins over the dashboard, and his shoulder brushed against hers. Her stomach fluttered. She turned her head and looked at the path that led to the back porch—such a short distance, and then the night would be over.

The seat creaked. She shivered as the cool night air replaced the heat from Ezra's body. The shay dipped and his boots crunched on the gravel. Moonlight cast his shadow before him as he walked around Star, and then he was there, looking up at her, holding out his hand.

"I've brought you safely home."

His smile stole into her heart, settled there. She placed her foot on the iron rung, took a breath and put her hand in his, trembled at his touch.

"You're shivering." A frown replaced his smile. "I'm sorry. I should have thought to provide a lap robe."

"Not at all. I was quite warm in the shay." Heat warmed her cheeks at the admission. She ducked her head, took his offered arm and walked beside him to the porch, dreading the moment they would part, wishing it were over.

"I enjoyed watching the Senecas' dance. Thank you for accompanying me."

"I'm pleased you asked me." His boot heels clicked against the wood of the steps, her hems swished softly. She glanced across the porch. Only a few steps more to the door. She gathered herself together, prepared to smile and bid him good-night. They stopped and she slipped her hand from his arm. He captured it in his.

"Thank you for a lovely evening, Callie."

His quiet words felt like a caress. He raised her hand and turned it over, pressed his lips to her palm, then turned and walked away. Cold air replaced the warmth of his hand. She curled her fingers over the spot of warmth where his lips had touched, pressed her closed hand to her chest and watched him stride through the moonlight to the shay. She leaned back against the door, looked up at the sky and smiled, then took a long, deep breath and went inside.

Chapter Thirteen

Sophia's sitting room door opened. Callie shaped the last lump of dough, plopped it into the greased pan and glanced up. "Good morning."

"Indeed, it is." Her aunt strode into the kitchen, the long skirt of her silk gown swishing. "Where is Agnes?"

"She's outside getting the milk and eggs and butter. And bacon." Ezra preferred bacon to sausage. She hummed softly, covered the dough with a towel and set it aside to proof, then began to peel a potato.

"I thought perhaps you would stay abed for a bit this morning—now that Agnes is here to help."

She shook her head and brushed back a dangling curl that tickled her forehead with the back of her hand. "I need to show her where things are, and how you like things done." She slid the potato into a bowl of water and started on another.

"Is that the only reason, Miss Songbird?"

She heard herself humming, stopped and looked up. Sophia's eyes glowed with fondness laced with a touch of amusement and sagacity. There was no reason to try and hide the truth from her—not that she could. "I couldn't sleep." Understanding flashed between them. Her cheeks warmed.

"I thought as much." Sophia smiled, reached across the worktable and covered her hand holding the potato with hers. "And I'm glad. It's high time you had a beau."

One of her own choosing—yes. She pushed the thought away. She would not allow her sour memories to taint this wonderful new happiness bubbling around inside her.

The door opened and Agnes stepped into the kitchen carrying a basket laden with dairy foods, eggs and bacon. "I brought along a wedge of cheese. I thought perhaps we could add it to some stirred eggs? Father is very fond of them that way."

"What a good idea, Agnes." Sophia squeezed her hand, straightened and turned toward the young woman. "I'm sure our guests will enjoy the special treat."

Did Ezra like cheese? Had she served him any? She cast back through the meals she'd prepared since he'd arrived. Meals he'd told Sophia were better than any he'd had in the fancy restaurants in the city. He thought she was a good cook—he'd told her so that very first day. A smile warmed her heart and touched her lips. She hummed softly and slid the knife around the potato slicing off a thin layer of skin.

Life couldn't be any better—at the moment. Ezra whistled "Amazing Grace" and drew the brush along the chestnut mare's back. He was certain Callie held at least budding affection for him. She had avoided his direct gaze during breakfast and dinner, but several times he had caught her stealing looks at him from beneath her lowered lashes. And, throughout the meals, whenever their gazes *had* met, that betraying, rose color had spread across her delicate cheekbones. Just as it had when he'd looked up and caught her gazing down at him when he'd freed her skirt hem last evening. A grin slanted across his mouth. He loved her blushes—loved even more that he caused them.

He crossed his forearms on the mare's back, fisted his free hand and rested his chin on it remembering the way Callie had looked standing there watching the Seneca dancers, with the firelight playing over her beautiful face and flickering in her violet eyes. Her eyes had seemed darker, warmer than ever when she'd looked at him.

The mare whickered low, thrust her muzzle against his ribs. He laughed and shot out his left leg to catch his balance. "All right! I'll finish grooming you. There's no need to push." He put down the brush and picked up the cloth, wiped it down her neck and resumed his whistling.

The mare whickered again, tossing her head. "Is that approval of my musical ability, or are you telling me that you like being groomed?"

The kitchen door of the hotel squeaked. His pulse jumped. He glanced out of the wide, double doors, open to allow the sunlight to brighten and warm the barn's interior. A tall and gangling young woman with a long-jawed, hawk-nosed face crossed the porch and started down the steps, an empty basket clutched in her hand. Disappointment drowned his hope of catching a glimpse of Callie. He'd forgotten about the new cook.

He turned back and finished wiping down the mare, then took hold of the chestnut's halter and led her toward the doors. "Let's get you watered, girl. Then you can go back to your clean stall and eat, and I can get washed up for supper." He stood stroking the mare's shoulder while she drank, his head full of Callie. Would she go out onto the porch with him when he made his request after supper? He wanted privacy when he asked her if she would allow him to escort her to church.

He took the mare to her stall and started for his room, stopping at the beat of hooves on the gravel way. A long shadow fell across the floor, followed by the span of horses that cast it. Their hooves fell in rhythm on the wide planks, and danced to a halt as a carriage rolled into the barn. It was a phaeton—one of the fanciest he'd ever seen.

He moved forward, spoke in a soft tone to the matched pair of black geldings standing with heads high, nostrils flared, and took hold of the reins of the nearest one. Joe came from his room and limped toward him.

"I want my horses rubbed down and stabled in stalls next to each other with an empty stall on either side." A tall, thin man dressed in a black suit with a snowy white cravat at his throat climbed from the carriage, lifted out a leather case and turned to look down his long, aristocratic nose at them. "Give them only your best grain— oats mixed with bran—three times a day. And fresh hay. See that they are well-watered and groomed daily." The man's haughty gaze swept his direction. "I expect my orders to be carried out implicitly."

He bit back a retort and turned his attention to the

horses. The man scowled, tugged at his suit coat then strode out the door.

"He ain't none to happy with you not bowing and scraping."

"Then he's going to have a very unhappy stay."

"That's what I figured from the look you give him." Joe chuckled and took hold of the reins of the other horse. "Let's get this fancy rig moved over to the side, then unhitch these beauties and get them in their stalls. As for him—" Joe threw a disgusted look toward the open doors "—I hope she gives him a room with old straw in the mattress and the stalks prick him all night!"

He looked over at Joe and grinned. "I could always give him mine."

Callie lowered the drop front of the secretary desk, smoothed her skirts, sat in Sophia's chair and eyed the exposed cubicles and drawers. Laughter bubbled.

"Is something funny, dear?"

She glanced over her shoulder and shook her head. "It's only that I always feel a little bit guilty, and ridiculously adult when I touch something in this room that was forbidden to me as a child." She turned on the chair. "Does Agnes need me?"

Sophia laughed, and stepped close. "No, dear. I only came in to get some ink. The well in my office desk is empty. And I've a new guest to sign in." Her aunt picked up the ink bottle, rested her free hand lightly on her shoulder and smiled. "And there is no reason for guilt, Callie—and no reason for you to ever again ask permission to use my desk or other things. Anything I have is yours, dear. This is your home now."

Tears surged. Her throat tightened. She caught Sophia's hand in hers and pressed it to her cheek, too overcome to speak.

Sophia cleared her throat, then gave a small laugh. "We shall never get our tasks done this way." She withdrew her hand, turned with a swish of her long skirts and strode toward the door. "I will leave you to write your letter while I go and tend to my guests. I should have hired a second cook *days* ago had I realized exactly how much it would free our time." Sophia paused in the doorway, smiled over her shoulder. "Give Sadie my love, dear."

"I shall." She nodded, stared at the empty doorway. *Thank You, Almighty God, for the blessing of Aunt Sophia's love.* She took a breath, blinked the moisture from her eyes and turned back to the desk. She pulled an inkwell and pen from one of the many cubicles, drew a sheet of writing paper toward her, then paused, ordering her thoughts. There was so much she had to say.

She dipped the pen in the ink, tapped the excess off against the lip of the ink well and began.

Dearest Sadie,
I have been remiss in not writing to inform you that I am no longer living at home with Mother and Father. I am in Pinewood.

She paused, knowing Sadie would be struck by an onslaught of terrible memories upon reading the village name, then took a breath and continued. The nib of the pen scratched lightly against the paper as she recorded all that had happened since her arrival, then added her hopes for the future.

The sun shifted. She slid the paper toward the light, thought for a moment, then sighed and added a final paragraph, though she knew it would bring her friend pain.

Before I close, I must tell you I chanced to meet your grandparents the other day on my way to the mercantile. Your grandmother is as sweet as ever. And your grandfather still pretends to that sternness we all know to be false. He is kindness itself. I hope to have a long visit with them soon. They miss you, Sadie.

I pray this letter finds you happy and satisfied in your teaching position there at the female seminary. Stay well, my dear friend, and write soon. I miss you.

My dearest love,

Callie

She blotted the writing, folded the letter, wrote the direction, capped the inkwell and put it and the pen away. Sealing wax candles were in one of the small drawers. She lit the wick of a red one at the lamp and held it over the loose end of the paper. A large drop of wax dropped onto the seam, sealing the letter.

She forwent the use of Sophia's stamp with its ornate capital S and tidied the desk, rose to hurry to the post office and post the letter. If only Sadie would come home. But she wouldn't of course. And who could blame her?

The door was pulled open. The bells tinkled their greeting. "Good afternoon, Miss Callie."

"Indeed, it's a lovely day, Mr. Totten." She smiled up at the widower everyone in the village knew wanted to marry her aunt, gathered her skirts and stepped by him into the dim, cool interior of the mercantile.

The blend of aromas that always made her want to take a deep sniff greeted her. She detected the sharper scent of lemon among that of the usual leather, coffee and molasses and skimmed her gaze over the long, wood counter. A slatted wood crate holding the yellow fruit nestled in a bed of curly wood shavings sat a short distance away. How far had they traveled by ship, canal boat and wagon? She eyed their plump firmness, walked to where the proprietor was stacking boxes of paint dyes and placed her basket on the counter. "I'll have six of the lemons, Mr. Cargrave. And a quarter-pound of cinnamon, please."

She crossed to the glass fronted nest of pigeonhole mailboxes, stepped to the narrow, waist-high opening in the center and laid her missive on the small shelf. "I've a letter to post, Mr. Hubble."

The stout, gray-haired man turned on his stool and squinted at her through the pair of wire-rimmed glasses that rode the end of his slightly bulbous nose. "Afternoon, Miss Callie. The letter is off to your parents in Buffalo, is it?"

"No. It's for Sadie."

"Ah." He nodded his gray head, tugged at his suspenders and came over to examine the letter. "I hope you told Miss Sadie her grandma and grandpa are lonely for her. Mr. and Mrs. Townsend aren't getting any younger. None of us are. Young people sometimes forget that."

She snagged her lower lip in her teeth to keep from springing to Sadie's defense, and watched him write the rate on the top right corner, then reached into her reticule and handed him the correct coins. He dropped them in a cashbox, turned and placed her letter in an open bag on the table.

She moved on to the shelves that held dry goods and notions, selected needlepoint wool in the green and rose Sophia had asked for and carried them to her basket.

"This going on Sophia's account, Callie?"

"Yes, thank you, Mr. Cargrave." She picked up her basket and walked to the door, listened to the bells jingle their goodbye and stepped outside.

The young man stepping into the entrance alcove froze. The next instant he was touching his hat brim and dipping his head in a polite greeting.

She looked away from his hazel eyes, bright with unabashed admiration, snagged her skirt in her hand and hurried down the wood walkway.

Callie hurried up the path to the back porch and climbed the steps, glanced over her shoulder toward the barn, turned and stared. She grabbed the porch post beside her and closed her eyes. *Please, Almighty God, please...*

She took a breath and opened her eyes. They were still

there—two perfectly matched black geldings with identical white markings, being watered by Ezra and Joseph. Her stomach clenched, knotted. She could be wrong. She'd only seen them a few times. *Please, Almighty God, please let me be wrong.*

She let go of the post and crossed to the door, knowing deep inside the prayer was useless. She wasn't wrong.

He was here.

Chapter Fourteen

Callie squared her shoulders, stepped into the kitchen and closed the door.

"My, that was quick." Agnes looked up from stirring batter in a bowl and smiled. The smile faded. "Are you all right, Callie? You look a mite peaked."

"I'm fine, Agnes." She dredged up a smile, placed the basket on the worktable and smoothed back the rebellious curls at her temples. "Mr. Cargrave had lemons. I bought enough to make meringues filled with lemon curd for dessert tomorrow."

"That sounds good."

She nodded, carried the needlepoint wool to Sophia's sitting room, found it empty and headed for the door leading to the hotel dining room.

Agnes gave her a quizzical look.

"I'll be back to help with supper." She hurried through the empty dining room, stopping in the doorway of Sophia's office. Her aunt was writing in the guest register. She stared at the book, clenched her hands and closed her eyes. *Please, Almighty God, please let me be wrong.*

She opened her eyes and moved forward into the small room. If she could get close enough to read the name of the last guest...

Sophia blotted her writing and closed the register, then looked up. "Why, Callie. I didn't expect you back so soon." Her aunt's eyes narrowed. "What's wrong, dear? You look pale. Are you ill?"

"No. I'm only—" She stopped and took a breath. She couldn't ask yet—didn't want her dread confirmed.

The knots in her stomach tightened. She pressed her hands against her abdomen, drew a slow breath and forced out the question she didn't want to ask. "Aunt Sophia, what is the name of the last guest to arrive this afternoon?"

"Why, it's Mister—"

"Jacob Strand. At your service."

The sound of his voice froze her lungs. She pressed her hand to her chest and turned toward the doorway of the entrance hall. He stood there in his expensive black suit with a black satin cravat at his throat, a pear-shaped pearl resting in a cup of glittering diamonds pinned to its center, and a gold watch chain dangling across his black velvet waistcoat. He was as dark and sleek and proud as his horses. But nowhere near as likable. She detested the man.

He smiled, and made her a deep bow. "I thought I heard your voice, my dear Miss Conner."

Her stomach churned. She put all of her dislike into her voice. "I am not your 'dear Miss Conner'."

"Not yet, perhaps."

Bile rose into her throat, prevented her from speaking. She swallowed hard and clenched her hands, longing to slap the smug smile from his face.

"You know my niece, Mr. Strand?"

"I am soon to be her betrothed, Madam."

She couldn't stop her gasp, the sense of panic that gripped her at his pronouncement. Sophia's hand lifted, resting on her arm. She drew a breath and glanced at her aunt. Sophia was gazing at Jacob Strand, a frosty glint in her violet eyes.

"I assume that sentiment is according to Miss Conner's father, Mr. Strand. However, my niece now lives with me, and her wishes will determine the matter. Her father has no authority here."

Her father has no authority here. The sick feeling eased. She was in Pinewood, and no longer alone in her struggle.

Jacob Strand smiled, tilted his head in a small, mocking bow to Sophia. "As you say, madam." He shifted his gaze to her.

Sunlight from the window glinted in his dark eyes, but could not warm the cold anger in their depths. "Will you join me in the sitting room, Miss Conner? There is a small nook there that will afford us *privacy* while we discuss our future."

His contemptuous treatment of her aunt set her to trembling in every part of her body. She glanced at his offered arm, lifted her chin and looked him full in the eyes. "There is no need for privacy, Mr. Strand, as there is nothing for us to discuss. We have no future." She turned around, flashed a look of love and gratitude to Sophia and strode from the office.

"You have my niece's answer to your suit, Mr. Strand. Will you be leaving us now?"

Sophia's voice stopped her headlong rush from Jacob Strand's presence. She held her breath and waited for his reply to her aunt's question.

"I shall be staying on, madam. Perhaps I can change Miss Conner's mind...or yours."

Change Aunt Sophia's mind? How could he do that? She clutched at her stomach, breathing hard to stop her pounding heart. She had heard that silky tone in Jacob Strand's voice before. And he did not speak empty words.

Ezra closed the door behind them and frowned as Callie moved over to the porch railing, wrapped her arms about herself and stared in the direction of the barn. The sun was still bathing the valley with dusky light and the air had not yet chilled. Was she ill? "Would you like me to get your cape, Callie?"

"I beg your pardon?" She glanced at him over her shoulder, her face taut, her eyes unfocused.

"Your cape. I'd be happy to get it for you. You seem chilly."

"Oh. No. Thank you, Ezra. I'm not cold." She turned her head back around. "I love this time of evening when everything is settling down for the night. If you listen, you can even hear the river water brushing against the banks. It's so...peaceful."

She didn't act at peace. She acted restive and overstrung. He walked up beside her, turned and rested his hip on the railing so he was facing her and slipped the boot toe of his dangling foot around the base of a spindle. "What's wrong, Callie?"

Her head jerked up. Her gaze met his, then slipped away. The mass of black curls captured with a green ribbon at her crown fluttered at the shake of her head.

"There's no use denying it. You didn't eat a bite of your supper, only pushed the food around on your plate. And you say you're not cold, but you're hugging yourself as if you're afraid you'll shiver apart if you let go." He took a breath, wishing she'd look at him.

"I'm not denying it. I simply don't want to talk about it."

Her voice was quiet, strained.

"I'd like to help—if I can."

He got his wish—she looked up at him. The vulnerability on her face and the sheen of tears in her eyes tested his self-control. He gripped the railing so hard his knuckles hurt.

"Thank you, Ezra, that's very kind of you, but there's nothing you can do." The helplessness in her soft voice wrenched at his heart. Her lips lifted in a tremulous smile. "Now, why did you ask me to come outside with you? What did want to speak about?"

He dragged his gaze from her mouth, fought down the temptation to pull her into his arms and hold her close and safe in his embrace until whatever was troubling her fell away. He rose from the railing and stood looking down at her. "I wondered if you would grant me the honor of escorting you to church tomorrow?"

She bowed her head, was silent so long he thought she wasn't going to answer, and then her black curls rose up and down in a nod of silent acceptance. "That would be lovely, Ezra." She turned and hurried across the porch, stopping with her back toward him and her hand resting on the door latch. "You may call for me here—at the kitchen door." Her voice broke.

"Callie—" He started toward her.

She yanked open the door and rushed inside.

"Please don't worry, Callie. Trust the Lord and—"

"And *what,* Willa? Everything will be all right?" She whirled away from the chairs, paced the parsonage sitting room to the entrance doorway, took a deep breath and walked back again. She had to make them understand.

"I did trust the Lord, Willa. I prayed and asked Him to have His way—and look what has happened! Jacob Strand has arrived to claim my hand in marriage!" Her throat closed. Tears burned her eyes. She looked at Willa and Matthew, standing so calm and relaxed beside the fireplace, and wanted to stomp her foot. Did they not realize her position? "He came to tell me Father has given his blessing to our *betrothal.*"

"And Sophia told him you were living with her now, and that your father has no authority here."

"Yes!" She jerked her gaze back to Willa. "But you don't know Jacob Strand. And you didn't see his mocking smile. He means to have me, and he is a very powerful man."

"No one is more powerful than God."

The answer was spoken in unison. She stared at them, then turned away.

Send For
2 FREE BOOKS
Today!

I accept your offer!

Please send me two free
Love Inspired® Historical
novels and two mystery
gifts (gifts worth about $10).
I understand that these books
are completely free—even
the shipping and handling will
be paid—and I am under no
obligation to purchase anything, ever,
as explained on the back of this card.

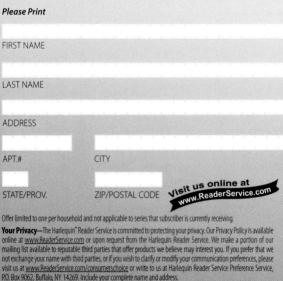

102/302 IDL FVZ5

Please Print

FIRST NAME

LAST NAME

ADDRESS

APT.#   CITY

STATE/PROV.   ZIP/POSTAL CODE

Visit us online at
www.ReaderService.com

Offer limited to one per household and not applicable to series that subscriber is currently receiving.

Your Privacy—The Harlequin® Reader Service is committed to protecting your privacy. Our Privacy Policy is available online at www.ReaderService.com or upon request from the Harlequin Reader Service. We make a portion of our mailing list available to reputable third parties that offer products we believe may interest you. If you prefer that we not exchange your name with third parties, or if you wish to clarify or modify your communication preferences, please visit us at www.ReaderService.com/consumerchoice or write to us at Harlequin Reader Service Preference Service, P.O. Box 9062, Buffalo, NY 14269. Include your complete name and address.

◄ Detach card and mail today. No stamp needed. ◄ © 2012 HARLEQUIN ENTERPRISES LIMITED. ® and ™ are trademarks owned and used by the trademark owner and/or its licensee. Printed in the U.S.A.

LIH-GF-13

Matthew stepped toward her. "Callie, I am not being glib and giving you a 'pastor's answer' to your problem. I am speaking the truth." Sincerity shone from his eyes, rang in his soft words.

Her stomach clenched, knotted. She pressed her hand against her abdomen, and fought down a surge of bile. "Then you are telling me it is God's will that I marry Jacob Strand?"

"I am telling you that if you put your trust in God, He will work things out for the best."

"I *did* put my trust in Him. And Jacob Strand has come for me." The words left a vile taste in her mouth. She drew a deep breath, turned and walked toward the door.

"Callie, *wait!*"

She turned to face her friend rushing after her. "No, Willa. There's nothing more to say. If it is God's will that I marry Jacob Strand, then He will have His way. As you say, there is no one more powerful than God." She squared her shoulders, clenched her hands and lifted her chin. "And I will lose. But I will fight Him every step of the way. I will not willingly marry that man."

She rushed across the small entrance, opened the door, slipped through and pulled it closed. Moonlight lit the walkway. She followed it to the street, crossed the hard-packed dirt, and made her way around the hotel. The gravel of the carriageway pressed into her feet through the thin soles of her slippers.

She headed for the path to the porch, refusing to give in to her despair. She'd had such high hopes when she went to the parsonage. And there wasn't a shred of them

left. There was only her puny strength against a powerful man and an all-powerful God.

She caught her breath, climbed the steps to the porch
and went inside, looking around the kitchen. Her home.
She would resist every effort to take her from it.

She crossed to her bedroom, prepared for bed by
moonlight and slipped beneath her covers.

*I wondered if you would grant me the honor of es-
corting you to church tomorrow?*

Ezra. Her defenses collapsed. Tears poured from her
eyes. A plea streamed in silent agony from her heart.
*Have Mercy, Almighty God, have mercy. I love him.
Please let me stay.*

She reached out and lifted the sprig of pussy willow
from the nightstand, clutched it close against her heart
and buried her sobs in her pillow.

Chapter Fifteen

Callie smoothed the bodice of her bottle-green dress, slipped on the twilled silk jacket and fastened the small buttons that marched from her neck to her waist. Thank goodness Aunt Sophia insisted on a simple breakfast for the guests on Sundays. And for Agnes, who had offered to make the gruel. She simply did not feel equal to cooking this morning. The muscles in her face tightened. It was certain Jacob Strand had slept well and felt no such fatigue.

She shook out the sections of the divided skirt of the jacket to hang straight over the gown's long, full skirt, peered into the mirror and straightened the points of the high collar, lifting her gaze. Her face was pale, and there were faint violet smudges beneath her eyes that testified to her sleepless night. Tears stung her eyes. She wanted to look her best this morning. For Ezra.

She swallowed hard and glared at her reflection. "No more crying, Callie Conner. If you stay strong and simply refuse him, Jacob Strand cannot win." It was pure bravado. She'd seen his eyes. Her hands shook as she adjusted the mass of curls atop her head.

Knuckles tapped softly. She whirled, staring at the door. Agnes was in her room upstairs. She took a deep breath and crossed to the door and pulled it open. Her held breath escaped at the sight of Sophia's maid. What had she expected? "Yes. What is it, Mary?"

"A message for you from the fine gentleman in room ten, Callie. 'Mr. Strand awaits your presence in the reading room.'" The maid gave her a curious look laced with envy and turned away.

"Mary—" She halted, shook her head as the maid turned back. "Never mind. I'll go speak with him myself." She cast a glance at Sophia's closed door. Her aunt was dressing for church, but she was there. What comfort that was. She was not alone.

She straightened her shoulders and walked through the empty kitchen, crossed the length of the dining room and stopped in the doorway of the small reading room beside Sophia's office.

Jacob Strand turned from looking out at the street, made her a small bow and smiled. "You look beyond beautiful this morning, my dear Miss Conner—as always."

She ignored the spasm in her stomach and lifted her chin. "Mary said you wished to speak with me."

Anger flashed in his dark eyes. "You are not normally so rude as to ignore my compliments."

Her heart pounded. She clenched her hands, made no effort to hide her disdain. "I am no longer forced to comply with my father's wishes. What is it you wanted?"

His mouth tightened. The knuckles of the hand holding his kid gloves went white. "I will overlook your discourtesy as a result of your surprise to see me here, my dear. But do not test my good graces too far." His eyes bored into hers. "I assume there is a church you attend in this *village*." His lips curled at the word. "I wanted to tell you I will escort you there this morning."

"No, Mr. Strand, you will not. I already have an escort." Oh, the joy of speaking those words, of knowing Ezra would soon be calling for her. She whirled away from the sight of Jacob Strand's furious face and hurried back toward the kitchen to wait for Ezra's knock on the door.

"Miss Conner!"

She froze at his imperious call, lifted her chin and turned. Jacob Strand stood in the doorway of the reading room, his features as cold and still as a statue's.

"Play your little games if you must, Miss Conner, but I assure you, it will not gain you or your father one cent more. I have paid all I intend to pay for you."

Her hands trembled, her insides quivered. She waited until she could speak through the painful tightness in her throat. "Return to Buffalo, Mr. Strand. I have neither regard nor respect for you, and I am not interested in your money." She held her ground as he stepped close, refusing to look away when he gazed down at her, his eyes glittering with malice.

"I shall return to Buffalo shortly, my dear Miss Conner. And *you* will accompany me. Your father has announced our betrothal, and I will not be humiliated in front of my friends."

"You have no choice—or friends. Only others like yourself who use each other to feed overweening pride."

His eyes flashed. His nostrils flared. "It is you who have no choice, Miss Conner. Unless you wish to see your parents lose their home." His voice was cold, deadly.

And now she knew the price her father had set for her hand. *Thank you, Aunt Sophia.* She took a steadying breath, buried her trembling hands among the folds of her long skirt and lifted her head high. "My parents have a home here, Mr. Strand. I am not for sale."

He smiled.

It was the most frightening thing she'd ever seen.

The hymns were only noise, Matthew's sermon a droning of words. She heard them, but they had no meaning she could grasp and hold on to. All she could think about was Jacob Strand. She had disliked him before, had disdained his smug satisfaction with the underhanded business practices he spoke about with his friends within her hearing, had hated that he treated her as a bauble to be purchased—but she had never been afraid of him until today.

Callie glanced at Sophia sitting beside her and listening intently to Matthew, and love and gratitude swelled her heart. If not for Sophia…

She blinked back tears, clasped her trembling hands in her lap and wished again that she were plain. Jacob Strand would never have looked at her if she were plain. But God had seen fit to make her uncommonly beautiful, and Jacob Strand had decided he must have her. Her stomach knotted. She closed her eyes, fought the need to look at Ezra sitting tall and strong on her right. She dare not, lest she lose all control and start sobbing.

Oh, Almighty God, please, please make Jacob Strand go back to Buffalo and leave me here in Pinewood.

There was a general stirring. A low murmur as people spoke to one another. Church was over. She opened her eyes, unclenched her hands. It was impossible for her to smile and chat about everyday matters. She leaned toward Sophia. "Please make my excuses to everyone. I don't feel well, and I'm going home."

"I'll come with—"

"There's no need, Mrs. Sheffield. I'll see her safely home."

She looked at Ezra standing beside the open pew door, and tried not to read anything other than polite concern into the look in his eyes. It was only her foolish heart that wanted it to be more…much more.

She gathered her skirt and stepped out of the pew, walked up the aisle beside him, conscious of his hand holding her arm, and of the looks and smiles of the villagers in attendance. He opened the door for her and they moved out onto the porch into the warm April air. She took a breath and glanced up at him. "Thank you, Ezra. I—"

"The groom, Miss Conner? This *stable hand* is your escort? He is the one you are using to try and make me jealous?"

She jerked her gaze to the bottom of the steps. Jacob Strand smiled and shook his head.

"It won't work, my dear. I have settled our betrothal funds upon your father and you'll not entice me to give you more." He touched his hat brim, made a slight bow and walked away, a gold-headed cane swinging from his hand.

She looked up. Ezra was staring after Jacob Strand. "Ezra, I'm so sorry. I—I don't know what to say." She strained the words from her taut throat. "It's not true."

Behind them the church doors opened and people filed out onto the porch. He glanced over his shoulder, looked back at her, his eyes shadowed, a closed expression on his face.

"You're quite pale. I think I'd best get you home."

His grasp on her arm tightened. He led her forward, helped her down the steps, then released her arm and walked beside her down the walkway to Main Street.

So polite. Ezra was always polite. But never before so silent and distant. She drew breath to explain, but looked up at the sound of hoofbeats. Jacob Strand's matched black geldings pranced by pulling his fancy rig, the cover folded down to showcase the man in all his expensive fineness. He dipped his head in their direction and smiled.

She glanced at Ezra. His eyes had darkened to a steely gray. The muscle along his jaw pulsed. "Ezra…"

He looked down at her and that closed expression returned to his face. "Sorry—the way's clear."

He took her elbow, his grasp so light she could barely feel it and stepped out into the street, an invisible but very real wall between them. It was clear any budding interest he may have felt toward her had died. She swallowed back her explanation along with the sobs clawing their way up her throat and lifted her hems off the hard-packed dirt.

* * *

Joseph cleared his throat. "You missed a good supper, Ezra. That Agnes is almost as good a cook as Callie."

"I wasn't hungry." Ezra glanced over his shoulder to where Joe leaned on the stall door then stepped in front of the bay. "Callie didn't cook tonight?" Was she with that *popinjay?* He gritted his teeth, tightened his grip on the handle of the bucket he carried.

"Nope. Must be she's feeling under the weather."

Or out riding with her *betrothed.* The thought was like a hot coal burning in his gut. He held his gaze from the empty stalls where the black geldings were stabled.

Joe squinted at him. "What's eating at you, son? You look sour as milk left in the sun to curdle."

"Nothing I want to talk about." He dumped the measure of grain into the manger, patted the bay's neck and moved toward the door.

Joe backed up, pulling the door along with him. "I know how that is. Let me know if I can help."

He nodded, caught the stall door Joe sent swinging toward him, shoved it the rest of the way closed and secured the latch. "There is something. I'd like to go for a walk. I've got some thinking to do." He set the bucket on top of the grain chest, looked at the old man who had become more friend than boss. "If that's all right with you."

"You've earned a night to yourself and more besides, son. I'll take care of whatever needs doing here."

He nodded his appreciation, strode to the open doors, grabbed his jacket off a peg and stepped outside and turned to follow the path to the river. It was harder to see it now with the grasses growing.

He headed for the band of trees by the river, their new leaves bright green in the fading light from the sun slipping behind the foothills in the west. The ground of the open field was firm beneath his long strides, the boggy areas all dried up. He stepped onto the trail, welcomed the darkness from the enclosing trees, the silence broken only by the flow of river water.

How could he have been so wrong? He jammed his hands into his pockets to keep from driving his fists into the nearest tree. It was that *popinjay* he wanted to punch until that arrogant, sneering look disappeared.

But what good would that do? She would still be betrothed to the man. He kicked a stone off the path, sent it sailing out into the river and watched the ripples spread. To think that Callie had used him to try and gain more money for her father and herself! He snorted out a bitter laugh. It was usually *his* money women were chasing after. Of course, Callie didn't know about his wealth. Good thing, because she'd had him completely fooled. He'd been on the brink of asking her to marry him—was only waiting to be sure the affection she had shown toward him was real.

Real. *Ha!* Miss Callie Conner was quite an actress. Better than any he'd seen on stage. And Sophia Sheffield—she had certainly played her part well. He'd felt there was some reason she was letting him pay court to her niece when she believed he was lying to them. Now he knew what that reason was—money. It was always money. Why hadn't he believed his instincts during that conversation she had with him, as he did in business?

He gave another snort and ripped a piece of loose

bark from a tree beside the path. No need to puzzle that out. He was aware that no one in Pinewood knew of his wealth, and he'd relaxed his guard. And he'd been so besotted by Callie's beauty and her sweetness—

He clenched his hand. The bark crumbled beneath the power of his grip. He uncurled his fingers and dropped the shreds to the ground, staring down at it. That's all that was left of his life here in Pinewood—shreds. It was time to go home. To go back to the city, and the people he *knew* were using him for their gain.

A bitter grin tugged at his mouth. He would ask to borrow his writing needs from Sophia Sheffield. There was a certain justice in having her supply him with the means to write Tom Mooreland for funds to pay his way home.

He filled his lungs with air, blew it out, brushed his hands together and pivoted, the shredded bark disappearing into the soft dirt of the path beneath his boot as he started back the way he had come.

Chapter Sixteen

Ezra hadn't looked at her once during breakfast. Not once. Not even a quick, stolen glance. He'd eaten his meal, discussed the day with Joe and Sophia and left.

Callie wiped the flour from her hand and reached for the cup sitting at the end of the worktable. Not that the tea helped the sick feeling in her stomach. But at least the warm brew felt good sliding down her throat. She took a swallow, put the cup down and scooped up a spoonful of the butter and maple sugar mixture she'd made. It helped to be busy.

How foolish she had been to attach any meaning other than a lonely and polite young man's impulsive gesture to that sprig of pussy willow Ezra picked for her. And of course he would ask her to accompany him to the Seneca dance. He was a stranger in Pinewood. He knew no one to ask but her. But the way he had looked at her…

No. It meant nothing. And even if he had had a budding regard for her, Jacob Strand's lies had destroyed it. That was obvious. She swallowed hard and blinked back a rush of tears. How she detested that man! She would never agree to marry him. *Never!* She shoved the butter and maple sugar mixture into the center of the cored apple resting on a square of dough and dropped the spoon back into the bowl.

"Have I done something wrong, Callie?"

She jerked her attention from her thoughts and looked across the work table at Agnes, saw the worry in the young woman's eyes and shook her head. "Why no, Agnes. Why do you ask?"

"You're frowning. I thought maybe I'd made a mistake or something." Agnes set her finished dumpling in the baking dish and reached for another cored apple.

"No, not at all, Agnes. You're a wonderful cook. I was only...thinking."

"About Mrs. Sheffield having a restaurant?"

She stared at Agnes's excited expression. Jacob Strand's coming had driven the restaurant idea right out of her thoughts. How selfish of her. She forced a smile. "It will mean more work for us, but I think it's a lovely idea."

Ezra's idea. The thought had her swallowing back tears again. "I'm sure once they become accustomed to the notion, the ladies of Pinewood will be coming here to meet for tea with their friends." She ducked her head, pulled the dough up around the apple she'd filled, moistened the corners with a bit of milk, pinched them together and put the dumpling in the dish.

"Callie." Cora's head poked around the dining room door. "The gentleman from room ten wants to talk with you. He's in the reading room again."

How many times must she refuse him before Jacob

Strand would give up? An image of that smile flashed into her head. She took a breath to steady her voice. What could he do? Her parents would have a home here with Sophia. His power over her was gone. "Thank you, Cora. Please tell Mr. Strand I've no time to speak with him."

Cora's head bobbed and disappeared.

"If you want, I'll finish the dumplings so you can go and talk to the gentleman, Callie. I don't mind the work."

There was kindness and envy in Agnes's voice.

She shook her head. "I don't wish to speak with Mr. Strand, Agnes. I'd rather be here cooking with you."

Curiosity flared in Agnes's brown eyes. She ignored it and reached for another apple.

What a day. The hotel was full. Mr. Totten had brought back four new guests on his late afternoon trolley run to Olville. And two more had come in on horseback. Sophia was right. The warm weather brought out the travelers. Her aunt was still busy overseeing the settling in of all the new guests. Callie slipped out the door, wrapped her arms about herself and drifted down the porch steps to stroll about the field, too restless to stay within the confines of four walls.

She glanced toward the barn, hoping. He was not outside watering horses. There would be no "chance" meeting. She veered her thoughts from that dangerous path, her emotions too strained to withstand more of her foolish, broken dreams. It was safer to think about the hotel.

Thank goodness for Agnes. It had taken both of them to prepare enough additional food to feed the late influx of guests. She made a mental note to tell Sophia they would have to increase the amount of milk, butter and cheese she bought from Mr. Hoffman. And the size of their orders from Brody's Meat Market must be increased as well. Pride swelled. Her aunt's hotel brought increased profits to all of Pinewood's businesses.

A soft breeze swept across the meadow, ruffled her hair. A dog barked. Happy, perhaps? Out for an evening romp with Joshua before the boy's bedtime? She tucked the curl tickling her ear back under the ribbon that was supposed to confine them to the top of her head, and glanced in the direction of the parsonage. How blessed Willa was. Envy rose.

It's not that I don't want Willa to be happy, God—I do. It's only that I want to know Your hand of blessing upon my life as well.

She choked off the words pushing upward from her heart and turned to look at the pink and gold rimming the clouds above the hills beyond the river. She was afraid to ask for a husband and children—the husband she wanted—when she was refusing Jacob Strand's offer of marriage. Not that God didn't already know.

She kept her back toward the barn, refused to think or speak the name in her heart lest something terrible happen. *Have Your way, dear God.* She'd offered the prayer, and Jacob Strand had arrived. She was frightened to offer another.

Tiny white and blue flowers clustered at her feet, trailed off through the meadow grasses, the purple beauty of violets scattered here and there among them. At the edge, the white heads of adder's-tongue bowed and bobbed in the breeze. She bent to pick a violet. Her hands shook.

She straightened and looked at the sinking sun. The idea of disobeying God after yielding to His will was terrifying—but the thought of being wed to Jacob Strand was unbearable. *Please forgive me for not honoring my word. You know the repugnance I feel for Mr. Strand and his lifestyle. He is a man who professes belief in You, yet lives his life according to his own lights. Surely, surely, You cannot wish me wed to such a man. Oh, Lord, You are all-powerful. Please, please save me from Jacob Strand.*

Shadows of darkness lengthened across the sky. The pink and gold of sunset dimmed. She turned to return to the hotel. Jacob Strand was striding toward her. He stopped in the middle of the path where it curved around the buttery and smiled.

She read the message clearly. He was waiting for her to come to him. And she had no choice. This time. She lifted her chin and moved forward on the path.

Ezra wiped off the nib of the pen, put the stopper in the inkwell, set the borrowed writing tools on the blotter and rose. He glanced across the empty kitchen at the stove, braced himself against the memory of Callie in his arms when he'd caught her close to keep her from being burned, and shoved his chair under the table.

Mister Thomas Mooreland
American Founders Bank
Broadway
New York City

He stared down at the direction written in his bold, slanted hand. The muscle in his jaw pulsed. He picked up the folded and sealed letter, opened the door and stepped out onto the porch. Darkness was claiming the sky. It suited his mood.

He trod down the stairs and stepped onto the path that led toward the barn.

"Why did you not come when I sent for you? What takes up your precious time, my dear Miss Conner? Picking flowers?"

"I *like* violets. And I told you, I am—"

Callie. And that *popinjay?* Ezra jerked to a halt. Their voices were coming from the path that led to the field. They must be returning from a walk. To the deer path where he'd first revealed his heart by giving her the sprig of pussy willow? An unfounded sense of betrayal hit him, but he was in no mood to be reasonable. The muscle along his jaw jumped. His hands fisted.

He glowered and looked around, feeling trapped. He couldn't go back to the porch—and if he kept going toward the barn he would have to pass them. He glanced at the crushed letter in his fisted hand. It did not bode well for a meeting with Callie's betrothed. Neither did his thudding pulse.

He hurried forward, stepping off the path into the deeper shadowed area behind the buttery and wished he were anywhere but there.

"I summoned you because I wanted you to go for a ride with me. My new rig is—"

"I'm certain it's the finest available, Mr. Strand. Your pride would permit nothing less. However, I am not interested in your fine possessions, or your wealth, or you. And should you summon me again, you will receive the same answer. I have no time for you."

They were coming closer. Their voices were louder and he could hear their footsteps during the pauses in their conversation. He felt like an eavesdropping sneak. How he wished he had the right to confront the man. He backed farther into the darkness, felt the stones of the buttery wall press against his shoulder. If they would take a few steps more he would be able to slip around the corner and escape into the darkness where he wouldn't have to listen to Callie manipulating the besotted fool for more betrothal money. She was good at it—pretending no interest in the man. He could almost feel sorry for him—almost.

"That would not be wise, my dear. I am—"

"Do *not* call me 'your dear'!"

That did not sound like playacting. He straightened and peered through the darkness toward the path, waiting for them to come into view.

"Enough!"

The footsteps stopped. He tensed, strained for any sound.

"I am out of patience, Miss Conner. The next time I request your company, you will come immediately. Is that clear?"

"Unhand me."

The underlying fear in Callie's voice set him moving. He ran around the buttery, stepped onto the barn path and whistled a tuneless melody as he strode toward the hotel.

He stopped a few steps from them, dropped his gaze to Callie's hand rubbing her other wrist. "Good evening."

The man fastened his gaze on him, his dark eyes glittering with anger. "Go back to your horses, and don't interfere with your betters. We are having a private conversation."

"Your conversation is over. Callie was about to go inside." He ignored her gasp, took her elbow and urged her toward the steps.

"Ezra, *wait*." She dug in her heels, looked up at him. "I don't want—"

"Stay where you are, my dear!" The man stepped close, his gold-headed cane lifted in his hand. "And you—" the cane swept his direction "—take your hand off my fiancée!"

He deflected the head of the cane with his free hand, tightened his grip on Callie's arm and gave her a little push out of harm's way. She caught her breath and raced up the steps. He turned.

"You have the *gall* to interfere with—"

His lips formed a tight smile. He couldn't help it. He was so hoping Callie's betrothed would swing that cane his way again now that Callie was safe and his hands were free.

The man's gaze narrowed on his mouth, lifted to his eyes then dropped to his hands hanging loose at his sides. He stepped back, tugged at his waistcoat and curled his lip. "I will not accommodate your obvious wish for an altercation. A gentleman does not indulge in fisticuffs with a ruffian."

"A *gentleman* does not manhandle a lady."

The insult bit deep. The man's nostrils flared, his lips drew back over his teeth. "You do not know to whom you are speaking!"

"Neither do you."

"You *dare* to challenge me, you upstart? I'll have your job! And see to it you never find another!" The man strode out to the gravel way, disappeared around the corner of the hotel.

He stared after the coward, his hands clenching and unclenching, his pulse slowing.

"Please don't be concerned about Mr. Strand's threat, Ezra. Aunt Sophia will never dismiss you at his say-so. And he has no influence here in Pinewood." Callie's soft words trembled on the night air.

He turned and looked up at her. She was standing at the top of the stairs beside the porch post—a shadow figure with a bowed head, garbed in a gown turned black by the night. He wished he could see her face clearly, read what was written there and know the truth.

"I'm sorry I stepped in between you and your betrothed that way, but—"

"He is *not* my betrothed!" Her head lifted. Even in the darkness he could see her hands fold into small fists at her sides. "Father may have accepted money from Jacob Strand for my hand, but he will have to return it and give up his grand brick house on Perry Street. I will never wed that man. *Never!*"

Her voice quivered, broke. He heard her take a breath, saw her head turn toward the corner where Jacob Strand had disappeared. His heart lurched. She'd been telling the truth all along. What a fool he'd been to doubt her. "Callie..."

She looked down, and he could see tears glistening in her eyes. He started up the steps.

"I *loathe* that man, Ezra. And all of the other wealthy, arrogant men that were bidding for my hand, as well."

Wealthy? He halted, his heart pounding.

"That's why I ran here to Aunt Sophia. I cannot abide those men or their self-serving, deceitful ways."

Deceitful. The word stabbed deep, held him there, halfway up the steps.

"They are liars, the lot of them. And they always have an underhanded, selfish reason for the deals they make and the stories they tell. They think their wealth and prestige sets them above everyone else—that their money can buy anything, even a wife. Well, I am not for sale!"

She whirled around, her long skirts swishing against the floor as she ran across the porch and rushed inside.

Deceitful.

The slam of the door drove the word deeper. He stood on the steps while the silence and the darkness settled around him, then turned and walked down to the path, picked up the crushed letter he'd tossed to the ground and headed for the barn. He'd finally found a woman who would love a man for himself, not his purse—a woman his heart longed for. And now, the deception he'd indulged in to find her might cost him any chance he'd had to win her heart.

I cannot abide those men or their self-serving, deceitful ways. They are liars, the lot of them!

Her words twisted like a knife in his heart. He should have trusted his instincts about Callie's goodness and told her the truth from the beginning. He swallowed against the sick feeling in his gut and stared down at the letter in his hand. He had to tell her who he really was and ask her forgiveness.

And God's.

Conviction swelled. What a fool he was. He looked up at the black sky strewn with stars. "Forgive me, Lord, for not trusting You to provide the answer to my dilemma instead of trying to work things out with my scheming. I vow I will never again deceive or lie to gain my way, but will put my trust in You. And, please give me the words that will make Callie understand, because I'm not giving up until I've earned her forgiveness and her respect. And, Lord, I promise You, I will always love and honor and cherish Callie with my whole heart if You will bless me with her love."

He stepped off the path and strode beyond the barn to the river and tore the letter to pieces, the ripping sounds loud in the silence. He watched the bits of white paper darken and disappear in the water, turned and headed back for the barn. It was in God's hands now. Tomorrow, Callie Conner would meet the real Ezra Ryder.

Chapter Seventeen

She was a coward. All during breakfast she had avoided looking at Ezra, afraid to face him after her outburst last night—afraid of the disgust she might see in his eyes. And just now, she'd told Mary to tell Jacob Strand she would not speak with him instead of facing the man herself.

A shudder ran through her. She frowned and scooped the pieces of carrots and turnips out of the bowl into the iron pot dangling over the fire. The tantalizing aroma of simmering ham rose from the disturbed broth. Her stomach clenched in rebellion. She was unable to even entertain the idea of eating this morning. Jacob Strand had truly frightened her when he'd gripped her wrist so forcefully. It had taken all of her self-control to not throw herself into Ezra's arms when he'd come striding toward them out of the dark.

She stepped around Agnes, rolling out dough to be fashioned into tarts for supper, and slipped the bowl into the pan full of soapy hot water, swished the cloth around it then slipped it into the rinse pan. Ezra had seemed so…

confident last night. He had not appeared at all intimidated by Jacob Strand. It had been quite the opposite.

She snatched up the towel hanging over the edge of the dry sink and pulled the bowl from the water, paused, and remembered the glitter in Jacob Strand's eyes, the snarl in his voice.

You do not know to whom you are speaking!

Neither do you.

What had Ezra meant? He had made his reply with such authority—

The door squeaked open. She abandoned her thoughts, and smiled as Sophia entered. Her smile died. "What's wrong, Aunt Sophia?" She put the bowl on the shelf, absently wiping her hands.

Sophia placed her basket on the table and glanced around the kitchen. "Cole Aylward just stopped by on his way to deliver shingles in Olville. Cora's mother is not well. Her father says she's to come home immediately."

"Oh, poor Cora."

"Yes." Sophia removed her hat, smoothed back her hair. "Callie, please go and tell Ezra to hitch up the shay and bring it around to the back immediately. I'll go tell Cora and help her gather her things." She started for the door, looked back over her shoulder. "And tell Ezra if he pushes Star, he can have Cora home within an hour. He can rest Star on his way back."

She nodded and hurried out the door and off the porch onto the path, lifted her hems and ran toward the barn. The doors were open. She slowed, brushed back the curls shaken free by her quick dash and stepped into the cool, dim interior. She blinked to adjust her eyes, heard a sound and looked up.

Ezra was in the loft forking bedding down into an empty stall, his broad shoulders straining the fabric of the blue shirt he wore, the muscles in his forearms, exposed by his rolled-up sleeves, knotted and stretched. Her pulse skipped at the sight of him. "Ezra."

He froze, and glanced her way.

"I've a message from Aunt Sophia." *Coward. Afraid to face what you feel. Afraid he'll think little of you after your tirade last night.*

He stuck the fork in the mounded hay, swung over the edge of the loft, dangled there a moment then dropped and came to stand in front of her. "What is it?"

His eyes. Her heart thudded. She looked down, focused on the piece of straw clinging to the front of his shirt. "Cora's mother is unwell. You're to hitch up the shay immediately and take her home." Her fingers twitched to reach out and pluck off the bit of hay, to feel the coarseness of the fabric of his shirt against them. She looked up and met his gaze, warm and deep and— Warmth crawled into her cheeks. It was safer to look at the bit of straw. "Aunt Sophia says to push Star on the way and get Cora home as quickly as possible, then rest Star on the way home."

She turned. His hand caught hold of her upper arm— gently, but there was power in his long, callused fingers. She fought the urge to turn into his arms, to feel their strength around her. She took a breath and looked up at him. "Yes?"

"I want to talk to you, Callie. Will you go for a walk with me along the deer path at dusk?"

His voice was warm, quiet. His intent gaze steady on hers. Her pulse throbbed in her throat. She prayed her quivering knees would continue to support her and nodded. "I would like that."

"Good. I'll call for you at dusk."

He smiled, and she almost fell. Traitorous knees. She nodded, made a careful turn and walked, step by cautious step, from the barn.

A bird in the tree outside her window chirruped a happy song. Callie smiled, straightened from the mirror and went to the window to try and spy the cheerful creature among the leafy branches.

She whistled at the bird as Daniel had taught her, but received only silence in reply. She was out of practice. "All right, stay hidden in your leafy bower!" She laughed, then whirled back across the small bedroom to finish tying the bow of the wide ribbon restraining her curls. Not even their obnoxious habit of pulling free to fall on her forehead and dangle down her neck dulled her happiness. Ezra would be returning soon. She would watch him drive to the barn. And then, this evening after supper—

Hoofbeats! Her stomach flopped. Could he have returned so soon? She ran to the window—drawing back at the sight of the matched blacks prancing and tossing their proud heads. The horses halted, the phaeton they pulled rolling to a stop. She jerked her gaze to the driver. Joe. Breath gusted from her.

The elderly groom climbed slowly from the fancy rig, tied the reins to the hitching post and limped back toward the barn. The hood of the phaeton was down. Her face tightened. No doubt Jacob Strand was going for another posturing ride for the benefit of the residents of Pinewood. She turned away from the window, lest he see her there when he walked to his rig, and returned to the mirror. She would not allow Jacob Strand to ruin her day, to spoil her anticipation of what was to come.

Ezra wanted to talk with her. The mere thought of being with him alone brought a restless, breathless excitement. She adjusted the loops of the bow and straightened the ends, smiled at the slight trembling in her fingers. Ezra wanted to walk with her—on the *deer path*. She glanced at the sprig of pussy willow on the nightstand. Her stomach fluttered. His choice of place *must* mean something special. And his voice and his eyes when he had asked her! Surely that look in his eyes meant he found her…attractive.

She turned her head left then right, studied her reflection. He'd never said he found her pretty, or tried to kiss her—not even when the opportunity was there. An image of him holding her close by the stove flashed into her head followed by the memory of him bending over her in the tilted shay, his face so close to hers. Perhaps tonight…

She stepped back from the mirror and wrapped her arms about herself. What would it feel like to have Ezra embrace her? To feel the strength of his arms about her, his lips pressed to hers? She smiled and closed her eyes.

Knuckles tapped against the wood of her door. Heat

rushed into her cheeks. "A minute!" She pushed away the dream, and walked slowly over to open the door, giving her cheeks time to return to normal. "Yes? What is it, Agnes?"

"There's a man here who wants to speak to Mrs. Sheffield, and I can't leave my doughnuts to fetch her." Agnes pivoted and rushed back to the stove.

She walked over to the stranger standing just inside the kitchen door. The man's eyes had that glazed look men wore when they first saw her. She lifted her chin. "May I inquire as to why you wish to speak with my aunt, sir?"

"Um…er…" The man's head gave a sharp shake. He cleared his throat. "It's about a sign she wants made."

"Oh. Yes. For the restaurant." Excitement tingled. "Wait here please. I'll get Mrs. Sheffield."

She exchanged an excited smile with Agnes and hurried into the empty dining room—a room that would soon be filled with patrons all day. The excitement grew. She glanced into the living room and smiled at the guests sitting and conversing with one another. Sophia was not among them. She hurried toward her aunt's office, her head swarming with ideas for table decorations and special menus, and froze at the sound of Jacob Strand's voice. Why was he with her aunt?

I shall be staying on, madam. Perhaps I can change Miss Conner's mind…or yours. Bile rose into her throat at the remembered words. Her pulse raced.

Not Aunt Sophia, Lord, please. Don't let Jacob Strand harm Aunt Sophia. She gathered her skirts close so their rustle would not betray her presence and edged closer.

"…is being unnaturally obstinate about seeing me, but it will do her no good. I will not increase the amount I am paying her father for her hand one cent."

"My niece is not interested in your money, Mr. Strand. And she has made it clear she does not wish to entertain your suit. As you will not leave willingly, I am telling you to leave my hotel today."

"*You* are telling *me?*" Jacob Strand gave a disdainful snort. "My patience is at an end, madam! My plans are made. You will go to your niece *now,* and you will advise her to come back to Buffalo with me as my betrothed. We will journey to Dunkirk tonight. And we will wed tomorrow, after I take her to her parents' home where she will change into suitable attire. Now please hurry. My conveyance is waiting outside."

Her heart jolted. It was there—right outside her window. The strength leached from her body. She leaned her head back against the wall and closed her eyes. *Almighty God, help me! Please help me.*

"How convenient, as you are leaving my establishment *now.* And you are leaving alone."

"You will not advise your niece to marry me?"

"I will not."

Tears sprang to her eyes. She pressed her hand to her constricted chest and sagged against the wall, waiting. It wouldn't work. She knew Jacob Strand, he was too proud to lose.

"I believe you will, madam."

The certainty was there, in his silky tone. She turned her head toward the door, strained to hear over the pounding of her heart.

"…outstanding loan on this hotel. Unless you go to your niece this instant and advise her to marry me, I will return to Buffalo, buy your loan from the bank and then return to throw you both out into the street. Unless you do as I say, not only will Miss Conner no longer have a home here, you will be homeless as well."

No, God, please—

"Do what you will, Mr. Strand. I will never tell Callie to marry a man as vile and contemptible as you."

"Very well, madam, if that is your decision. I advise you to prepare to live elsewhere with your niece. For when I return as owner of this hotel, I intend to burn it to the ground."

So cold and emotionless. So uncaring of the damage he would do to so many by his vengeful act. And it would be her fault. She never should have come to Pinewood.

"No." Fury replaced her fear. She shoved away from the wall and stood in the doorway, her hands clenched and her chin lifted. "You will not ruin Aunt Sophia's life. I will return to Buffalo and marry you. And I promise you, I will do my utmost to make you regret it the rest of your life."

"Callie, no! Don't go with him! Don't marry him!" Sophia rushed toward her.

Jacob Strand stepped between them, his eyes glittering, his mouth tight.

"Don't touch her." She looked full into those dark, mean eyes and issued her ultimatum. "If you want me for your wife, don't you dare touch her."

She turned and walked through the entrance hall to the front door and stepped out onto the porch, blocking

Sophia's cries from her mind. A door slammed. Jacob Strand's footsteps sounded behind her.

The sun shone bright upon her as she strode to the phaeton and climbed to the seat. She'd never been so cold in her life.

Jacob Strand freed the reins, climbed in beside her and cracked his whip. The horses leapt forward.

Sophia was rushing down the front porch steps as they swayed out onto Main Street. She faced straight ahead, thankful she couldn't hear her aunt calling to her over the thundering beat of the horses' hoofs.

Chapter Eighteen

Star's hooves thudded against the plank floor of the barn announcing her eagerness to be home. The shay left the gravel way, bumping over the sill. Ezra eased his taut hold on the reins and glanced toward the empty space on his left. The phaeton was gone—and the black geldings. No doubt Jacob Strand was out riding around showing off his fancy rig again. Or, perhaps, after last night, Strand had gone back home to Buffalo—though he wasn't the sort to give up when he wanted something, and Strand wanted Callie. He'd be glad to see the last of the man. And not only because of Callie. Strand's presence was like a dark blotch on the village.

He scowled, draped the reins over the dashboard when Star halted and tossed her head. He'd met many men like Strand, arrogant, unscrupulous thieves that hid their sly deeds beneath the law, good manners and elegant trappings. His good fortune was that he had an ability to recognize them for what they were, thwart their underhanded ploys and make them accept a straight, upright deal. It seemed Callie had that same ability. He'd seen that in her suspicion of him when he arrived. What would she think of him when he told her the truth? His gut clenched.

Lord God Almighty, please give me the words to make Callie understand that I'm not like—

"I'll take care of Star." Joe stepped into view, looked at him over the top of the mare's broad back. "Mrs. Sheffield said she wanted to see you soon's you got back."

"What about?" He jumped from the shay and walked forward, rubbing the mare's muzzle. "Good girl. You've earned your feed today."

The older man shrugged, ran a gnarled hand down Star's neck. "Don't know. But she sounded upset, and it takes a lot to rile Mrs. Sheffield. You'd best go find out what she wants."

He nodded, his mind sorting through possibilities. "It might be something to do with opening the restaurant."

"Could be." Joe turned and began unhitching Star.

He gave the mare a last pat and strode out of the barn toward the hotel, glancing at the kitchen window. Was Callie watching? His pulse quickened at the thought, his stomach tightening. He'd sure be thankful when tonight was over and this push-pull of apprehension and anticipation had ceased. He was a man of facts and wasn't accustomed to dealing with emotions and uncertainty. But Callie was worth it. Glory, how he loved her!

He broke into a whistle and lengthened his stride, took the porch steps two at a time and crossed to the door, frowning at the squeak when he opened it. He made a mental note to check the hinges for rust and stepped inside.

Callie wasn't in the kitchen. He swallowed his disappointment and looked at Agnes. The young woman looked a little harried. "Mrs. Sheffield wanted to see me."

Agnes nodded, spooned ham and vegetables onto a plate and reached for another. "She's in her sitting room."

He caught a whiff of ham, frowned as his stomach grumbled at not having been fed since breakfast and stepped around the dining table to Sophia's door. His pulse sped at the muffled sound of voices. If Callie wasn't in the kitchen serving up dinner for the guests, she was likely with her aunt. Odd that the door was closed.

He raised his hand and knocked. The voices stopped. The latch clicked. He stepped back as the door opened.

"Ezra! Thank God, you're back! Come in."

He stepped into the room, stared at Sophia, taken aback by the woman's puffy, red-rimmed eyes, her tense features. He glanced at the young woman standing by the settee, noted the same puffy, red eyes and tense features on Willa Calvert's face. *Callie.* His throat tightened, squeezed. He closed the door and turned to Sophia. "You wanted to see me?"

The older woman nodded. Her mouth worked. His sense of foreboding deepened.

"Callie's gone—with Jacob Strand."

The words slammed into him with the force of an enraged stallion's kick. His heart lurched. His gut knotted. He stared into her eyes and read the distress, the anger and the helplessness in them. *Learn the facts.* He took a firm hold on his roiling emotions and cleared his throat. "What happened?" His voice came out tight, but calm.

Sophia searched his face, straightened her shoulders and placed her hand on his arm. "To understand, you have to know that Callie came here to Pinewood to escape Mr. Strand and others who were bidding with her father for her hand."

He forced back the dark anger uncoiling inside him and nodded.

"Mr. Strand won Callie's father's blessing." Bitterness laced Sophia's voice. "Knowing of Callie's effort to escape his offer for her hand, Mr. Strand made some inquiries before he came after her." Sophia's eyes flashed violet sparks. "He found I have a loan—with the hotel offered as surety of payment—with the Bank of Buffalo. When Callie refused to speak with him this morning, he came to me and ordered me to advise Callie to marry him. I refused and—" Her voice broke. Her fingernails dug into his arm.

"And he threatened you with the loan." The dark ugliness gave way to a clear, cold calmness at her nod. This was familiar ground, but he needed more details. "What exactly did he say?"

"He told me if I did not persuade Callie to return to Buffalo with him and marry him immediately, he would go buy the note. Then he would throw both Callie and I out into the streets, and burn the hotel to the ground. I told him to do what he must, but Callie overheard—"

"And she went with him." *I will never wed that man. Never!* His hands fisted. Callie hadn't fully realized the viciousness of her opponent.

"Yes. To save me." Sophia blinked tears from her eyes, straightened her back. "That's why I wanted you to come see me when you returned. I need you to feed Star well, give her a good rubdown and then hitch her back to the shay. Willa is going to take care of the hotel, and I am going after Callie and bring her back."

"How do you intend to do that?"

Her head lifted. "They are stopping in Dunkirk for the night. I'll overtake them and convince Callie that I will provide a home for us until we can start a restaurant. Humble though it may be, it will be better than her spending her life with that vile man!"

"No, Sophia."

He jerked his gaze to Willa Calvert, watched the young woman move to Sophia's side, wary of her purpose.

"You will tell Callie that you *both* have a home with Matthew and me as long as needed. And that it doesn't *matter* if Jacob Strand purchases the hotel and burns it to the ground, because everyone in Pinewood will help you rebuild the Sheffield House." Willa's small chin jutted. "We may not be able to stop Jacob Strand from burning the property in revenge for Callie refusing him, but he cannot stop us from rebuilding it!"

The people in Pinewood were a revelation to him. How wonderful to have friends who cared nothing about wealth, but willingly shared what they had with you and quickly stepped forward to help in time of need. He'd been a fool to judge these good people by the actions of those he knew in the city who both openly and covertly pursued wealth as their goal in life at whomsoever's expense.

"That won't be necessary, Mrs. Calvert."

He looked from her startled, puzzled expression to Sophia, watched the worry and fear in her eyes yield to a look of speculation, a spark of burgeoning hope. "Strand said Callie was to wed him immediately on their return to Buffalo—is that correct?"

"Yes. Tomorrow. After he took her home so she could change into proper attire."

He nodded, then reached for the door latch.

Sophia reached out and gripped his arm. "You're not going to hitch up Star, are you, Ezra?"

He looked down, shook his head. "No. I'm going to Buffalo—to stop a wedding. A man on a saddle horse can travel a lot faster than a woman in a shay."

She stared, the spark of hope flickered, blazed brighter. "*What* saddle horse?"

"The one David Dibble is going to sell me." He turned from her astonished look, pulled open the door, strode through the kitchen, outside and across the porch. He cleared the steps in one leap and hit the path running, the length and power of his strides eating up the distance to David Dibble's livery.

"Mr. Strand requests that you join him for supper, miss. He says unless you do, you'll have nothing to eat." The maid's mouth tightened. "He's ordered that we're not to bring supper to your room."

Callie nodded, tightened her hand on the doorknob. "Tell Mr. Strand my answer is no—he'll be dining alone." She closed the door behind the maid and threw the bolt. She'd had to endure Jacob Strand's presence beside her in the phaeton—and she had no choice but to wed him tomorrow—but tonight, his threats held no power. To-night she would shun his company and be alone.

She turned from the door and looked around the tiny corner room.

A room on the top floor should discourage any thoughts you may entertain about running off, my dear.

How little Jacob Strand knew her. She eyed the narrow porch outside the window. It ran the width of the inn, and there was a tree at the corner of the building. Thanks to Daniel's lessons, it would be a simple feat for her to climb onto a branch and scramble to the ground. It was not the height of the room that held her prisoner—it was the rest of Jacob Strand's words.

Of course, should you do so, it would not bode well for your aunt. You see, I intend to purchase that bank note on her charming little hotel after all. It should serve nicely to ensure that you obey me and treat me with respect. Never threaten me again, my dear.

Her fingers twitched. She'd wanted to slap that smug smile off his face. *Oh, Aunt Sophia, I never meant to endanger you. I didn't know—* Sobs shook her. They clawed and crawled their way up her throat, filled her mouth. She buried her face in her hands, clamped her lips together and forbid them release.

Oh, God, help me. Deliver me from Jacob Strand.

But how could He? She drew a shuddering breath and lowered her hands, squared her shoulders. Not even God could make Sophia's bank loan disappear. If He was even real. She had prayed God would have His way and all of this had happened. And none of it was what she'd been taught was acceptable by a Holy God. She was trapped—ensnared by the machinations of a despicable man—and without hope.

Ezra.

His name hovered on her lips, brought intense longing, crushing pain. Tears stung her eyes, and made hot, wet paths down her cheeks. She drew a deep breath and then another, forced the image of his face from her mind. She must not speak his name, must not think of him. He would live forever in her heart, but she must bar him from her thoughts or she would not survive.

She wiped the tears from her face and stepped to the window, looked out at the shimmering green water of Lake Erie. Swift-moving, rolling waves with frothy, white crests raced to shore and threw themselves with reckless abandon upon the sand. Flocks of seagulls swooped through the air inches above the turbulent lake, dipped and snatched sustenance from the roiling surface. The white bodies of the raucous birds bobbed in an awkward dance as they landed, pecked at some enticing morsel among the grains of sand, then flapped their black-tipped wings and soared into the air to avoid an onrushing swell of water.

She wrapped her arms about herself and watched the brave seagulls and the tumbling waves, emptied her mind of all else. She must learn to live each day without hope, and to never, *never* think about tomorrow.

The dusky pink and gray sky deepened to purple. The lighthouse on the point of land jutting out into the lake blazed to life, sent its warning beam sweeping over the restless, rippling waves in intermittent flashes. The air cooled and the sky turned an inky black. The seagulls disappeared.

She shivered in the night chill, leaned her forehead against one of the small glass panes and wished the birds would return.

His progress had slowed to a walk, the night too dark to permit any speed. Stars twinkled in the sooty sky, but too few to give him any length of vision. The sliver of moon slipped in and out among dark clouds, hiding its silver face, refusing him aid.

Ezra leaned forward and stroked the neck of the long-tailed bay gelding, delighted by the power and strength in the muscles that bunched and stretched as the horse climbed the hill. He'd told David Dibble he needed a mount with staying power, and Dibble had certainly provided one.

He straightened and squinted through the darkness trying to make out a dark form a short way ahead. A bush? Or a hungry, marauding bear? He glanced down at the bay, took his cue from the lack of fear and relaxed in the saddle.

He'd been ready to promise David Dibble anything for the horse—fight him for it had it been necessary—though the older man looked tough as leather. The truth was, the man's rugged exterior covered a warm and generous heart—and he'd already heard about Strand's threat to Sophia.

He shook his head and pulled his shirt collar up against the cold night air. This experience was teaching him a lot about life in a small town. Dibble had handed him a bridle, led him to the bay then saddled the horse without any talk of payment. "You bring Callie back. We'll see to her welfare and Sophia's. And we'll take care of that 'strutting rooster,' should he follow you back. We don't take kindly to people threatening one of our own—especially decent women like Callie and Sophia."

And there had been at least a dozen people lining the wood walkway in front of the block of stores who had nodded silent support as he rode by. He would never forget the brave waves and grim faces of Sophia and Willa, standing side by side on the front porch and watching as he rode out of town.

He urged the bay to better speed as the land leveled out. He was going to enjoy living in Pinewood. As soon as he stopped this wedding, made sure Strand would never threaten Callie or her family again, and won her for his own.

Chapter Nineteen

The bay's ears pricked forward, its pace quickened. They must be approaching Lake Erie. Ezra sniffed the air, listened for the wash of waves on the sand, but they were too far away for him to smell or hear the water.

A large bird's wings flapped overhead, loud and close enough that he ducked, though the owl or hawk was no doubt after one of the small animals that rustled through the grassy fields that bordered the road. He straightened and looked toward the whirring sound now off to his right, but could see only darkness and rode on, the clop of the horse's hooves against the dirt road a discordant interruption of the surrounding silence. How many animals crouched in the darkness and watched his passing? A wry grin twisted his mouth as he eased back against the cantle. There were probably more than he cared to know about.

The sliver of moon that had played hide-and-seek all night slipped from behind a cloud in the inky, star-strewn sky and cast a stingy, silver gleam over the fields and the road ahead. A beam of yellow light flashed on his left, disappeared, flashed again. The lighthouse. His heart thumped. He remembered that light flashing the night he was robbed. The Dunkirk stage inn was not far ahead. He'd caught up to them.

He leaned forward and strained to see through the meager moonlight, caught a glimpse of a looming shadow as the light flashed out over the lake again. He drew a breath and relaxed back in the saddle, held himself from urging the bay into a reckless speed. If he remembered correctly, the haystack he had awakened in after the attack was beside the stables. That would place the building a little behind and to the right of the hotel. He reined the bay that direction and found what he was seeking.

The waves lapping against the shore, and the pounding of his pulse in his ears were the only sounds as he halted beside the fancy phaeton sitting under the shelter of a slanting roof attached to the stables. He twisted in the saddle, looked up at the windows reflecting the flashing light and pushed his clenched fists hard against his thighs to keep from running inside and pummeling Jacob Strand to within an inch of his life. That would not solve the problem. There was a better way.

He slipped from the saddle, led the bay to the water trough and stared at the hotel while the horse drank. Was Callie awake? Could she sense his presence? Did she hope he would come after her? He set his jaw, turned and gripped the reins close, then patted the bay's neck. "Let's go, fella. We've got more traveling to do."

He mounted and looked again at the windows. "Don't despair, Callie. I promise you it will be all right." His whisper hovered on the air. He tapped the bay with his heels and headed him back onto the road to Buffalo.

Bank of Buffalo. There it was. An impressive building. Ezra eyed the cold, gray-granite structure warmed to a golden glow by the morning sunshine and dismounted. He tied the bay to the hitching post, glanced down at his rough clothes and ran his hand over the stubble on his face, wished for a suit and a razor. It would be a lot easier to convince the banker of his identity if he were properly groomed, but difficulty had never stopped him. And he'd never before had such pressing, imperative reasons for winning.

Callie. How long did he have before Jacob Strand made her his bride? He set his jaw and hurried up the granite steps.

"Mr. Strand ordered the gown made for you, dear. Isn't it lovely? The rose-and-leaf ribbon trim on the tiers of the skirt is simply exquisite!"

Callie's stomach churned. She watched her mother lift the luxurious cream-colored silk gown off the bed and walk toward her, swallowed hard.

"He borrowed one of your dresses for size so the gown would fit perfectly. And he even had matching petticoats made. He's such a thoughtful, considerate man."

She bit back the words she yearned to say and stood silent as the silk gown whispered over her body. It would do no good to express her contempt for the man she would soon wed. Nothing could help her now. Bile surged into her throat. She swallowed hard, then took a deep breath.

"I don't know why you look so…grim, Callie. Really dear, you should be positively beaming! Every young woman in the social circuit had been trying to win Mr. Strand's affections, and he has chosen you. You are a very fortunate young woman." Her mother bent to settle the ruffled tiers into place. "Why, you will live in the largest home, have the most servants and the very best of everything! And you shall never have to cook another meal."

Her mother straightened, shook her head. "I can't imagine what Sophia was thinking of, having you cook for the guests in that hotel of hers."

"Aunt Sophia did not *have* me cook for her guests. I *offered*." The words burst out. Jacob Strand's threat that she not speak of what had transpired at the hotel did not extend to defending her aunt, or her desire to cook and feel useful instead of parading around in fancy gowns for the sole purpose of winning a rich husband so she could continue parading around in fancy gowns.

"Well, Sophia shouldn't have permitted it." Her mother reached out, took hold of her wrist and lifted her arm. "Look at your hands—they've become dry and… well, never mind. They will soon soften again."

Her mother turned her toward the padded bench in front of the dressing table and gave her a little nudge. "Sit down and rub some cream into your hands while I tie this headband of silk roses around your hair, Callie. We haven't much time. Mr. Strand told your father to have you at the church within the hour."

Her stomach heaved. She clapped her hand over her mouth, ran to her dressing room and bent over the washbowl.

A large brick home on Perry Street—that's what Callie had said. *Almighty God, please...let me be on time.*

Ezra reined in the bay, leapt from the saddle, wrapped the reins over the hitching post and ran up the brick walk. He lifted the lion's head knocker and rapped it against the plate, resisted the urge to open the door and rush inside.

The handle turned. The door whispered open. A maid dressed in black scanned her gaze over him. "Deliveries are made—"

He stepped inside before she could close the door on him. "I'm here to see Callie. Get her immediately."

The maid gaped at him, no doubt confused by his authoritative manner. "Miss Callie isn't here. Her father and mother took her to the church. She's—"

His heart lurched. His gut clenched. "Where is the church?"

"Why, I—"

"Quickly, woman!" He snapped out the words. There was no time for politeness.

"Down the street." The maid pointed. "Turn right at the corner. The church is in the middle of the next block."

He pivoted out the door, jumped off the stoop and raced down the sidewalk, tugged the reins free and leapt into the saddle. He kicked the bay to speed, reined him around the carriage ahead, and galloped to the corner. The bay wheeled right at his touch, thundered down the street and sat back on his haunches when he tugged on the reins.

He leapt from the saddle, dropped the reins and ran up the brick walk, jumped to the stoop and shoved open the double doors.

The interior was dim after the sunshine. He blinked, ran toward the sound of a muffled voice, and stiff-armed another set of double doors. They burst open upon a wide, carpeted aisle. Five people stood in front of an altar at the other end.

Jacob Strand whirled about. The man who had been speaking stopped, and gaped at him. The other man and woman turned and looked his way. Only Callie stayed facing front, hopelessness in the slope of her shoulders.

Fury shook him. He strode down the aisle, his bootheels thudding loud against the carpet in the silence.

Recognition flashed into Strand's eyes. "What are you—"

"This wedding is over."

Callie's back stiffened, her shoulders lifted. She turned, met his gaze, and the love he so longed for shone in her eyes.

"Ezra."

His name was a whisper, a hope fulfilled. He stepped close, took her hand in his, felt it tremble. "I've come to take you home."

"You'll do no such thing! Take your hand off her!"

"Who is this man?"

"What right have you to interrupt these sacred proceedings!"

He ignored the men, and looked into Callie's beautiful violet eyes now shimmering with tears. "Let's go."

Her lips quivered. She withdrew her hand, shook her head. "I can't."

"Very wise, my dear." Jacob Strand smiled, then glanced at him. "Go home to your horses." He turned to the preacher. "Proceed with the ceremony."

"I said there will be no wedding." He fought back the anger, the desire to drive his fist into Jacob Strand's sneering face and focused on Callie. "You don't have to marry Strand, Callie. You—"

She shook her head. "I do. Aunt Sophia's hotel—" Her voice broke.

"It's all been taken care of. The loan is paid." *Please, God, let that be enough until I have a chance to explain—*

Jacob Strand snorted. "That's impossible. The loan was outstanding when I left for Pinewood."

Please, God... "The loan was paid this morning."

"By whom?"

The words were a sneering challenge. He looked into Callie's eyes reading the confusion, the hope, the desperation in them and knew he was out of time. He had to tell the truth—even if it cost him her love. "By me."

"You!" Jacob Strand laughed. "And did you buy the note on her father's house, as well?"

He looked at him.

Strand's laughter died. His eyes narrowed, his nostrils twitched as if smelling danger. "Who are you?"

"My name is Ryder—Ezra Foster Ryder—of New York City."

Strand stiffened. "Ezra *Ryder*. Of New York City? Are you—" He cleared his throat. "Are you the Ezra Ryder who owns the Ryder Custom House?"

He dipped his head.

"And the American Founders Banks, and the Founders Insurance Company?"

"That's correct." He let Strand think about that a moment, then spoke in a calm, quiet tone. "You know, it is never a good idea to use one home as surety on another—it puts them both in danger."

Strand's face paled. "My King Street property..."

"*My* King Street property until you pay off the indebtedness."

He heard Callie's gasp, but kept his gaze fastened on Strand.

"And Conner's property?" Strand's voice had lost its confidence. The man was defeated and knew it.

"Mr. Conner's home has been freed of all encumbrance."

He turned. Callie was staring at him as if she'd never seen him before. His heart sank. "It's time to go home, Callie. Sophia is waiting."

He took her arm and led her up the aisle, her parents following. Her silence, and the paleness of her face, tore at him. He guided her through the first set of double doors to the second set, led her through them and out into the sunshine.

She stopped, drew a shuddering breath and pulled her arm from his grasp. "You lied." There was a world of hurt in her voice.

He clenched his hands to keep from reaching for her. "No, Callie. I never lied."

Her eyes accused him. "No, you only deceived me. I suppose in your world there is a difference." She started down the brick walk.

He grabbed her arm, stepping close. "Callie, please. I can explain—"

She wrenched her arm from his grasp. "I'm certain you can, Mr. Ryder. Men like you *always* have an explanation for the sly, self-centered and dishonest things they do! Well, I am not interested in your convenient, mendacious explanation. Why would I believe it?" She started down the walk, turned back, her chin high, her eyes glistening with unshed tears. "And, so you will know—I intend to purchase Aunt Sophia's note from you. I will earn the money somehow. I have no desire to be beholden to you or any other man who thinks they can buy or manipulate a woman!"

"Callie, that's not—"

Her chin jutted higher. "You'll have to excuse me, Mr. Ryder, I've a stage to catch. I'm going back to Pinewood—alone." She whipped around, strode past Strand's fancy phaeton and climbed into her parents' carriage.

Her mother followed her. Her father stopped beside him, cleared his throat. "Well, it seems you have a... fondness for my daughter, Mr. Ryder. I shall expect you to call upon me soon. We have matters to discuss."

He stared at the nattily dressed older man, read the avaricious gleam in his brown eyes, pivoted on his heel and strode to the bay, working to keep control. It wouldn't do to punch his future father-in-law. And that's what the man would be, for he had no intention of letting Callie walk away from him—not after he'd seen that love for him in her eyes.

He grabbed the reins, mounted the bay and rode off toward the bank. He had more business to take care of.

Chapter Twenty

He hadn't even tried to stop her or change her mind—hadn't followed her to the carriage and demanded that she listen to him. He'd just gotten on that horse and ridden away. And now he was gone. Somewhere. Probably on his way back to New York City.

Callie rubbed at the ache in her temples, stepped into the kitchen and crossed to the stove. The stage was slow, but she still had arrived in Pinewood yesterday. Ezra should have easily beaten her home from Buffalo riding horseback, but he hadn't. He was not at supper last night. And Joe hadn't seen him.

The sick, hollow feeling that had kept her tossing and turning and pacing through the night intensified. She blinked her puffy, tired eyes, shook down the ashes, adjusted the drafts to clear away the wisps of smoke, caught a spill afire and lit one of the lamps above the work table. The lamp swayed, its golden circle of light chasing shadows on the wall the way it had the day he'd pulled her close to keep her from burning herself.

She swallowed hard and threw the spill in the stove,

added wood to the glowing embers. The woodbox was almost empty. She clenched her hands and turned away.

Must *everything* remind her that he wasn't there? And why should she care? What did she expect? She pressed her lips together, swiped at the curls on her forehead and carried the iron teakettle to the pump at the washstand. Ezra had never said he cared for her. He'd never even said he thought she was pretty! And when he'd arrived at the church, he'd only said he'd come to bring her home. She'd assumed it was because he loved her—because she so wanted that to be the reason. And because of that sprig of pussy willow.

Tears gushed from her eyes like water from the spout. She released the pump handle and wiped the moisture from her cheeks. He'd often said he was indebted to Sophia for her kindness in giving him a job when he'd come begging. She should have known that's why he'd come to rescue her from Jacob Strand—for Aunt Sophia. It wasn't because of her at all. And she didn't want it to be. She was glad he was gone. She was simply concerned about the note he now held on the hotel. How would she ever earn enough money to pay it off? And how much time did she have? She'd overheard enough conversations between Jacob Strand and his friends to know there was a time limit on loans, and that it was important to pay them off before that time was up. And where would she send the payment? To one of the *banks* Ezra owned?

She squeezed the metal handle, longing to slam the teakettle down on the stove, but she couldn't have that satisfaction. Agnes and Sophia were still abed. And why was she so discomposed anyway? She didn't want Ezra

Ryder around her. The man was a liar! They were well rid of him.

The pounding headache that had sent her early to bed last night throbbed. She set the teakettle on the front stove plate and grabbed the skirt of her apron, pressed the fabric against her eyes to stop another rush of tears. She would not cry over a man the likes of Ezra Ryder. She would not!

Bootheels struck the porch floor.

She froze.

The latch clicked. The door squeaked open.

"I must be early. I don't smell any coffee brewing."

Her heart pounded furiously. She wanted to run and hide in her room. She wanted to run into his arms and sob out the fear that had gripped her—the fear that she would never see him again.

"Something wrong?"

"Smoke." It wasn't really a lie. The smoke *had* made her eyes smart…more. She lowered her hands, smoothed down her apron and watched Ezra unload the stovewood he carried into the woodbox. Anger replaced the hollow emptiness. How could he look and act so *normal,* when she was so…*not* normal?

"What are you doing here?" The words did not come out as cool or as steady as she'd tried for. She lifted her chin. "Not that you don't have the right. You own the hotel now. Until I can earn the money to buy back Aunt Sophia's loan."

His back stiffened. He brushed bits of bark and dirt from his shirt, turned and started toward her, his gaze fastened on hers. Her breath caught at the anger darkening his eyes.

"My name is Ezra Ryder, Callie—not Jacob Strand. And frankly, I do not care for you ascribing the man's selfish and underhanded motives to me. I do not *own* this hotel. Your aunt owns it—free of encumbrance. I presented her with the cancelled note and a signed relinquishment of collateral when I arrived late last night. As for what I'm doing here…"

She held her breath, hoped.

"…I'm doing my job."

She dug her fingernails into her palms, breathed deep against the sudden, rending pain in her heart. Her foolish, *foolish* heart that refused to listen to her head. "I hardly think a man of your financial accomplishments needs work."

"That's true. However, I did need work when I arrived." His gaze softened. "If you remember, I'd been robbed of everything. I was injured—I had nothing to eat and nowhere to sleep and no way to contact my business manager for funds."

His *business manager.* There'd been no mention of him when he came. She clenched her hands. "And so you lied to me."

He shook his head. "And so I asked you for the meal and bed I sorely needed in exchange for work. And your aunt provided me with those things and gave me a job when I needed one. I would be the worst sort of ungrateful wretch if I simply walked away from my responsibilities. Besides, Joe needs help. The work is becoming too much for him. I can't leave my job until there is some-one hired to replace me."

His gaze bored down into hers, and she could not deny the sincerity with which he spoke. But, oh how much easier it would be if he weren't so kind and generous. If he weren't so considerate of Joe, and grateful and thoughtful of her aunt. It undermined her resolve.

"As for you, Callie Conner…"

Her heart skipped.

He stepped closer, leaned down. Flames in the depths of his blue eyes flickered like the lighthouse beam at Dunkirk that flashed its message of warning into the dark. *Danger…danger…danger…*

Her knees quivered and her mouth went dry. She stepped back, felt the worktable and groped for its support.

"…You should go back to bed and let Agnes prepare breakfast."

His voice was low, soft. His breath warmed her cheek. She looked into his eyes, so close, so— His palm cupped her face, his thumb brushed across her cheekbone and her determination to resist him dissolved into a form-less wisp of nothingness.

"You look tired."

She closed her eyes, drew on her inner strength and slipped sideways along the table, opened her eyes and stepped around the end to safety on the other side. "I'm fine. And I've work to do."

She walked the long way around the table to fill a large bowl with water. The space between the stove and worktable was too narrow to be comfortable with him standing there, and he showed no signs of moving. She put the filled bowl on the table, set a basket of potatoes beside it and wished he'd stop looking at her, and that the horrible need to cry would go away.

"I know there isn't time now, Callie, but I want to explain why I didn't tell you about myself."

His voice was as warm as his touch had been. She steeled herself against it, snatched up her paring knife and a potato and began to work. The teapot hissed out steam. She ignored it. She was not going to go to the stove and chance getting that close to him again. If only he would leave her kitchen—leave her life.

"Will you come for a walk on the deer path with me at dusk?"

The image of him picking that sprig of pussy willow flashed into her head. Her throat clogged with the tears demanding to be released. Walk with him? On the deer path? *Never!* She would not ever walk there again. She cleared the lump away and put all the coolness in her voice she could muster. "There is no reason for you to make me any explanation, Mr. Ryder. I would not believe it. And, that, of course, means there is no reason for a walk." She took a chance and looked up at him. "Now, if you'll please allow me to work…"

He held her gaze with his, then when she thought she could bear it no longer, he dipped his head.

"As you wish, Callie, but I'm not going to give up. I need to explain, and you're going to listen. Tonight or next week or next month, it makes no difference. I'm a patient man—and a persistent one. One day you will agree."

"Your patience will do you no good." She dug her fingernails into the potato, fought to keep her voice steady. "There is no acceptable explanation for deception, Mr. Ryder, and I'll not listen to yours. Go back to New York City."

He walked around the table, stood so close she could feel the warmth radiating off him, see the flicker of those tiny sparks smoldering in the depths of those blue eyes.

"That will never happen, Callie. All I want is here in Pinewood. I'm not leaving." He turned and walked to the door, gave her another look that shook her to her toes. "I'll see you at breakfast."

She held her place, waited for the door to close behind him. The latch clicked. She dropped the potato and knife onto the table, ran to her bedroom and closed the door. She hurled herself onto the bed and buried her weeping in her pillow.

"Good morning, boy." Ezra scratched beneath the big bay's black mane, stroked the proud, arched neck. "You need a name. How about...Reliable, because you surely proved to be so on our night ride to Buffalo."

The bay nickered, tossed his head.

"Seems like he's agreeing."

He glanced at Joe, smiled his gratitude for the man's extension of friendship. Things had been strained between them since he'd come back from Buffalo and told Joe who he really was. "Seems that way, so Reliable it is." He slipped a halter on the bay so he could lead him out to the watering trough. "Do you know this Otis Gordon fellow Mrs. Sheffield has hired to take my place helping you?"

Joe nodded, leaned back against a stall. "I know him. He's a good hand with horses. I reckon he'll be taking my place, and I'll be the one doing the helping." He scrubbed a gnarled hand over his stubbled chin, narrowed his eyes at him. "Truth is, it's been that way with you—you've just been too kind to say so."

"Joe, that's not—"

"Yes, it is. You been doing the work around here, Ezra. I've been helping out when Mrs. Sheffield called on you to do something else. With this rheumatism crippling me, I can't keep up with all the work there is to do around this place anymore. And I ain't blind nor dumb—I can read the writing on the wall."

He looked at the elderly groom, saw the frustration and worry in his eyes. "It's a lot of work all right." He chose his next words carefully, heeding Sophia Sheffield's warning that Joe would have no part of anything that he thought had a whiff of charity about it—even if he was dead wrong—and he would be. "Do you know anyone else like Otis? You know, someone who's good with horses? I'm going to need someone."

"*You?* What for?"

"I'm going to build a place."

Joe nodded. "I figured you was going to stick around. Still, you're the best hand with a horse I've ever seen—you don't need no help."

He grinned. "Thank you, Joe. I take that as a real compliment coming from you. But, I'm going to be returning to business, and I won't have time to care for

Reliable and the carriage mare I bought." He led the bay toward the open doors, taking hope when Joe followed.

"That phaeton of yours ain't nowhere near as fancy as the one that Strand fellow had—except for that purple color." Joe grinned, and his eyes danced with a teasing light. "That's right pretty."

And he'd bought it because he thought Callie would like the color. It reminded him of the dress she'd had on the night of the Seneca festival dance. He shoved the memory aside and pulled his face into a mock scowl. "It's called *plum*."

Joe's grin widened. "Looks purple to me."

"As I was saying…" He loosed his grip on the halter and let the bay drink. "I want someone I can trust to take good care of my horses. I thought about offering you the job, but I don't want to take you from Mrs. Sheffield. I owe her a lot and stealing her head groom would not be fair to her." He stroked the bay, kept his expression mildly curious as if waiting for Joe to supply him with a possible name. His charade wouldn't fool the canny old man, but it would save his pride and allow him to accept the offhand offer on his terms—if he wanted to.

The elderly man studied him, then nodded. "Like *I* was saying—I been reading the writing on the wall. I can't take care of this big barn and all the guests' horses and rigs the way it should be done anymore, and me and Mrs. Sheffield both know it."

Joe stepped forward, ran his gnarled hand over Reliable's broad back. "I figure I could care for a small stable and a couple of horses with no trouble."

"Then you will come to work for me?" He had no

trouble looking relieved. He'd been afraid Joe would say no.

"Soon's I'm sure Otis can handle things here, and you need me."

"Good." The bay lifted his head, blew. "C'mon, boy, let's get you back in your stall. I've got to clean my things out of the equipment room before Otis comes."

"You moving into the hotel?"

There was amusement in Joe's voice. He fixed his gaze on him. "I am. Why?"

"Cause Miss Callie ain't going to like that, and she can be right spirited and stubborn as I recall. Course, I've seen you being a mite stubborn, too." Joe chuckled low in his throat and led the way back into the barn. "This is gonna be right fun to watch."

Chapter Twenty-One

"What has you so upset?"

Callie spun about and frowned at Willa sitting so calm and serene in the chair by the window. "I've been *telling* you, Willa! Have you not been listening?"

"Of course I have." Willa held Joshua's shirt sleeve a little closer to the sunlight coming in through the small panes and took another stitch in the tear. "You told me that Ezra came to Buffalo and stopped your wedding to Jacob Strand just in time—for which I assume you are grateful?"

"Well, of course I am. I detest Jacob Strand!" She batted her long skirt out of the way of the tea table leg and strode toward the entrance door at the other end of the room.

"...And that Ezra paid Sophia's loan at the bank."

"Yes!" She half hissed the word. The yellow-striped cat stretched out on the carpet leapt up and hunched its back, the fur on its neck and back rising.

"...And that now Sophia has hired a new stable hand, and Ezra has moved into the hotel."

"*Yes.*" The cat hissed and ran from the room, darting up the stairs. "I'm sorry, Tickles." She called the apology after the furry, yellow blur of motion, whirled about and started back toward Willa. "And Ezra is acting as if he *owns* the place—which he does."

"Oh?" Willa frowned, then took another stitch. "I thought you said Ezra gave Sophia a...a relinquishment of..."

"—collateral. He did. But there has to be a reason he's—" She stopped, glared. "Must you sit there and *sew.*"

Willa lifted her head and smiled. "Would it make you feel better if I paced with you?"

"Yes! No! And I'm not *pacing.* I'm merely—"

"—too agitated to sit down?"

She huffed out a breath. "Wouldn't you be? Ezra struts into the kitchen anytime he pleases—dressed in his fine suits and fancy shirts and waistcoats—then sits there drinking coffee and talking plans with Aunt Sophia."

"Ezra doesn't seem a strutting sort of man to me."

"That's not the point." She scowled and tugged at the loose waist of her dress. "This gown is too big."

"It wasn't the last time you wore it. You must be losing weight." Willa glanced up. "Is your appetite off?"

She stiffened, placed fisted hands on her hips and stared down at her friend. "Stop it, Willa. I know what you are doing, and it won't work. We are not discussing my appetite *or* the lack thereof, we are discussing my problem."

"Ezra."

"Yes!"

"Which brings us back to what I asked before." Willa laid her sewing aside and fastened her gaze on her. "I repeat—what has you so upset, Callie? What is it you object to? That Ezra rescued you from a disastrous marriage to a man you cannot abide? Or that he paid off Sophia's loan and gave her back her hotel free of debt? Or perhaps it's that he now wears fine clothes and drinks coffee while talking with his friend? Villainous acts, indeed."

The starch left her spine. She turned away to hide the tears stinging her eyes. "You may think me foolish, but there is a reason he's done those things, Willa. I know there is. I just don't know what it is."

"Then why don't you let him tell you? You said he asked—"

She whipped around, jutted her chin into the air. "He's a *deceiver,* Willa. How can I believe him? You and Aunt Sophia, Joe, everyone…you're all willing to simply forget his deception and accept him as he is now. But someone has to be on guard against him. I *know* wealthy men like Ezra Ryder. They always have selfish motives for the things they do. There is always a sly reason—"

"Callie Rose Conner! That is so unfair and unjust. Shame on you. You are allowing your experiences with the arrogant and prideful men your father sought out to be your suitors to color your judgment. All men and women—from the wealthiest to the poorest—have reasons for the things they do or don't do. And those reasons are often self-serving, though not always selfish. There is a difference. You had a reason for coming to your Aunt Sophia that was self-serving, but not selfish.

How do you know that Ezra did not have that same sort of reason for keeping silent about who he is?"

She stared at Willa, taken aback by the lecture. "Very well. Let us ascribe a 'pure' motive to Ezra's original deception and set it aside. We now know he owns banks, and an insurance business, and a custom house, and who knows what else in New York City. Why does he stay on here in Pinewood? Why does he not go back to his businesses and his life there? There has to be a *reason*. And I don't want Aunt Sophia hurt."

"Sophia? Or you, Callie? Will you not listen to Ezra's explanation because you're afraid to let him into your heart?"

She gasped, then turned to go. "Think what you will."

Willa's hands gripped her shoulders, held her. "Listen to me, Callie. I understand that fear. I almost lost Matthew because I was afraid to trust him. I was afraid if I let him into my heart, he would turn out to be like my father and Thomas. Don't make that mistake. Oh, Callie…give Ezra a chance."

"A chance for *what?*" She swallowed away the tears flooding the back of her throat. "I don't know why Ezra is staying here in Pinewood, Willa—but it's not because of me. He's—he's never— That is…" She took a breath to steady her voice. "He's always polite and…nothing more. He's never even told me he thought I was pretty." The times Ezra had the opportunity to take her in his arms and did not flooded her mind. "I don't know what he is after in Pinewood, but I know it's not me. I'm concerned that it has to do with Aunt Sophia and the hotel.

Why else would he want to explain his deception and gain my approbation."

She stepped out from under Willa's hands and walked to the entrance struggling to stifle the ache in her heart. "Remember me to Matthew. And give Joshua and Sally my love."

She let herself out of the parsonage and started down the walk to Main Street, pausing at the sight of two tall, trim, well-dressed men standing in the large empty field beside the church. Ezra and Matthew. What were they doing?

She stood a moment and watched them walking about and waving their hands through the air, nodding and shaking their heads, then hurried to cross the street before they noticed her. She was in no condition for another confrontation with Ezra Ryder.

Ezra rode north along the road leading out of the village toward Olville. He held Reliable to a walk, eyed the open acreage dotted with trees on the side of the road opposite the river. He hadn't cared for the Allegheny's floodwaters flowing so close to the Sheffield House stables when he arrived.

He rode a short distance, stopped and twisted in the saddle to glance back over his shoulder. The land as far as Oak Street was empty of buildings. On the far corner of the street was the village park with the gazebo, and beyond it, farther back along Main Street was the Pinewood Church with the parsonage behind it. On the river side of Main Street stood the Sheffield House. Perfect. Both were in plain sight, and within easy walking distance.

He turned back and looked out over the flat acreage to a spot where a group of elm trees towered and imagined a house set in the middle of them with a stable behind it. And behind the stable, a barn—there, at the place where the land began to rise in a gentle slope to the high, forested hill that backed the property. A perfect pasture.

He smiled and reined the bay that direction. "Let's have a run out to that hill, fella. I want to see if there's any water on this land." He nudged Reliable with his heels, sat deep in the saddle and enjoyed the bunch and thrust of the strong muscles beneath him as the bay's flashing hooves ate up the distance.

Sunlight glistened on water that flowed over a rock bed in a narrow brook that ran parallel to the high hill. The bay took the small stream in a smooth leap, threaded through the trees that marched alongside it and raced on.

"Whoa, boy. Ease up now." Ezra slowed Reliable then drew the gelding to a halt at the base of the forested hill and scanned the thick growth of trees that covered it. The whisper and chuckle of water over rocks caught his attention.

He slid from the saddle and led the bay to the edge of the woods, walking toward the sound. Water seeped from between layers of slate that formed a shelf high above him, then splashed down onto a tumble of rocks and slate that formed a small pool, overflowing into a rill that ran toward the field. He'd found the source of the small brook.

The hush of the woods settled over him. He stood watching the water, thought about the delight of a young boy coming upon such a place and exploring the surrounding woods. He wasn't sure about young girls—his sister had been timid. But from the tales Callie told of her childhood adventures with Daniel and her friends, not all girls were like Iris.

His pulse quickened at the thought of being wed to Callie—of the children they would have together. "Please Almighty God, grant that Callie will allow me to explain why I let her believe I was a laborer. Please touch her heart with understanding and forgiveness, and grant that she will give me her love and allow me to love her all of my days." He whispered the prayer into the vastness of God's creation, listening to the sounds in the stillness.

Birds twittered, hopped along the branches of the trees, disappearing into their hidden nests. A soft breeze stirred the leaves high in the treetops. Beside him there was a quiet rustle of vines and ferns disturbed by small creatures, and on the forest loam beneath the giant pines climbing the hill, the quiet tread of dainty hooves.

The bay twitched his ears forward. He placed his hand on Reliable's muzzle and waited.

A doe stepped out from among the trees at the far side of the small pool, lifted her head and tested the air, then moved on to the water. Two more deer followed. He watched them drink then wander off a short distance and disappear among the trees.

Their own deer path.

The thought settled deep in his heart, brought an unshakable surety of God's blessing. *Thank You, Lord.*

He walked the bay back to the edge of the field and climbed into the saddle. "Let's go, boy. I've got some property to buy." He tapped his heels and let the geld-

ing run over the tree-dotted fields that would soon hold
the home he would build for Callie and their children.

Callie frowned at the scrape of a chair's legs against
the floor upstairs and glared up at the ceiling. How was
she to sleep knowing Ezra was awake and, no doubt,
working out the details of his *plan*—whatever it was.
And why had her aunt given him room number two when
he requested it because the window looked out upon the
barn and the river? Sophia knew perfectly well room
number two was above her bedroom. Of course, to be
fair, Sophia did not know it would matter. It *shouldn't*
matter.

Footsteps crossed the floor above, then stopped.

She tensed, listening to the silence. Finally! She
flopped over onto her side and burrowed her fisted hand
beneath her pillow. He must have—

Footsteps went back across the floor. The chair
scraped. He coughed.

She whipped back the covers, lunged from the bed,
jammed her feet into her slippers, snatched her dressing gown from the foot of the bed and stormed out into
the kitchen.

The trimmed lamp gave barely enough light to see
by. She shoved her arms into the sleeves of her dressing
gown, tied the bow closures and opened the back door.
No squeak. Ezra had fixed it the day Otis came. He
seemed to know how to fix everything. Probably from
growing up on a—

No! No! *No!* She would not think about him as a
young boy helping his parents on their farm. He had

grown into a deceiving man of business and that is the way she must think of him.

She eased the door shut and sat on one of the settles flanking the door. The one she and Willa had sat on that day Aunt Sophia had scolded them for taking Daniel's homemade raft and going out on the river. What a fool-hardy, dangerous thing for them to have done. The Lord had surely been with them, bringing them safely to the bank when the piece of branch Daniel used for an ore had broken in two. They could just as easily have been caught by the current and swept downriver to sink and drown.

She rested her head against the high, wood back and closed her eyes. *Have Your way, dear God.* She had stood here on the porch and prayed that prayer, and God had brought her to safety again. He had rescued her from sinking and drowning in a marriage to Jacob Strand as surely as He had saved her from the Allegheny's waters.

"Thank You, Almighty God. Thank You for saving me from Jacob Strand. I am so very, very thankful." She whispered the words, opened her eyes and stared into the black night, held her lips from uttering the rest of the thought. *But why, why did You have to use Ezra? Why did You bring him here? Now, it's my heart that's in peril.*

The breeze picked up. Raindrops pattered on the wood shingles of the roof, spattered on the steps and walkway. She curled into the corner of the settle, tucked her dressing gown over her feet and leaned her head against the wood wing. She would wait here until she was certain he was abed—then perhaps she could sleep.

Chapter Twenty-Two

"I went riding yesterday afternoon."

Callie stiffened, glanced at the reflected flames of the overhead lamps dancing on top of the black coffee Ezra swirled in his cup. *Please don't let him make conversation, Lord. Please—*

"I found a nice piece of property—well-watered, well-timbered, and with lots of good pastureland."

Property for what? She pressed her lips together to hold back the question and slapped the air bubbles out of the lump of bread dough she was shaping.

She stole a look at him from beneath her lowered lashes, frowned and slapped the bread again—harder. How was she to ignore him when he leaned there against the worktable drinking coffee, his suit coat hanging open, that tapestry waistcoat laying against his flat stomach and his long legs stretched out and crossed at the ankles. He looked so comfortable, so relaxed, so *well rested.* And her walking around with lavender crescents under her dull, dry, burning eyes, all because he was in room number two.

"Excuse me." She snatched up the prepared pan sitting close to where his lean hips pressed against the table, thought about brushing his dark brown suit coat with her floury hand. It would serve him right for being where he wasn't wanted, wasn't supposed to be—especially before dawn. Guests were not permitted in the kitchen. Of course, guests did not pay off your loan and give you back your hotel free and clear. Her stomach knotted. *Dear God, please reveal the reason for Ezra's subterfuge—and for his largess.*

"Want to know what else I found on the land?"

How did he *do* that with his voice? He hadn't moved an inch but it felt as if he were right beside her. She blew out a breath, and groped around in her head for an answer other than the "yes" she wanted to give. "I'm busy."

She turned to the shelf beside the stove, shoved the pan of dough beneath the towel covering the other loaves already sitting there to proof in the warmth. What was taking Agnes so long? All she had to do was bring the eggs, bacon and milk from the buttery. She turned back to the worktable, began cleaning up the spot where she'd worked with the dough.

"Yes. I can see that you're busy." He drained his cup, straightened and took a step.

Good. He was leaving.

"I'll get my own coffee." He moved toward the stove.

Oh, no. She'd been caught with him in that confined space before. She darted to the opposite end of the worktable, circled around it and stood in front of the step back cupboard, her heart pounding, her mind filled with the memory of him drawing her close. Tears welled, stung her dry eyes.

She took down plates and cups to set the table. It was getting crowded with Otis and Ezra. Why didn't he go eat in the dining room with the rest of the guests? She grabbed flatware out of the drawer.

"Good morning, everyone. Doing my job, Callie?" Sophia stepped into the kitchen, smiled and took the dishes from her.

She wiped her empty hands down the front of her apron skirt and pushed at her wayward curls. Now, what could she do? Where was Agnes? She glanced toward the door.

"What is this?" Sophia put down the dishes and picked up a rolled piece of brown paper.

"That's a sketch I drew last night."

So that's what he had been doing. Curiosity pricked. A sketch of what? She edged closer to see without letting Ezra know of her interest, saw him start toward the table and turned back toward the cooking area.

"It's a building."

Sophia's comment slowed her steps. Had this to do with the property he had mentioned? She stepped more quietly, listening.

"Yes. I thought perhaps you might like to see it, as you inspired the idea."

"Me?"

The door opened wide. Agnes leaned against it, holding the basket of food. Otis edged by her, glanced at them over the load of stovewood in his arms and dipped his head, stepping to the woodbox.

She smiled and nodded, and tried to hear Ezra over the sound of the stovewood being dumped into the box.

"...talking with people. They all were very—"

"I'm sorry I took so long, Callie. I...waited to hold the door for Otis."

She tamped down the urge to shush Agnes, and looked up. The plain young woman's cheeks were flushed, her eyes glowing. She looked almost pretty. *Oh, please let her be pretty in Otis's eyes.* What a difference the favorable regard of the right man made in a woman's heart, and to her countenance. And the lack of the right man's favorable regard, also. "I understand, Agnes." She forced a smile, then strained to hear Ezra's conversation with Sophia. "Let's get breakfast started."

She pulled the slab of bacon from the basket Agnes set on the table, and poised her knife over it.

"...safe will set here, behind my office. That's this room."

Safe? She slid the knife through the thick slab, hissed as the blade caught her fingertip. His office? She dropped the knife and stuck her fingertip in her mouth, ignoring the stinging. A safe and an office. Was Ezra—

"And what is this room?"

She glanced at the spot where Sophia touched her fingertip to the piece of paper Ezra held flat against the table, but could make no sense of the lines partially hidden by her aunt's hand.

"That is the accountant's room."

"And this is the counter where the teller will be?"

"Yes."

A bank. Ezra was going to build a bank in Pinewood.

Why? She closed her eyes to block out the image of Ezra's strong, broad hands holding the drawing pinned to the table and tried to think back to all the conversations she'd overheard between Jacob Strand and his friends. There had always been an underhanded reason for their ploys. Surely one of those reasons would be—

"You look pale, Callie. Is the cut bad?"

She opened her eyes and looked into Agnes's concerned gaze.

"Why don't you go tend to it, then rest for a bit? I'll finish breakfast."

She started to protest, thought better of it and nodded—it would give her time to think. "Thank you, Agnes. I won't be long."

She started for her bedroom, but halted as Ezra stepped in front of her.

"You've hurt yourself?" The concern in his eyes and voice made her stomach flutter. *Foolish woman.* It was just his way.

Sophia hurried around the table. "Callie, dear, I didn't know you'd hurt yourself. What happened? Let me see."

She tucked her bleeding finger into her palm and shook her head. "It's nothing—a scratch only. Excuse me, please."

She pulled her long skirt close and swept around Ezra into her room, closed the door and leaned back against it, her finger forgotten. A bank? In a village as small as Pinewood? What sort of scheme was Ezra planning?

The old sign screeched in protest as it was pried from the place it had occupied for almost twenty years.

"Gracious, I feel as if I'm betraying an old friend."

Callie smiled at her aunt, then turned back to watch the new sign being lifted into place and nailed to the fascia board of the porch roof. "The touch of red at the edge of the black border is very attractive and eye-catching, Aunt Sophia."

"It does look nice."

"It's right pretty, Sophia."

"When does the restaurant open?"

Callie's heart swelled with pride as Sophia turned and smiled at the friends and neighbors gathering at the edge of the road. "The restaurant will be open for breakfast tomorrow morning. We will serve all day and close after supper."

"Only imagine—our very own restaurant in Pinewood."

"I can hardly get my mind around it."

"Well, I won't have any trouble getting my mouth around a good piece of pie or cake."

Callie joined in the laughter as the rotund barber who had left his shop to come and watch the sign being hung patted the white apron over his belly. "We'll be happy to accommodate you, Mr. Fabrizio."

"Such a change—a restaurant. And I heard we're going to have a bank, too. Whoever would have thought it?"

"We can all thank Mr. Ryder for both. He is bringing new prosperity to Pinewood." Sophia made a gracious little wave toward the side of the crowd.

She glanced that way, and saw Ezra standing watching

the carpenter. His gaze slipped over the crowd, met hers. Her pulse skipped. She turned back to face the hotel.

"That's it, folks. The sign's up there good and proper." Daniel Dibble waved his hammer through the air at the burst of applause, then backed down the ladder.

She glanced at Sophia chatting with the well-wishers around her, smiled and walked across the gravel carriageway. She would have to write Sadie about this moment. She lifted her skirt hems to climb the three steps to the walkway, winced at the touch of the fabric against her sore fingertip.

Boots struck the planks behind her. *Please let it be Mr. Fabrizio.* It wasn't. She recognized the sound of Ezra's footsteps, felt his presence. She braced herself, fixed a polite smile on her face. He stepped into view beside her, and stayed there.

"That's quite a celebration going on back there. Your aunt is regarded with much love and respect by the people of Pinewood. And I can certainly understand why."

Her breath caught at his smile. She glanced toward the mercantile, quickened her steps. "With all that's happened, I don't believe I have ever thanked you for bringing the restaurant into being. I'm certain it will ease Aunt Sophia's concerns over finances. Not that you haven't already done that." She gave him a sidelong glance, then looked straight ahead.

"All I did was suggest the idea for the restaurant, Callie. Sophia's planning and hard work brought the idea to fruition. And it's your cooking talent that will make it successful."

"Nonetheless, the idea was yours, and it has helped

Aunt Sophia. I'm grateful." She couldn't feel that way about his paying off the loan. It made her uneasy. If she could only figure out what he hoped to gain by it. She paused, gave him a polite nod of farewell and stepped into the recessed entrance to Cargrave's Mercantile.

He stepped in behind her, leaned forward and pushed open the door. Bells jangled, mimicking the jangling of her nerves.

A trembling took her at the feel of his arm against hers, the closeness of his face. The space was so small she could feel his warm breath on her cheek. If she moved the smallest bit… She clenched her hands and froze in place, afraid to even breathe.

"I'll see you at supper, Callie." He turned and walked away.

She closed her eyes, took a moment to compose herself, then gathered her skirts and stepped inside, thankful he hadn't come into the store. His presence was too…disconcerting, and it seemed there was no place she could go to be away from him.

She closed the door, and pushed all thought of Ezra away. The man was becoming an obsession. She stepped to the post office and smiled at the postmaster sitting on his stool. "Good afternoon, Mr. Hubble."

"Afternoon, Callie." He glanced at her over his thick shoulder. "You've got a letter from your parents. I hope everything is all right."

"I'm sure it's fine. There's nothing from Sadie?"

"Nope, not today."

She sighed and stepped to Sophia's box, removed the letter nesting there and turned back toward the door.

"Callie, dear!"

She looked down the narrow aisle in front of the dry goods shelves, smiled and hurried forward. "Mrs. Townsend, how good to see you again." She leaned down and kissed the woman's plump cheek. "I'm sorry I haven't come out to visit yet, but—"

"Hush, dear. Don't you apologize. I heard what happened." Sadie's grandmother stretched out her pudgy hand and patted her arm. "I'm simply thankful that nice young man of yours came after you and brought you back home."

Heat crawled into her cheeks. She glanced toward the group of men talking at the counter and lowered her voice. "Mr. Ryder is not *my* young man, Mrs. Townsend."

"Well, of course he is, dear, or he never would have chased after you. Papa thinks quite highly of him."

Papa? She'd never heard Mrs. Townsend refer to her husband as Papa.

"Papa says Mr. Ryder is going to build a bank, and that it will be a wonderful thing for Pinewood."

Her face stiffened. "I'm sure—"

The woman's smile vanished, her eyes clouded. "I wish Mr. Ryder would bring Sadie back home."

She looked at the elderly woman's eyes, caught her breath. "Mr. Ryder doesn't know Sadie."

"Truly?" The clouded eyes cleared, a smile curved Rachel Townsend's plump lips. "Then you shall have to introduce them when Sadie comes home next week. Now, tell me, Willa, which of these silks do you like better— the green or the blue? I want to make Sadie a new dress for her birthday and I've only a few days."

Willa. And Sadie's birthday was in December. Sadness gripped her throat, squeezed her heart. She looked down at the woman who had been a grandmother to them all and cleared away the tightness so she could speak. "Sadie always looked lovely in green."

"Oh, that's right. Thank you for your help, dear. I'll buy the green." Rachel Townsend smiled and hurried over to the counter.

Tears choked her. She watched as Manning Townsend stepped out of the group of men and took his wife's plump arm. "Are you finished with your shopping, Rachel?"

"Yes, quite finished, Mr. Townsend. Put the green silk on Papa's account, Mr. Cargrave. And this bottle of rose water, also." Sadie's grandmother took the bottle into her pudgy hand, smiled up at her husband and walked with him toward the door.

Manning Townsend looked back over his shoulder at Alan Cargrave and nodded. The proprietor wrote a figure in his account ledger.

I'm concerned about Mrs. Townsend, Callie. She seems easily confused. Willa's words flowed into her mind. She blinked back the welling tears, stared down at the green silk fabric still lying on the shelf and forced air into her constricted lungs. *She had to tell Sadie.*

She clasped her letter tight and hurried out the door, too heartsore to appreciate the merry tinkling of the bells. She gathered her full skirts and slipped into the narrow passageway between the mercantile and Brody's meat market, followed it to the back steps, then hurried along the path behind the stores. It was the way she'd taken when she was a child and wanted to be alone.

She stepped out from behind Mr. Fabrizio's barber shop onto the hotel's graveled way and glanced toward Main Street to check for any approaching carriages or riders. Ezra was across the street in the open field by the church.

She stepped back into the shadow of the store and watched him pacing around. Was that the property he had talked about this morning? No. It couldn't be. He'd said he'd found that property when he'd gone riding. So what—

He was going to build his bank there. Right across the street from the hotel. Her stomach flopped. She would see him every day—unless it was all some sort of ruse and he went back to New York City whenever he'd gotten what he was after. What could it be?

"Let's go, Belle! Get moving, Sal!" Leather creaked, hooves thumped against the hard-packed dirt of Main Street. Two teams of horses plodded out from in front of the hotel building hauling Totten's trolley.

More guests? She sighed, pushed the concern away and hurried to the hotel. She was becoming too brain weary to cope with the problem, and she had a supper to prepare.

Ezra leaned his shoulder against the window frame and stared out into the darkness. He'd had to admit defeat and leave the kitchen without talking to Callie after supper and he didn't like it. But she and Agnes and Sophia had all been too busy preparing for the restaurant opening tomorrow to welcome his presence. Not that Callie ever did.

He frowned, shifted his position and jammed his hands into the pockets of the coarse twill pants he'd put on for a quick ride out to their land. He refused to think of it as anything else, though Callie sure wasn't making his courting easy. The truth was, he wasn't even sure she was aware that he *was* courting her. She seemed more annoyed than pleased with his attention. And she was certainly standoffish—especially in the early morning when there was always a few minutes when they were alone together.

A wry smile touched his lips. Those moments were torture for him. And she was not indifferent to him, either—of that he was certain. The way she had practically run around that worktable when he'd come close to her this morning proved it. And that moment at the mercantile entrance… It was becoming harder and harder to keep from taking her in his arms and telling her that he loved her. But she had to accept him and trust him first. One of these days she'd give in and let him explain his deception, and then—*please, God*—forgive him. Then his *real* courting of her could begin.

Meanwhile, he'd continue to spend time with her. And to explain his plans to Sophia in the kitchen where she couldn't help but overhear. She had definitely been curious about his plans for the bank this morning, though she'd tried hard not to show it.

He stiffened, pushed away from the window frame and stared at the splotch of lamplight spilling out into the night from a downstairs window. It hadn't been there a moment ago.

Someone was in the kitchen.

Callie.

He headed for the door.

Chapter Twenty-Three

The kitchen was empty, silent and dark. Callie sighed, the soft sound blending with the whisper of her silk dressing gown and the soft pat of her slippers against the plank floor. She placed the scissors and the piece of soft cotton cloth on the worktable, lifted the lamp from the shelf by the stove and turned up the wick. The flame flared, then settled to a steady burn.

She put the lamp back in its place, stared at the golden light glinting against the dark window panes and heaved another sigh. Once again she was up and prowling around in the quiet while others slept.

The painful pulsating in her finger drew her back to her purpose. She took the small crock of Indian salve from the shelf, looked down at it in her hand. It would take the redness and the throbbing from her finger, but there was nothing she could do about the turmoil in her mind and the ache in her heart.

The golden light shimmered down the dark blue silk of her gown as she moved out of its bright circle and set the crock on the table. She had to tell Sadie about her grandmother. And she would. She'd tried earlier. She'd gone to Sophia's desk and took out the writing supplies, sat and stared at them thinking about the hurt her words would bring to Sadie. In the end, she'd put the supplies back, closed the desk and left the room.

The horrible feeling she hadn't been able to shake off even during the hustle and bustle of preparation for the restaurant's opening tomorrow took her by the throat, and squeezed. She had to write the letter. She simply couldn't do it yet—the sadness was too new, and a few days wouldn't matter.

I wish Mr. Ryder would bring Sadie home.

The tears she'd been fighting blurred her vision. She picked up the cloth, awkward to hold with her forefinger stuck out straight to protect her pulsating fingertip, and reached for the scissors.

Footsteps echoed through the empty dining room and approached the kitchen door. *Ezra.* She jerked her head up, spun toward her bedroom, turned back. It was too late to hide.

He strode into the kitchen and came to stand beside her, the lamplight playing over his handsome features, touching the curve of his lips when he smiled. Her heart skipped, her pulse stumbled.

"I saw the light from the window and thought I'd come make sure everything was all right."

He was dressed in his laborer's clothes and smelled faintly of horse and the outdoors. He must have been riding or visiting Joe in the stable. She looked up at him, acutely aware of her own appearance, of the dressing gown and the jumble of curls hanging down her back. Heat burned her cheeks. "Everything is fine."

She tried to sound cool, dismissive, but it didn't come out that way. The man so unnerved her. She tore her gaze from his, snipped at the material. The scissors bit, then slipped—the material too loose in her awkward grip. She tried again.

"What are you doing?"

He stepped closer, peered over her shoulder. Her stomach fluttered. She drew breath to answer, but lost it again when he reached out, grasped her hand and drew it toward him.

"That is more than a scratch, Callie."

She nodded, tried to slip her hand from his grasp, gave up when his grip tightened slightly. "I was making a bandage..."

"I'll do it." He took the cloth from her hand, held out his free one.

She surrendered the scissors, too discomposed by the tenderness in his touch to protest.

"I used to watch my mom do this when I'd injured myself one way or another." He positioned the cloth and scissors, glancing at her hand. "I'd better make this narrow—your hands are small."

Compared to his broad, strong ones. She listened to the efficient snip of the scissors, watched the narrow strip of cloth fall away and reached for the salve. He beat her to it.

"This should make your finger feel better. I know it took the pounding ache from my head wound when you tended me."

When she'd thought he was an injured logger. The remembrance of his deception helped her composure—until he took hold of her hand again. She willed her hand not to tremble as he applied the salve. She failed.

"Am I hurting you?" He looked up, ensnaring her gaze with his.

"No." She looked down at their joined hands. That wouldn't explain her trembling. "It's a bit tender is all."

"I'll be gentle." He wiped the salve left on his finger on the strip of cloth, then laid the cloth against the cut and wound it around her finger. "Hold that please." He picked up the scissors and split the end of the strip down as far as her finger, twisted the two pieces at the base, looked up at her and nodded.

She moved her fingers back out of his way. He pulled the two ties in opposite directions around her fingertip and tied them below her fingernail. "A rather clumsy bandage I'm afraid, but it should help."

"It's better than I could have managed myself. Thank you." She looked at his hand still holding hers and was afraid to try and pull away lest he tighten his grip. Would he draw her close? Enfold her in his strong arms? The trembling spread, weakening her knees. She groped for something to say, something that would not betray the feelings he stirred in her. "Your mother taught you well."

He nodded and lifted her hand. "She also taught me that a kiss always makes the hurt better." He touched his lips lightly to the bandage, and looked up. His smoldering gaze locked on to hers. "I never want to see you hurt, Callie. And you never will be, by me." He bowed his head, pressed his lips to her palm then turned and walked away.

She stood frozen in place, her hand pressed against the pounding pulse at the base of her throat and listened to his footsteps fade, knowing that it was too late for her. She loved him. How could her heart be so wrong?

Ezra shoved his fingers through his hair, huffed out a breath and trotted down the front porch steps, strode off up Main Street. That had been the hardest thing he'd ever done! His heart was still pounding. He didn't dare stay in the hotel lest he storm back into the kitchen, and pull her into his arms.

But he couldn't—not until she listened to him and gave him her trust. That had to come first. Who knew what sly, nefarious purpose she would ascribe to his courting her if she did not learn to trust him first?

His stride lengthened, his hands fisted. He was getting sick of this frustration. What more could he do to show Callie she could trust him? To prove to her he was an honorable man—a man of his word?

He swerved onto the property he'd purchased, stopped and stared at the dark shadow that was the cluster of towering elms.

Go back to New York City. He could still see the flash of sparks in Callie's beautiful violet-blue eyes when she'd spoken those words. But the sparks had died, smothered by doubt at his answer. *That will never happen, Callie. All I want is here in Pinewood. I'm not leaving.*

He looked at the elms, their top leaves kissed by silver moonlight, their trunks lost in the darkness of their own shadows. He walked closer, studied the lay of the land. *Their* land. It was time to show Miss Callie Conner he meant exactly what he'd said.

Moonlight filtering through the branches of the tree outside her window made silver and black patterns on the floor. Callie put the cloth and scissors back into her sewing box, removed her dressing gown and slipped into bed, her fingertip curled into her palm to protect it.

There was no sound of movement overhead. She straightened her finger and stared at the bandage. He'd been so gentle with her. It was amazing that his strong hands could be that tender. She couldn't imagine Jacob Strand or any of the other Buffalo men who had courted her bothering themselves over her cut, let alone tending it. Was Willa right? Was she allowing her experiences with them to cloud her judgement of Ezra? Was she wrong to suspect his motives?

She turned onto her side, slipped her hand beneath her cheek and closed her eyes.

Papa says Mr. Ryder is going to build a bank, and that it will be a wonderful thing for Pinewood.

We can all thank Mr. Ryder for both. He is bringing new prosperity to Pinewood.

She frowned, opened her eyes and stared at the blotches of moonlight on the floor. It made no sense at all that a man with his prestige and wealth would not return to his businesses and fancy lifestyle in New York City. If she could only discover what he hoped to gain by staying here—*if* indeed he did stay—she would be able to protect her aunt from any hurt he might cause her.

All I want is here in Pinewood. I'm not leaving. That's what Ezra had said when she'd told him to go back to the city. But she knew better than to put her trust in a man's words.

A floorboard squeaked overhead. A door closed. Footsteps crossed the room.

Ezra. No wonder it had been quiet upstairs. He'd been gone. Where would he go this time of night? She sat up and heard muted whistling, the scrape of a chair. More drawing? What was it to be this time—a store, an insurance company—something else to excite the people of Pinewood?

She rose and slid her feet into her slippers, grabbed her dressing gown and shrugged into it on her way to the porch. She swallowed back tears, and crossed to the railing. The light from his lamp was a soft golden glow in the thin moonlight. She turned and walked to the end of the porch.

"Almighty God, I don't understand what is happening. I'm so confused and…and heartsick—" Her whisper broke off. She caught her breath and pressed her hand against the tightness in her chest. "I asked You to have Your way before, and I ask it again now, for I can trust neither my heart nor my mind. And I certainly cannot trust Ezra Ryder's words."

The tears welled, spilled down her cheeks. "Oh, why does he stay? What is he after? Your Word says You know the hearts of men. Please, please reveal the truth to me that I might know beyond doubt. Amen."

She lifted her hands and wiped the tears from her

face, felt the brush of the bandage ties against her skin. The salve had helped—her finger had stopped paining her. If only there were a salve for her heart.

Chapter Twenty-Four

"Where is Agnes?"

Finished. Callie added the plate she'd dried to the stack sitting on the worktable, hung the towel on its peg to dry and looked at her aunt. "I noticed Otis was watering the horses at the trough, so I sent her to the barn with the last two pieces of molasses cake. Joe loves my molasses cake."

"Why, you little matchmaker! I hope it works." Sophia laughed and picked up the plates, carried them to the step back cupboard and set them on the shelf. "My accounting for the day's restaurant receipts is finished. I was unsure of exactly what to record so it took me longer than I expected. I'd still be working on them if Ezra hadn't shown me what to do."

Ezra. Why did her heart have to jump every time someone spoke his name? "He's very helpful to you."

"Yes." Sophia fixed her gaze on her.

She turned and dumped the pan of rinse water into the bucket on the shelf beneath the washstand to hide her face.

"We've all had a very busy day, but you especially

so, Callie. I came to help as soon as I was free. Have you more to do?"

"No, I'm finished." She untied the strings of her apron, slipped it off and draped it over its peg. "Agnes is going to set the bread dough for tomorrow. I can't do the kneading very well with a bandage on my finger."

"How *is* your finger? Is it better?"

"Yes, much better. It's tender to the touch, but it no longer pains me." She held up her hand and wiggled her finger as proof.

Sophia stepped close, took hold of her hand. "How did you tie the bandage on the back of your finger that way?"

"I didn't. Ezra bandaged it for me." She couldn't stop the betraying heat that climbed into her cheeks at the memory. Or the tears that clogged her throat.

"I see."

She looked into her aunt's keen gaze and withdrew her hand. "There is nothing to see, Aunt Sophia. My finger pained me so I couldn't sleep, and I came into the kitchen for the salve. Ezra noticed the light and came to make certain there was nothing wrong. When he noticed my plight he helped me, that's all."

"Then why are you blushing?"

Because I have a foolish heart that wants to make more of a kiss on the palm than was meant. "I was in my dressing gown and my hair was down."

"Oh, my. Poor Ezra."

She stared at Sophia. "What does that mean…'poor Ezra'?"

Sophia shook her head. "It means only that Ezra is a young man and you are a very beautiful young woman."

That would explain the look in his eyes when he'd kissed her palm.

"Shall we go into the sitting room and relax, dear? We've been too busy the last few days to have a chance to chat."

Her stomach churned. She pushed back a curl at her temple and nodded. "Yes, I've much to tell you." Her voice faltered. She took a breath. "I had a letter from Mother yesterday. I...didn't read it until this morning."

Sophia stepped through the sitting room door, paused and looked at her. "Penelope said something that disturbed you."

"Yes. Mother said she and Father were taking ship for London—that they would be well on their way before I received the letter." She walked to the window and looked outside. *I asked You to reveal the truth to me, Lord, and You have. Please help me to get through this without breaking down.*

Sophia's satin dress rustled as she stepped close, her hand touched her arm. "Are you concerned for their safety, dear?"

"No..." She clenched her hands, took a breath to stop the swirling nausea. "I'm concerned because Mother asked me to thank Mr. Ryder for them. It seems Jacob Strand bought Father's *blessing* on our 'betrothal' by paying off a loan the bank held on Father's house. Only instead of giving Father the paper clearing the debt as agreed, he used the house as partial surety for a loan when he purchased a property on King Street. Ezra bought that loan."

Shivers took her. She closed her eyes, wrapping her

arms about herself. "I remember that being mentioned at the church when Ezra came after me, but not clearly. Everything happened so fast, and I was so confused and upset—" Tears stung her eyes, seeped between her lashes. "But I was telling you what Mother wrote. Ezra sent Father a relinquishment of collateral letter which freed the house of all encumbrance, thus allowing Father to borrow the money for their trip to London. They are grateful to Mr. Ryder for his largess, and—" Her voice broke, tears flowed down her cheeks. "—and Father sends his blessing on Mr. Ryder's courtship of me."

"Oh, Callie dear, don't cry." Sophia clasped her arms, turned her around to face her. "Let Ezra explain—"

"That he is *buying* me—the same as Jacob Strand and all the others tried to do?" She stepped back out of Sophia's grasp, squared her shoulders and lifted her chin. "The only difference is that Ezra is paying a higher price. He had to pay off the loan on the hotel, as well as the one on Father's house. I suppose I should be flattered, but I'm not. I am *not* for *sale!*"

"Callie dear, you're wrong—"

"Tell that to Father and Mother who are so thankful for Mr. Ryder's request for Father's blessing." Her voice quavered, her stomach clenched so painfully she could barely breathe. "I not only do not want to listen to Mr. Ryder's glib explanations—I never want to see him again—though that is impossible with him living here. I can only pray that he will give up his fruitless pursuit of me and leave." She started for the door.

"Callie, wait!"

She shook her head and kept walking. She wanted to

run…to cry out the agony tearing at her heart, but there was no place for her to go. Ezra was much smarter than Jacob Strand—Ezra had won Aunt Sophia's regard.

She skirted the dining table in the kitchen, stepped out onto the porch and looked toward the river path—the deer path. Not there. He had ruined that for her, also.

She clenched her hands and walked around to the front of the hotel, looked across the street to the parsonage. No. Willa thought she was wrong about Ezra, also. And the children were there.

She stepped into the street, nodded to the driver of a passing wagon and angled past the church and the park. She crossed Oak Street and walked on toward the tree-dotted field that bordered the road as far as she could see.

She turned into the empty land, her elongated shadow caused by the setting sun going before her. She had asked for the truth, and she had received the truth. How could she love such a man? How could she? A sob burst from her throat, and tears gushed from her eyes.

She snatched up her hems and ran toward a cluster of elms, heedless of the tall grasses grabbing at her skirts and stockings, threw herself down on the ground in the shadow at a tree's base and cried out her anguish where no one could witness her pain.

"Where did she go?"

"I don't know, Ezra. I looked in her room and checked with Willa. She hadn't seen her."

He looked into Sophia's eyes dark with distress and shook his head. "Don't worry, Sophia. No harm will come to her."

"I know. It's only that this isn't like Callie."

"I think I may know where she is."

He hurried to the kitchen and out the back door, leaped the steps and trotted past the buttery, his mind filling with the memory of that night he'd rescued her from Jacob Strand.

I loathe that man, Ezra. And all of the other wealthy, arrogant men that were bidding for my hand, as well.

What had he done? He ran down the path through the field toward the river, his feet pounding, his lungs straining.

They think their wealth and prestige sets them above everyone else—that their money can buy anything, even a wife. Well, I am not for sale!

What a bumbling fool he was. What had he been thinking, sending that relinquishment of collateral in the same post with his request for permission to court Callie. *Of course* her father would interpret it to mean he was buying his blessing. That's the way the minds of men like that worked. He knew that. He'd come up against them in business deals often enough. And now Callie thought he was the same.

He ducked beneath a branch and ran along the deer path to the place where he'd picked the pussy willow sprig for Callie, stopped and stared at the empty space.

"Callie!" He moved forward, quietly now, his heart pounding, his breath labored. "Callie, can you hear me?"

What made him think she would answer him if she did hear? He clenched his hands, held his breath and listened for any sound of movement. There was nothing.

He looked up at the sun sinking behind the hill. It

would be dark soon. He thought about bears and bob-cats and other wild animals.

"God, please keep her safe. And please allow me to explain to her... I love her, Lord. You know I love her."

How far would she go? How far would her anger drive her? He set his jaw and continued up the path, a sick, hollow feeling in his gut as he looked for her shoe prints in the soft forest loam.

There was a quiet rustling in the grass. Callie lifted her head off of her crossed arms, and blinked her burning, swollen eyes. Night had fallen.

She pushed herself to her knees and sat back on her heels, wiped the moisture off her cheeks, too tired to do more. The rustling came again. A snake? Some loathsome creeping creature? A skunk?

She rose to her feet and looked around but could see nothing in the darkness beneath the elms. It was brighter in the open area between the trees and the road. She brushed off her bodice and sleeves, shook out her long skirts and started through the grass, drained but determined. She would repay Ezra Ryder every cent. She would find a way. Perhaps she could find employment teaching at the female seminary with Sadie. She hated the thought of leaving Aunt Sophia and Pinewood again, but if she must, she would.

She stepped onto the road, heard the thud of bootheels against the dirt and looked up. A tall, broad-shouldered man was striding toward her. She froze in place.

"Callie, are you all right?"

Matthew. She drew in a breath and started forward again. "I'm fine, Reverend."

"Sophia came by to see if you were with Willa. She said you'd gone off by yourself—somewhat upset."

She looked into his warm, compassionate gaze and forced a smile. "I'm sorry if I caused Sophia and Willa concern. I needed a little time to myself."

He nodded and fell into step beside her, escorted her across the street and to the carriageway. "Willa asked that you come see her tomorrow."

She stopped and looked up at him. "Thank you for seeing me home, Reverend." She let her smile say the rest. "Please tell Willa I may be too busy to come tomorrow as the restaurant takes more of my time now, but I will come as soon as I'm able."

"I'll tell her." He smiled and dipped his head. "Good night, Callie. May the good Lord bless you and grant you His peace."

She supposed the Lord had blessed her—with the truth. Perhaps His peace would follow, though she couldn't imagine it with the turmoil inside her. She turned and walked to the porch, climbed the steps and paused.

Sophia rose from the settle by the door.

She walked to her aunt and kissed her cheek. "I'm sorry if I worried you, Aunt Sophia. I had to be alone for a while."

Sophia's hand grasped hers and squeezed. "As long as you're all right, Callie."

She dredged up a smile, thankful for the shadows that

hid her swollen eyes. "I will be. Now, if you'll excuse me, I'm tired and I'm going to bed."

Sophia hugged her then stepped aside. "Of course, good night, dear. I pray you sleep well."

She nodded and opened the door, then turned back. "Are you coming in?"

Sophia shook her head and resumed her place on the settle. "Not yet, Callie. Ezra went to look for you. I'll wait and tell him you are home safe."

Her breath left her. She nodded, stepped inside and closed the door.

Chapter Twenty-Five

The kitchen was silent, the light from the trimmed lamp on the shelf by the stove only bright enough to reveal the emptiness echoed by the hollow in his gut. The message was clear. She didn't want to see him.

"I'm not giving up, Callie." Ezra whispered the promise into the silence, walked to the back door and went outside.

The peaceful sounds of the unseen creatures preparing for the dawn stood in stark contrast to the unrest in his spirit. He frowned, walked to the steps then stopped, constrained by the urgent need in his heart. He gripped the porch post beside him and looked up at the graying sky, turned and walked to Callie's window, cleared the tension from his throat. "I know you're awake, Callie."

He braced his hands against the frame and raised his voice. "I erred badly in sending that post to your father, but my intentions were pure. I wanted his blessing to court you, as would any man. Will you refuse my court merely because I am wealthy?"

The silence offered no reassurance. He left the porch

and took the path to the carriageway. His logger boots crunched against the gravel as he strode out to Main Street, thudded against the hard dirt as he crossed.

The waning moonlight silvered the landscape. A sense of urgency quickened his steps. The men would be arriving with the dawn, but he couldn't wait—he had to start now.

He moved into the field by the church, trod over the flattened grasses until he reached the stakes linked together by heavy string. Moonlight glinted dully on the blades of the shovels waiting there. He picked one up, aligned the blade with the string, placed his boot on the shovel's shoulder and pushed. The blade sliced into the ground. He worked the handle back and forth to break the grip of the roots, tossed the scoop of dirt aside and started again.

Minute by minute the trench grew longer, deeper, the pile of discarded dirt higher—every shovelful a testimony to his veracity and honor. He was not leaving Pinewood. And the trench, the pile of dirt and the blisters forming on his palms, was the proof.

Footsteps. Callie stiffened. She'd been right to stay abed. Ezra was there in the kitchen as if nothing had happened—and he had to know. Sophia would have told him.

The hurt washed over her anew, wrenched at her heart. She fisted her hands and snagged her lower lip with her teeth to keep from crying out.

The kitchen door opened, closed. His footsteps crossed the porch, stopped.

No, Lord, please—make him go on so I can rise. I have work to do. She held her breath, strained against the silence, waiting. His footsteps drew near, his voice floated through her open window, the words clear, unmistakable. Her heart stopped. Her lungs quit working. His intentions were pure? The post was a foolish mistake?

Her breath gusted from her lungs. She rose and stepped to the side of the window, caught a glimpse of Ezra washed in the thinning moonlight as he left the porch. He was dressed in his logger clothes. Where was he going? She closed her eyes and leaned back against the wall. She was so tired of all this doubt and confusion. But how was she to know the truth? Every time she thought she had the situation with Ezra figured out, something happened to turn things around the other way.

Let not your heart be troubled, neither let it be afraid.

The Bible verse dropped into her mind, clear and uninvited. She jerked upright, her heart pounding. Was she afraid? Is that why she refused to listen to Ezra? Was it righteous indignation—or fear of what would happen if she let him into her heart? If she dared to *trust* him?

Conviction settled deep in her heart and spirit. She released the air pent in her lungs. She had to do it. Somehow, some way she had to find the courage, the grace to listen to what Ezra had to say.

Callie pushed the damp curls off her forehead with the back of her hand and wished she could go outside and stand in the breeze and see for herself what was going on—the shouts of the drivers encouraging their teams, the protesting scrape of the stone boat skids against the street and the rumble of the wagons passing by the hotel.

Ezra was building his bank. She now knew for a certainty that much of what he'd said was true.

She sighed, dropped the mixing fork and grabbed up the spoon, scooped the biscuit topping onto the prepared rhubarb in the dish. All day the guests had crowded the windows or stood on the front porch to watch the activity then clustered in little groups to discuss it. And the villagers who came to the dining room did the same. The whole *place* was abuzz with the goings-on. And she had to stay in the kitchen. For the first time it felt confining. That, too, had changed. The kitchen had been her escape, her sanctuary when she arrived.

She brushed the flour dust from her hands, glanced out the side window. Where was that cinnamon she needed? Agnes had probably gotten caught up in all the hubbub. She should have gone after it herself, then she would have been able to see Ezra at work. Perhaps that would give her the courage she needed to face him.

She opened the oven, drew back from the blast of hot air, shoved in the dish and closed the door. It was time to start baking in the cool of evening. She'd have to discuss it with Agnes when she—

The porch door opened. "Thank goodness, Agnes! I need that cinnamon for—" She gasped, stared at Ezra's pale face, at the blood running over his temple and cheek and dripping onto his shoulder.

He lifted his hand and wiped the drops from his jaw. "I think I need some of that salve."

His smile went straight to her heart, set it fluttering. She gathered her wits about her. "Sit down, Ezra." She reached for the teakettle, poured warm water into a bowl and snatched up a clean cloth. "What happened?" She grabbed the crock of salve and carried everything to the table.

"One of the men jumped out of the way of a tumbling rock and my head happened to be in line with his shovel."

The cut was at his hairline, on the left side of his forehead. There would be no standing behind him this time—not even to the side. She doused the rag, wrung it out and swallowed hard as he moved his legs out of her way and tipped his head back.

She stepped close to the front of the chair, acutely aware of his legs on either side of her skirts, of his broad chest so close in front of her. *Please, please don't let my hands tremble.* The edges of the cloth quivered. Why did she bother to ask?

She wiped the blood from his forehead and cheek, doing her best to hold her mind blank, to avoid looking into his eyes. That would be her undoing. The man wanted to explain his deception to her and clear his conscience, that didn't mean he *cared* for her. She rinsed the rag and dabbed at the cut, concentrated on getting the bits of dirt out.

"Callie…"

His long, strong fingers encircled her wrist—so gentle, so warm. She swallowed hard, stared at the cut and stood perfectly still. One small tug and she would be on his lap, in his arms. Oh, how she wanted to be.

He cleared his throat. "Sophia told me about the letter

from your Mother, and I know you're angry and upset. I also know you're captive right now and that it would not be fair of me to take advantage of that." His gaze burned up at her, his grip on her wrist tightened slightly. "Will you come for a walk with me tonight? Will you let me explain everything to you? I'd like to start again, with nothing but truth between us."

The warmth and sincerity in his voice crumbled the last of her defenses. She gathered her courage and nodded. She would give him his chance. She wanted so much for him to be the upright man she needed him to be.

"I'll call for you at the kitchen door at dusk." His voice was soft, gruff. He kissed the tip of her bandaged finger and released her wrist.

She caught her breath and opened the crock of salve.

One moment in time. One brief moment. How quickly a person's life could change forever. Callie left Sophia issuing instructions to Joseph and walked to the sitting room, sat at Sophia's desk and took out the writing supplies. She had to write Sadie now, while she was still numb from the shock.

She dipped the pen in the ink and pulled the paper forward.

Dearest Sadie,
My friend, I have bad news. Your grandfather was
in the village watching the foundation for a new
bank being laid up when a seizure took him and he
collapsed. He is now here at the hotel and Doctor
Palmer is tending him.

Your grandfather has awakened, but is unable to walk or use his right arm. His speech is slurred, also, though he has his wits about him and is able to answer questions. Doctor Palmer is hopeful that your grandfather will strengthen and not suffer another such attack, but he cannot say for certain.

Aunt Sophia has sent Joseph for your grandmother. I know not what will happen then for—

Oh, Sadie, your beloved grandmother is not well in her mind. She is very forgetful, and often confuses people and blurs the past with the present. The one thing she seems to remain absolutely clear about is you. She misses you terribly, Sadie.

Please know, my dear friend, that because Doctor Palmer believes your grandmother's condition renders her unable to manage your grandfather's care, both Grandfather and Grandmother Townsend will have a home here at the Sheffield House as long as is needed. Aunt Sophia, Willa and I will give them both our best care and our fond love.

I am so very sorry to write you such sad news, Sadie. My heart aches for you.

Aunt Sophia sends her love.
My warmest love always,
Callie

She sealed the letter, cleared and closed the desk, then stood looking at the letter in her hand, thinking of what had happened, and of the years of happiness Sadie had missed with her family because of fear.

"Blessed Lord, please don't let me miss my moment because I'm afraid." She whispered the prayer into the silence and hurried from the room.

Chapter Twenty-Six

The western sky was filled with a glorious burst of pink and gold rays that streamed between fluffy white clouds and dared the oncoming dusk to dim their beauty. A soft, warm breeze played with the grasses in the fields and the leaves of the trees. It was a perfect night. *Grant that it might be so, Lord.*

Ezra smoothed back his hair, straightened his blue cotton shirt and knocked on the kitchen door, his heart pumping as if he'd tried to outrun Reliable.

The door opened and Callie stepped outside and looked up at him. There was something different in her eyes... A man could lose himself in their beauty. Pink spread along her delicate cheekbones, her long, thick lashes lowered. He came to his senses. "Shall we go?"

She nodded and glanced up at him as they crossed the porch. "Am I permitted to ask our destination?"

He shook his head, took her elbow and helped her down the steps and onto the path to the carriageway. "It's a surprise."

"As is this." She stopped, stared at his horse tethered to the hitching post. "I thought we were going for a walk."

"We are, but there is wild, unkempt ground where we are going and I didn't want you to ruin your gown."

"How thoughtful." She glanced up at him, looked back at the horse and nibbled at the corner of her mouth. "I've never ridden horseback."

He jerked his gaze from her mouth, smiled reassurance as he freed the reins. "I'll walk beside you and lead him, but if you'd rather not, I can take him back to the stable and—"

"Oh, no, don't do that. I think this is a…moment." She gave him a smile he felt to his toes.

"A moment?" He tugged at the reins, and they started toward the road, Reliable plodding along behind.

"It's nothing." She stopped at the street, and glanced up at him.

"This way." He took her elbow and led her across the street, turned north. "You must be relieved that Dr. Palmer believes your friend's grandfather will be all right."

"Yes." She gave him a quizzical look.

"Sophia told me." They crossed Oak Street, approaching the edge of the field. "Do you think your friend will come home?"

"I don't know. Sadie—" She stopped as he turned off the road into the field. "Is this where we are going?"

"Yes." He looked down into her eyes. She took a breath and looked away. Disappointment struck. Foolish of him to think he could surprise her with his discovery. She had spent her childhood years here. "Are you familiar with this land?"

"I've been here…once."

Her voice sounded small and tight. Something had changed. He tried for a lighter touch. "But never on horseback."

"No." She smiled, looked down at the ground around them. "These grasses are all trampled. And there are ruts…"

"Do you want to ride?"

She shook her head. "Not yet. I'd rather walk as long as the grass is down…"

She was curious. He followed as she moved ahead along the trampled path. *Please, Lord.* She stopped again, stared ahead.

"What is that—there by those elms?"

"Those are stones for a foundation." He tightened his grip on the reins, moved up to stand beside her. "The lumber for framing will be delivered tomorrow." Confusion clouded her beautiful eyes. He waited for her questions.

"You own this land?"

"Yes."

She looked toward the elms, the piles of stone. "Is this the surprise you wanted to show me?"

"Part of it."

She threw him another curious look and walked on, her long skirts floating over the flattened grasses. "What are you building?"

"A home." That stopped her. She turned and looked at him.

"*Your* home?"

Ours. The word pushed at his tongue, but he held it back. He couldn't say it yet. "I told you everything I wanted was in Pinewood, and that I wasn't leaving. I meant it." He stood quiet beneath her searching gaze, let her read the sincerity in his eyes.

"I didn't believe you." Her voice was little more than a whisper.

"I know. But I never lied to you, Callie."

She drew a deep breath, turned and walked over to where the stakes linked with heavy twine drew the outline of the house. "Why did you deceive us?"

"To protect myself."

She turned and looked at him.

Please, Lord, give me the right words. He let the reins slip to the ground and walked over to stand in front of her. "You told me you came to Pinewood to escape the wealthy men who thought they could buy anything—even a wife."

She stared up at him, waiting.

"I came for the opposite reason, Callie. I came to escape the people who befriended me, and the women who pursued me for no reason other than my wealth."

Her eyes widened, her soft full lips parted in a small gasp.

He pressed his point. "It's not comfortable to always have to suspect someone's motives—to never know if a person likes you for yourself or because they are hoping to gain by your friendship. And I was heartily sick of fending off women who cared not a fig for who I am, but only for the lavish lifestyle I could give them."

She nodded, then looked down at the string outline of the house. "I know women like that."

"I needed to distance myself from that for a while, so I came to Pinewood where only my cousin knew who I was. The rest you know. I bought laborer's clothes to disguise myself, was attacked and robbed and left to die. I made my way to Pinewood only to find my cousin was gone. And then I met you. The most selfless, kind, talented, sweetest woman I had ever known. And I was attracted to you, Callie—more strongly than I have ever been attracted to any woman. But I'd made up my mind that if I ever courted a woman it would be one who would love *me,* not my wealth. I've learned not to trust anyone. And while I thought you were genuine and honest, I couldn't know."

She turned toward him. "And so you let your deception continue."

"Yes. Until I knew you better." He stepped closer, held her gaze with his. "I was going to tell you when Strand showed up and forced my hand. Can you forgive me, Callie?"

She looked down and nodded. "I forgive you." She brushed her hands down the front of her skirt and looked up. "I'm sorry I refused to listen to you, Ezra. It was wrong of me. Please forgive me."

There was an openness, a *trust* in her eyes that stole his breath. "Always, Callie." He looked away, cleared his throat. "Now, let me show you my surprise." He glanced up at the lowering sun. "We'll have to hurry."

Callie listened to Ezra's breathing, to the thud of the horse's hooves, the chuckle of the water over rocks in the creek they crossed, the night song of the birds in the trees on the high hill ahead. She concentrated on the bunch and stretch of Reliable's muscles beneath her, the rhythm of his gait, the warm breeze on her face and the flutter of the curls that dangled on her forehead and memorized it all, for she never wanted to forget this moment.

Having Ezra's arms around her was like nothing she had ever experienced. He was holding the reins, not her, it was true. Still, the warmth, the strength, the *safety* of his arms was beyond her ability to imagine, beyond the wish of her heart. She longed to rest back against him.

"Here we are. Whoa, boy."

Ezra's deep voice floated by her ear, faded into the sounds of dusk, the sounds of a world preparing for the coming night.

He dismounted, and cool air replaced his warmth against her back.

"Ready?"

"Yes." His strong hands gripped her waist. She put her hands on his shoulders, felt the play of his muscles as he lifted her down. She shook her skirts into place and stared up at the massive trees covering the high hill. Where was he taking her?

"All set." He turned from tying the reins to a bush and took her hand, led her into the woods. "It's not far. Mind the branches."

She nodded and walked a little behind him, far too aware of his hand holding hers. "Do I hear wat—"

"Sh, no talking."

His barely audible whisper put her in mind of Daniel leading them on adventures into secret, silent places. She smiled and stepped more quietly.

It *was* water. The sibilant whisper became louder in the hush of the woods. She peered around Ezra's broad shoulders, spotted fingers of sunlight filtering through the trees and sparkling on the water washing over layers of slate that formed a shelf high above them. The cascade fell onto a tumble of rocks and slate that formed a small pool. The runoff escaped into a rill that ran toward the field.

She couldn't stop the gasp.

He turned, looked at her.

She mouthed *It's beautiful!*—and felt her heart turn over at his smile. She caught the soft sound of a deer's tread and looked between the branches of the large pine beside them. A buck, head high, antlers glistening in the sunlight pranced into the open, blew once, twice, then stepped to the water. A doe followed after him. They drank their fill, then wandered off into the trees.

She turned her head toward Ezra. He was looking down at her, his blue eyes smoldering with a smoky gray haze. "You are so beautiful—so incredibly beautiful." Her heart stumbled.

He cupped the side of her face, his palm hot against her skin and lowered his head.

He drew her close. She closed her eyes and leaned into his embrace, slid her arms up around his neck. His lips brushed her forehead, trailed heat down her cheek and claimed her mouth.

The birds stopped twittering. The breeze stopped playing among the leaves, and the water halted its whispering glide over the stones. There was nothing in her world but Ezra. Nothing at all.

Too soon he lifted his mouth from hers. She pressed her head against his chest and listened to his ragged breathing, the thundering of his heart. His chin pressed against her hair.

"I love you, Callie. And none of this means anything to me without you. Will you marry me?"

She listened to his husky whisper and knew that forever, this would be their moment. "For all time." She lifted her head, stretched up on her toes and met his kiss with her love.

Epilogue

He was here. Callie listened to his footsteps, turned and hurried toward the entrance hall, stopped when Ezra filled the doorway, a little shy when their gazes first met. Would this feeling of wanting to rush into his arms ever leave her?

She gave into the urge and ran to him. He caught her close, kissed her until there was nothing but the two of them, their hearts beating as one.

Ezra stepped back, blew out a breath.

She gave him a cheeky smile, full of her feminine power.

He shoved his hands in his pockets, leaned back against the door frame and grinned, his eyes that smoldering blue that made her stomach flutter and her knees go weak. "I want you to smile at me that way tonight and every night for the rest of our lives."

He leaned forward, held his face so close to hers she could feel the warmth of his breath like a feather on her skin. "Because you are the sweetest, most beautiful woman God has ever created. And I'm the most blessed man alive because you love me."

Her pulse skipped; heat flamed in her cheeks. She wasn't the only one with power. She tossed her head and spun away.

He laughed, lunged and pulled her into his arms. "I didn't know you were coming here today. I thought you and Sophia and Willa would all be busy doing whatever it is women do to prepare for a wedding."

She leaned against him, reveled in the hard strength of his arms around her. "I can't stay away. I love our home. I can't wait until we move in tonight."

"Nor I." He grasped her upper arms and held her a little away from him. "I got you a wedding gift. Want to see it?"

She peered up at him. "You've already bought so much, Ezra." Curiosity got the best of her. "Is it more furniture?"

"Nope. Come with me. I'll show you."

He took her hand, led her from the sitting room, through the entrance hall, past the dining room and library and into the kitchen. She couldn't resist stretching out her free hand to touch her new stove. She couldn't wait to cook their first meal as husband and wife.

He opened the door and led her out onto the side porch. She glanced toward the village, at the parsonage and her aunt's hotel and smiled. She would spend a lot of hours on this porch. Ezra had thought of everything.

"There it is."

She glanced down. A pussy willow bush nestled in a

circle of fresh dirt in the corner where the porch joined the house.

"I stole it."

She jerked her gaze to him.

"From the deer path."

Tears slipped down her cheeks.

He cradled her face in his hands, brushed the tears away with his thumbs. "I fell in love with you that day, Callie. When I saw you standing there looking so sad, so vulnerable, I knew I would give my life to love you and protect you and make sure you never looked sad again. I'm going to do my best to live up to that. And should I ever forget, the bush will remind me."

He pressed his lips to hers in a gentle, tender kiss that was also a promise. She gave hers in return, then sighed and laid her head against his chest. "It was the sprig of pussy willow you picked for me that day that caused me to know I loved you."

She looked up at him and smiled, remembering. "I lost it on our walk back to the hotel and it threw me into turmoil. I couldn't settle or rest, so I waited until I was certain everyone was sleeping, took a lamp and went back and found it. I have it still. I'll keep it always."

The church was brimming with people. The villagers crowded in and pushed together in the pews to make room for others.

Ezra, tall and handsome in his black, swallowtail wedding suit with a snowy frill at his neck, stood at the front of the aisle with Matthew, ready with his Bible in his hand.

Willa, lovely in a dark green silk gown that brought out the red in her chestnut hair, stepped into the church and nodded. She walked down the aisle as the organist began to play and took her place, smiled at Ezra, then locked gazes with her husband.

"You look beautiful, Callie. Seems like God put an extra squirt of violet juice in your eyes today." Daniel grinned down at her, offered his arm. "Ready?"

She went on tiptoe and kissed his clean-shaven cheek. "Thank you for doing this, Daniel."

"For giving you to another man to protect and take care of?" He leaned down and planted a kiss on her cheek. "My pleasure, squirt."

She smiled at his childhood name for her and slid her hand through his offered arm, the delicate white lace of her glove a sharp contrast to the rough wool of his brown suit. "Well, two of us are married and off of your hands now. Only Sadie and Ellen remain."

Daniel's grin faded, and he gave a little nod.

She lifted the skirt hem of her long, white satin gown with her free hand and they stepped through the doors.

A murmur rose, a stirring as people twisted in their seats or craned their heads to see them.

She skimmed her gaze over all her friends and neighbors, but not her parents. She smiled at Ellen and her parents, felt her face stiffen at the sight of Ellen's newest suitor, Harold Lodge, heir to the Lodge shipping line.

She pushed away old memories, and smiled at the sight of Agnes sitting with Otis, and Joe looking uncomfortable in his Sunday clothes. She sent a silent message of love to her aunt sitting so straight and proud with her lovely violet eyes glowing behind a shimmer of tears. Rachel Townsend gave her a sweet smile and a sadness swept over her, a wish that Sadie and her grandfather could have come to share this special moment with her.

She moved down the aisle, shared a look that carried a lifetime of friendship with Willa, smiled at Matthew, then looked at Ezra—so handsome and confident, so thoughtful and caring, so *honest* and true. Her love forever.

Thank You, Lord, for showing me the truth and for having Your way.

Daniel stopped, then stepped back.

Ezra came to her, his gaze went to the sprig of pussy willow she had added to the cluster of silk roses tucked among her riot of black curls and he smiled, took her hand in his. Together they turned to face the altar.

* * * * *

*If you enjoyed this book by Dorothy Clark,
be sure to look for the next story
in her* PINEWOOD WEDDING *series,
coming in October 2013
from Love Inspired Historical!*

Dear Reader,

In my letter at the end of *Wooing the Schoolmarm*—the first book of this Pinewood Weddings series—I promised to tell Callie's story. I have done that in *Courting Miss Callie*. I hope you enjoyed reading about this young woman who was determined to be valued for who she was rather than for her outward beauty alone. And about Ezra, who was so tired of being used because of his wealth. What pleasure I had in bringing these two young people together and using their love to overcome their fears and their learned skepticism and to trust again—first and foremost in the Lord and His loving, watchful care, and then in each other.

How lovely it would be if we could all gather at the Sheffield House for one of Callie's delicious meals. Alas, that is impossible. But we can all meet again in Pinewood when Sadie Spencer comes home. And she will. She has asked that I tell her story next, for her strong love for her grandparents compels her to defy her deep fear and return to Pinewood to meet their need.

I do enjoy hearing from my readers. If you would care to share with me your thoughts about Callie and Ezra's story, or about Pinewood village and its residents, I may be contacted at dorothyjclark@hotmail.com or www.dorothyjclark.com.

Until Sadie comes home to Pinewood,

Dorothy Clark

Questions for Discussion

1. Callie Conner and Ezra Ryder are both driven to leave their present lives and flee to Pinewood. What drives them to do this? What is at the root of Callie's problems? Of Ezra's? How are they the same or different?

2. Callie is hurt and angered by her parents and the unhappiness their decisions brought her in the past and will continue to bring her in the future if she obeys their wishes. Was the action she took right or wrong, in your opinion? Why?

3. Callie is disgusted by Ezra's deception. Yet she herself commits the same offense. What blinded her to that fact?

4. Callie finally yields and gives her situation over to God. Does she truly yield at that moment? Have you ever given a situation/problem over to the Lord and then continued to try to solve it yourself? Did that work well?

5. Ezra wants relief from the phony friendships and affections offered by those who want to profit from his wealth, and so he forms a plan and flees to Pinewood. How does that "innocent" plan box him into a corner? Does he have a better choice?

6. Callie sends several prayers to the Lord, then becomes upset when they aren't answered. Are those

prayers in line with her first prayer that the Lord have His way? Why or why not?

7. How does the Lord use Callie's and Ezra's decisions/ actions to bless not only them, but others?

8. The scripture verse I used for this book is as follows: "A good name is rather to be chosen than great riches, and loving favor rather than silver and gold." Do you feel that verse is appropriate? Do you agree or disagree with the truth expressed?

9. Callie is badly hurt, and that makes her defensive and stubborn, even in the face of her beloved Aunt Sophia's advice. Have you ever stood firm instead of yielding?

10. It is Callie's and Ezra's reactions to others' actions that cause them problems. Could they handle their problems in a better way? How?

COMING NEXT MONTH
from Love Inspired® Historical
AVAILABLE MARCH 5, 2013

THE COWBOY'S UNEXPECTED FAMILY
Cowboys of Eden Valley
Linda Ford

With her own business in a fledgling frontier town, Cassie Godfrey will be self-sufficient at last. But her solitary plans are interrupted by four young orphans—and one persistent cowboy.

THE HEIRESS'S HOMECOMING
The Everard Legacy
Regina Scott

Samantha, Lady Everard, will lose her fortune if she isn't married by her twenty-fifth birthday. William Wentworth, Earl of Kendrick, seems the perfect solution, but he thinks the scandalous Everard family is nothing but trouble.

A TEXAS-MADE MATCH
Noelle Marchand

Ellie O'Brien has always prided herself on making matches, but when her childhood friend Lawson Williams comes back to town, the citizens of Peppin, Texas, decide to return the favor.

BOUND TO THE WARRIOR
Barbara Phinney

After the death of her husband, Ediva Dunmow is determined to keep her villagers safe. When the Norman knight she's ordered to marry proves to be gentle and faithful, can Ediva begin to trust God once more?

Look for these and other Love Inspired books wherever books are sold, including most bookstores, supermarkets, discount stores and drugstores.

LIHCNM0213

REQUEST YOUR FREE BOOKS!

2 FREE INSPIRATIONAL NOVELS
PLUS 2
FREE
MYSTERY GIFTS

Love Inspired
HISTORICAL
INSPIRATIONAL HISTORICAL ROMANCE

YES! Please send me 2 FREE Love Inspired® Historical novels and my 2 FREE mystery gifts (gifts are worth about $10). After receiving them, if I don't wish to receive any more books, I can return the shipping statement marked "cancel." If I don't cancel, I will receive 4 brand-new novels every month and be billed just $4.49 per book in the U.S. or $4.99 per book in Canada. That's a saving of at least 22% off the cover price. It's quite a bargain! Shipping and handling is just 50¢ per book in the U.S. and 75¢ per book in Canada.* I understand that accepting the 2 free books and gifts places me under no obligation to buy anything. I can always return a shipment and cancel at any time. Even if I never buy another book, the two free books and gifts are mine to keep forever.

102/302 IDN FVXK

Name	(PLEASE PRINT)	

Address		Apt. #

City	State/Prov.	Zip/Postal Code

Signature (if under 18, a parent or guardian must sign)

Mail to the Harlequin® Reader Service:
IN U.S.A.: P.O. Box 1867, Buffalo, NY 14240-1867
IN CANADA: P.O. Box 609, Fort Erie, Ontario L2A 5X3

Want to try two free books from another series?
Call 1-800-873-8635 or visit www.ReaderService.com.

* Terms and prices subject to change without notice. Prices do not include applicable taxes. Sales tax applicable in N.Y. Canadian residents will be charged applicable taxes. Offer not valid in Quebec. This offer is limited to one order per household. Not valid for current subscribers to Love Inspired Historical books. All orders subject to credit approval. Credit or debit balances in a customer's account(s) may be offset by any other outstanding balance owed by or to the customer. Please allow 4 to 6 weeks for delivery. Offer available while quantities last.

Your Privacy—The Harlequin® Reader Service is committed to protecting your privacy. Our Privacy Policy is available online at www.ReaderService.com or upon request from the Harlequin Reader Service.

We make a portion of our mailing list available to reputable third parties that offer products we believe may interest you. If you prefer that we not exchange your name with third parties, or if you wish to clarify or modify your communication preferences, please visit us at www.ReaderService.com/consumerchoice or write to us at Harlequin Reader Service Preference Service, P.O. Box 9062, Buffalo, NY 14269. Include your complete name and address.

LIH13

Matchmaker—Matched!

For Ellie O'Brien, finding the perfect partner is easy—as long as it's for the other people in the town of Peppin, Texas. When her handsome childhood friend Lawson Williams jokingly proposes, the town returns the favor and decides a romance is in order for them. But when secrets in both their pasts threaten their future, can the efforts of an entire town be enough to help them claim a love as big and bold as Texas itself?

A TEXAS-MADE MATCH

by **Noelle Marchand**

Available in March wherever books are sold.

Love Inspired

To Trust or Not to Trust a Cowboy?

Former Dallas detective Jackson Stroud was set on moving
to a new town for his dream job, until he makes a pit stop
and discovers on the doorstep of a café an abandoned
newborn and Shelby Grace, a waitress looking for a fresh
start. He decides to help Shelby find the baby's mother,
and through their quest he believes he's finally found a
place to belong, while Shelby's convinced he will move on
eventually. What will it take to convince Shelby that this is
one cowboy she can count on?

Bundle of Joy
by
Annie Jones

Available March 2013!

www.LoveInspiredBooks.com

LI87801